SCARRED PRINCE

A BRATVA ROMANCE

K.C. CROWNE

Created with Vellum

DESCRIPTION

My world was rocked the night I collided with a stranger.
A scarred Bratva Prince.
He left me with a taste of submission - *and his baby*.
Now Leo's back, and he vows never to let me out of his sight.

Our saga began when he came to my rescue.

And ended in a night of passion. Thrilling and intense.

But as quickly as he appeared... he vanished.

He left me with the sweet taste of submission... *and his baby*.

I was certain I'd never see him again.

Until today...

"I'd like you to meet our institution's most generous benefactor."

Then a familiar Russian accent takes my breath away, *"Good evening, Nikita."*

My whole body freezes.

Apparently my dark prince comes from a powerful Bratva dynasty.

And the guy he's been wanting to put underground this whole time? ***My father.***

Will Leo change his mind when he learns I have a secret of my own?

CHAPTER 1

NIKITA

The cold is unbearable.

The snowfall is getting thicker. I can barely see anything, and my cheeks burn.

My lips feel numb and hurt at the same time. My toes tingle, buried deep in leather boots and two layers of socks.

There's not enough clothing to help anybody survive out here in this weather.

Of all the nights, this had to be the one to find me stranded on the side of a road. In the middle of a snowstorm.

Dammit, I need a new car. My Beetle has seen one too many years.

The snow rises dangerously fast everywhere around me, while more keeps pouring from the blackened night sky.

It's late, and I haven't seen another car drive by in more than twenty minutes. I would've signaled them, and tried to hitch a ride back into Moscow, at least.

This is the last time I go to such extreme lengths to bail out my deadbeat father.

Had he not gotten himself in such a hot mess, I

wouldn't have had to drive back to my grandmother's house in Loza to gather the last of her silverware.

My father racked up such a debt with the Bratva that I'm having to pawn everything I own, including Grandma's dowry to pay those goons and keep my father breathing for a little while longer.

That is, assuming I make it back to Moscow on time.

That last text message he sent me sounded urgent.

I should've ignored it.

But here I am putting my life in serious danger.

I could run into some creep who would take me anywhere but home.

I could end up dead in a frozen ditch, my grandmother's silverware feeding said creep for a few weeks, at least.

I shudder at the thought.

Or maybe it's the below zero temperature that's got me trembling.

I check my phone again. Maybe an extra signal bar will miraculously appear on the screen if I look at it hard enough.

"No signal. Motherf..." I stop myself and put the phone away.

I'll literally die out here if I don't do anything.

I slip the gloves back on and grab everything of value from the car.

My papers, my purse, and the duffel bag holding my grandmother's things. That's pretty much it.

There's no other way. I need to follow the road south, and reach Abramtsevo before I freeze to death.

Not half-a-mile later, I'm blinded by a set of headlights so white and intense that I have to close my eyes for a moment because I can't make anything out in the glare.

My heart starts racing as I stand still in the middle of

this blizzard, listening as a car door opens and shuts. The wind howls and I can't hear footsteps crunching in the snow.

"Are you okay?" a man asks. He's not too far away but it's hard to see his face clearly.

"I'm okay," I manage with a trembling voice. "Just out on a walk."

"Are you insane?"

Finally, my eyes adjust and I can make out his frame.

He's tall. Taller than most men I've come across.

Broad shoulders, black hair.

The backlight of his car's headlights casts a sharp contrast, enveloping most of his massive frame in a deep shadow.

I should be scared, yet all I'm feeling is curiosity.

"It's a possibility," I say.

"What are you doing out here in the middle of this frozen hell?"

"My car broke down, obviously," I shoot back. "Just trying to make my way into town."

I can finally make out his facial features.

There's a prominent scar on his left eye that speaks of violence.

His eyes. Wow. The deepest green I've ever seen.

It feels as though he's looking right into my soul, stripping my defenses away, one layer at a time until I'm left naked and vulnerable before him.

A smile tests the corner of his mouth, but it's the twinkle in his eyes that has my pulse racing. "Good luck with that, you've still got a few miles to go, and I don't think you're going to make it in these temperatures."

"It's not like I have another choice."

He points back at his car. "The snowstorm is only going

to get worse." As if summoned, the winds grow harsher, blowing harder and turning each snowflake into a sharp razor blade slashing across my face.

It's getting harder to breathe.

My tremors intensify, and now this tall, dark and handsome stranger looks even more serious than he did a few seconds ago.

If that's even possible.

"I have a cabin just 500 feet away from here, down that country road over there." He points somewhere behind me, and I follow his gaze but I can't see a damned thing in this blizzard. "You can at least shelter in place until the worst has passed, and then I can give you a lift into town. Where do you need to get to?"

Damn, there's something about his low and raspy voice that's got my gears turning in all the deliciously wrong ways.

"Okay, first of all, you're a complete stranger. I'm not just gonna hop into your car and let you take me wherever," I reply, my fear getting the better of me. Or maybe it's just my common sense bypassing this muted but dangerous desire currently unfurling in the pit of my stomach.

"Second, I'm going to Abramtsevo."

"Is that where you live?"

"Yes." It's not, but since I'm already contemplating getting into his car before I freeze to death, the least I can do is make myself seem local. That way, he'll think twice about abducting a local girl.

"I'll drive you there myself when the storm quits," he says. "Where did your car break down?"

"Back that way. I don't even know at this point. I can't see a damn thing."

"Fine. I'll search for it in the morning and get someone

to tow it for you," he says. "But in the meantime, we should get you somewhere warm."

"I'll be fine."

I had to shout in order to make myself heard over this raging wind, its gale force making me wobble.

The man cocks his head to the side, visibly amused.

Who the hell am I kidding at this point? I will die out here if I don't accept his offer to help.

"Suit yourself. It seems you have an itch to freeze to death. I won't get in your way," he replies and starts walking back to his car. "Good luck."

A sense of urgency takes hold, and I find myself following him. "Okay. Just please don't be some kind of homicidal maniac."

"I'm an accountant."

That is literally the last choice of career I'd imagined for a big scary guy like him.

He nods at my duffel bag. "I can put that in the trunk for you."

"The back seat?"

"Can't let it out of your sight, huh?"

I shake my head slowly. He takes it and leaves it on the back seat, while I get in the front. As soon as he shuts the door, the heating system goes to work on each of my senses. I can feel myself thawing, melting into the warmed seat as a soft pop tune oozes through the stereo. Ahead, it's all white. Everywhere, it's all white. How the hell did I make it this far, in the first place? As much as I hate to admit it, he's right. I'll freeze to death out here.

"My name is Leo," he says as he gets behind the wheel.

"Hm. Thank you," I mumble, stealing a glance at him.

I can see the scar over his eye better in this light.

And the shade of green is different.

Lighter, almost milky. Whatever caused the scar must've caused this mismatch in color, too. But damn, he's good looking. That's for certain.

Sharp cheekbones, a five o'clock shadow that'll make a girl's fingertips tingle slightly. Mine are definitely tingling.

"Maybe I should watch my back around you. *You* could be a homicidal maniac, for all I know."

Guess I deserved that.

"My name is Nikita." I glance ahead. "Where's your cabin again?"

"You'll see in a minute."

Lo and behold, precisely one minute later, the country lane emerges on the right side of the road. I must have been too distracted by the storm to notice it before.

Leo takes a cautious right turn, and the car starts wobbling as we go over a series of hidden potholes until we reach the cabin—a small but sturdy looking thing wedged between ancient pine trees dressed in white.

"Well, it's a good place to bury dead bodies," I say once I'm out of the car.

"True. But I prefer to keep a couple of vats full of acid at the back. It's easier than digging holes in this hard ground."

I give him a cautious look but find his smile eerily reassuring as he points to the narrow front porch of the cabin. It's made entirely out of pine wood, with thick walls and a sloped roof, glass windows and flowerless pots hanging on both sides of the door.

"Come on, let's go inside," Leo says.

Quietly, I follow him up the steps and into the cabin.

He turns the lights on, and I close the door behind me. As soon as we leave the storm outside, the quiet takes over. Without the fireplace running, it's not exactly warm, but compared to what we just came from, it feels like a little slice of heaven.

I stand still for a while, watching Leo as he takes his thick coat off and starts a fire. My gaze wanders over the mantel, adorned with framed photos whose details I can't make out from here.

The whole living area has a cozy feel to it, the sofa and armchairs covered in plaid-patterned wool blankets and cream furs. There's a narrow hallway ahead, with two doors and a kitchen at the very end.

I'm guessing one bedroom and one bathroom beyond those doors. I can see the small espresso machine on the kitchen counter, along with other accoutrements that make this place feel like a home away from home.

I listen to the fire crackling as the orange flames grow brighter. Soon enough, the room gets warmer and I can finally take my hat, my scarf and my gloves off.

Leo stays close to the fireplace, watching me intently.

He looks different in this light.

Way bigger and infinitely hotter.

My core tightens as his gaze wanders up and down my body.

Is he checking me out?

My brain is being overridden by thoughts of fear mixed with sexual desire. Clearly, I don't how I'm supposed to feel about being alone with a stranger - especially one as breathtaking as Leo.

He adds another log to the fire, then goes into the kitchen while I move closer to the flames, drawn by the familiar warmth.

"I'll make us some coffee. That's all I have at the moment."

"You don't spend much time here?" I ask.

"Not as much as I would like," he says, louder from the kitchen as I listen to his movements, followed by the humming and gurgling of the espresso machine.

"When I get tired of the city life, I come up here and spend some time alone. It's good for the soul."

"I can imagine."

Leo comes back with two mugs of steaming hot coffee, offering me one. I take it, and his fingers slightly brush over mine in the process.

Wow, what was that? Thousands of tiny electrical tendrils shoot up my arm.

I suck in a deep breath before the first sip, the wonderfully bitter liquid tingling my tongue before it rolls down my throat.

The warmth spreads through my insides as I slowly relax.

"What were you doing out there?" he asks, his eyes never leaving mine.

"Just trying to handle some family issues," I reply. I don't feel like talking about why I was stranded in the middle of a snowstorm in the middle of nowhere.

I don't feel like thinking about my father and his increasingly worrying tendencies.

As if sensing my discomfort, Leo goes to a cabinet built into the corner of the living room and takes out a bottle of scotch.

"I hope you don't mind. I like to add scotch to my coffee," he says. "I'm not driving anywhere until the blizzard calms down, anyway."

"You think?"

"Look outside."

I do, all I see is white. A thick layer of white against the darkness of the night as the windows tremble, constantly puzzled by the growing winds.

We're going to get snowed in for a handful of hours, at least. If not for longer. The thought of being trapped in this place with a complete stranger should have me on edge, but there is something about Leo that soothes me.

There is also something about him that adds tension to the back of my neck, but it's enticing.

It's heavy and heady, burning hot under a layer of unanswered questions.

"You're safe here, Nikita," Leo says. "I'm not in the habit of abducting vulnerable women."

"Well it's probably too late to turn back now anyway, right?"

He chuckles. "What a shame."

"What is?"

He tilts his head to the side slightly and regards me, his intense dark eyes sweeping over me slowly. It's amazing how naked I feel beneath his observant gaze.

I feel like he can see right through me, can see every minute breath and small shift of muscle and maybe even read my thoughts.

Nervous excitement crackles inside me; the air around us is thick and tense. When I nibble my bottom lip, his eyes dart to watch the motion with an almost hungry darkness.

"A beautiful woman," he says, "all alone in a blizzard. Your boyfriend is a damn fool for letting you drive out in this madness all alone."

"Well that would be true if I actually had a boyfriend."

"I find that hard to believe."

He looks into my eyes more intensely.

I have to be honest with myself.

My body aches for this man.

My fingers itch to know what his hair feels like, if his body is as hard and muscular as it looks.

I crave his hands on me, his lips.

I want to lean in and press my mouth to his.

"Leo?"

"Hm?"

I lick my lips, hesitant.

I can tell by the way he leans forward and hangs on my every word that I'm not crazy. He feels it, too, this pull toward one another.

"I've never done anything like this before, but if we're going to spend the rest of this night together, I'd like to make it one to remember."

"You don't know how happy I am to hear you say that," Leo whispers and without any hesitation he brings his lips to mine, and slips his sweet tongue into my mouth.

Electricity pulses through me.

After a few heart pounding seconds, Leo pauses, pulling away a few inches.

A soft whine escapes me at the sudden lack of warmth.

"Are you sure you want to do this? "

"I'm sure," I rasp, tugging at his belt greedily. "I'm just letting you know I don't have a lot of experience, that's all."

"Sex with strangers?"

I roll my eyes. "Sex in general – except for..."

"I don't want to know. Don't worry. I'm going to show you how a real man fucks."

I shiver, my knees practically jelly. The wet heat between my legs is starting to grow unbearable. "Then what are you waiting for?" I mutter against his mouth.

It's all the permission he needs.

Leo takes my hand and leads me to a gorgeous bathroom, covered in marble.

He circles me in his arms and lifts me up on the countertop. I wrap my legs around his hips instinctively, clinging to him as his lips slot together with mine. His kisses are rougher, but I like it infinitely better this way.

He's rough and demanding, proof that he wants not just my mouth, but the very air I'm trying to breathe.

It's all-consuming and wonderfully dizzying.

Leo then carries me into the shower stall, the polished tiles cool to the touch. His big hands are surprisingly deft, peeling my clothes off piece by piece with amazing fluidity.

I don't even have time to feel awkward about it—because on some level this should be awkward.

But Leo leaves no time for doubt.

He looks at me like he's ready to devour, pressing hard kisses against my throat, down to my chest, squeezing my breasts while teasing my pebbling nipples with his teeth.

He sucks marks against my breasts, a hand slipping between my legs to gather up the slick heat there. A heady groan rips itself from my lungs when his fingers slide over my folds.

"Hurry up," I rasp. "Shouldn't you be naked by now?"

Leo rises to full height, peering down at me with a mischievous glint in his eyes. "It's called foreplay, my kitten."

He brushes the pad of his thumb over my sensitive clit, sending sparks flying through my body. Pleasure ebbs and flows through every fiber of my being, punctuated with his kisses and caresses.

I claw at his shirt, eager to see him naked and equally exposed.

The hard press of his cock against my thigh thrills me, hard and hot and doing its best to escape the confines of his pants.

He works me over with his fingers, teasing me until I'm on the edge of insanity, so consumed by pleasure I can't help but scream against his shoulder as I crash into my climax.

I accidentally bump the shower knob, turning on the high-pressure spray. We're drenched through in seconds, steam filling the already hot space.

"I'm sorry," I half-laugh. It's hard to feel genuinely bad now that his shirt is transparent, revealing the mosaic of dark tattoos beneath the white fabric.

Leo doesn't seem too upset. "That's fine. I'll just buy a new shirt."

He finally—finally—shrugs off his shirt while I reach between us and make quick work of his belt. Hooking my fingers over the waistband of his pants, I push down and marvel at the sheer size of him.

Good God, the man's massive. His cock springs free, hard and standing at attention. My knees give out, but he catches me and scoops me and turns me around, massaging his cock against my folds from behind.

"Take me," I almost beg him."

"What do you say?" He narrows his eyes at me, but I can see him boiling on the inside.

"Please, sir."

"Please, sir, what?"

"Please, sir, fuck me out of my mind," I say, barely recognizing myself anymore.

He thrusts himself deep inside me with all of his might, and what follows is a storm of passion and animalistic possession.

He pounds into me, deeper and harder as I'm stretched beyond belief, as every single nerve ending in my body screams, as a second orgasm urgently works its way through me. "I'm going to make you come again," Leo says.

He rams into me, deeper, harder, faster until it hurts so good that I rub myself most viciously, not stopping until the pressure reaches its peak, until he grabs a handful of my hair and pulls my head back, kissing me harshly as we both come undone, as I explode all over him and he explodes inside me, his cock filling me to the brim.

"You're mine tonight, Nikita," he whispers gruffly in my ear.

"I'm yours tonight," I reply. We're coming down from the heavens, now, yet I can tell from the ravenous look in his eyes that we are anything but done.

"You're mine for as long as I want," Leo says, his hold tightening on my jaw while I feel his cock growing again inside of me.

He cannot pull himself out. Why would he, when he's catching fire again, and my pussy is still clenching him tightly?

"Yes, sir," I reply, most satisfied as he releases my jaw and proceeds to massage my breasts, his hips swaying slightly.

It's going to be a long night, a sweet and decadent night as I will submit to this man with everything I've got.

He'll take me every which way, over and over, and I will welcome everything he's got to give me, in return.

I love his fingers running through my hair.

His fingers digging into my flesh.

His possessiveness.

His dominance.

The sheer size of his cock sheated inside me, filling me, fucking my brains out until I'm no more than a glimmering puddle of afterglow.

~

The following morning, Leo and I are dressed and back to business as usual. Our eyes speak volumes. Our bodies long for one another. My soul aches, muted underneath the layers of winter as we head back to his car and leave the cabin behind. We barely say a word to each other as the last of the snowflakes fall over a vastness of pristine white.

Once we're off the country road, those ancient pines quietly bidding us farewell forever, I give him a long look, admiring his profile while he keeps his eyes focused ahead. I remember kissing those lips. I remember him stretching my lips and deep-throating me like a beast last night. I remember him eating me whole and devouring every inch of me until we were nothing but shadows melting on the furry carpet in front of the fireplace, naked and covered in sweat.

I will remember it all forever, I think. I certainly don't want to forget a single second of this. My flesh aches in the sweetest way.

"You'll be safe here?" Leo asks as he drops me off at the train station in Abramtsevo. He gives me his coat to wear over my jacket. "It'll keep you warm."

"I'll be okay."

"Take it, Nikita. I don't want you freezing, not even for a minute."

I can't help but smile and decide not to refuse his coat. I put it on and get out of the car. "Alright then."

"You go straight home, okay?"

"Yes, thank you," I say, the duffel bag resting heavily on my shoulder. "Drive safe."

It's all I can say at this point. I'd ask him to stay, to take me to Moscow with him, but we agreed we'd be strangers again in the morning, and it's almost time to get back to reality. I've got a father in need of rescuing. A prima ballerina slot to earn. A life to build. It was fun, passionate, and intense. It was incredible to let myself be possessed and controlled the way I let Leo possess and control me.

Duty calls, however. And he knows it, too.

"I'll see you again, maybe?" Leo says, half-smiling from behind the wheel.

"Maybe," I mumble and shut the passenger door of his car.

Probably never again.

By the time I get home to Moscow, it's late in the afternoon. I scramble to get everything else of value that I can take to the pawnshop, and once I'm done, I take the duffel bag over to my father's apartment.

It's loaded with cash, this time, while my shoulders are loaded with tension, my mind loaded with anger and resentment. I am partially responsible, after all. He got in this sort of trouble because of me, because of my passion.

Upon reaching the front door, however, I notice something uncanny.

It's unlocked and slightly ajar.

I go in, greeted by silence and darkness.

"Dad?" I call out and turn the hallway light on first.

I gasp at the sight of a side table that was thrown over.

A broken vase and wilted flowers resting in a puddle of water on the floor.

Papers scattered everywhere. Droplets of blood smeared across the wall.

My father's phone tossed to the corner, the screen cracked.

Something happened here. Something awful.

CHAPTER 2

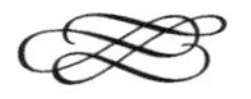

LEO

"Break his kneecaps."

My fingers twitch as I watch my younger brothers, Samuil and Roman, grab Erik Belov by either arm to hold him still while my half-brother, Damien, approaches with a crowbar in his hands.

I don't actually *want* to break Erik's kneecaps. It's an empty threat, one meant to spur a response out of him. Besides, I don't want to get blood on the carpet. Lord knows I'd never hear the end of it from Andrei. We're in his office. I'm just borrowing it while he's away.

"P-please!" Erik stutters. "Please, don't do this! I'll have the money for you by the end of the week—I swear!"

My fingers twitch again. I'm pretty sure I'm in need of a fresh nicotine patch. I gave up smoking two months ago at my sister-in-law's insistence going cold turkey has been a giant pain in my ass. I haven't picked up a cigarette yet, but no matter what I do, I can't seem to kick the craving. My tobacco addiction seems to rear its ugly head when I'm trying to collect on long overdue debts from deadbeat scumbags.

Like right now, for instance.

"We've been more than patient, Erik," I say slowly, my voice a low growl. "When you couldn't pay up at one of our gambling dens, my boys wanted to shoot you on site. Don't you agree that giving you the opportunity to pay us back later was more than generous?"

Erik Belov trembles. A thick layer of sweat paints his forehead with a sticky sheen, several thick beads of moisture dripping down his brow and cheeks. By my estimate, he's probably pushing sixty. His hair is thinning at the sides and bald at the top, what little he has left is a light gray. The man's complexion is blotchy—wrinkled and covered in sunspots. After I came back to Moscow following my mind-numbing snowstorm detour in Nikita's arms, I had Erik dragged out of his apartment and brought over here. He's been stewing for a few hours now, and I can tell he feels sorry for having crossed us.

But he'll find no pity from me. Anyone who dares to steal from the Bratva is a dead man walking. I gave him a second chance. It's not my fault he chose to squander it.

Erik quivers like a mouse. "I just need a little more time, One-Eye."

I cringe internally. One-Eye was a little nickname my sister-in-law, Sandra, lovingly gave me when we first met two years ago because I have, in fact, one good eye. My left was damaged in a knife fight ages ago, my vision reduced to nothing more than the slightest differentiation of shadows. It's a little on the nose, if you ask me, but the stupid nickname has stuck, and I frankly can't be bothered to try and change it.

Nikita didn't seem to care about it much. I'm still stunned by how responsive she was, by how surprised she was by her own willingness to submit. I shake the thoughts away, remembering where I am and what I'm supposed to do. *Back to the real world, One-Eye. That blizzard dream is over. She's gone.*

"Nine-hundred thousand rubles," I mutter. "Even if I gave you until the end of the week, where's a guy like you going to find that kind of money?"

"I'll think of something," Erik insists. "I'll sell everything I own, I'll borrow money from my family—I'll do *anything*. Please, I'm begging you."

I stay quiet, deliberately allowing him to stew in his own silence. I want him to understand just how serious this is. Because when it comes to money, I'm as serious as the plague.

In an official capacity, I'm the Bratva's numbers man. The accountant. I wasn't lying to Nikita when she asked me what I did for a living. There she goes again, crossing my mind. Every ruble, every kopeck... It all has to be accounted for. Business expenses, monthly profits, redistribution and laundering back into the system. That's my specialty. My bread and butter. Numbers are neat and logical. I find great joy in obsessing over every penny. An organization of our size is only as good as their bookkeeper otherwise everything falls apart at the seams.

I'm more than aware there's no glory in keeping diligent financial records. People think being a criminal is all about violence and firepower. Flashy cars, jewels, and women. Wannabe gangsters are only after the fortune, the parties, the lifestyle. But the truth of the matter is, you can't just take what you want and expect to get away with it.

To us, this is a business. A legacy that will hopefully last for generations to come. What differentiates my brothers and me from the run-of-the-mill street-dealing hustler is that we're *smart*. We cover our tracks. The police can't bring you in for a crime they can't trace back to you. *Follow the money*, as the old adage goes, but if I've done everything correctly—the cops will chase themselves in circles until the end of time.

I exhale heavily, giving Erik a cold glare down the length of my nose. Nine-hundred thousand rubles is peanuts to the Bratva—we make that amount in a day—but I can't very well let him off the hook. There's a lesson to be taught here. Erik has the misfortune of being made into an example. If word gets out that the Antonov-Nicolaevich Bratva is willing to forgive being stolen from if you piss your pants hard enough, it'll do irreparable damage to our reputation.

"Friday," I state firmly. "By seven pm. If I don't have that money in front of me..." I trail off, seeing no point in finishing my sentence. My threat feels much heavier now that it lingers in the air, unfinished.

"R-right," he stammers. "Of course. Thank you. Thank you so much."

I wave a hand dismissively, signaling to my brothers to take him away. Damien throws a black cloth bag over Erik's head, and Samuil throws him over his shoulder to carry him out.

Nothing bad is going to happen to the man. This is all for the sake of appearances and keeping our current location a secret. Nobody needs to know the Bratva works out of the Nicolaevich Brothers Taxi Company depot. We're just going to toss him into the back of one of our vehicles, drive around the block a couple of times so Erik's all turned around, and then we'll send him on his merry way until Friday.

"Well, *One-Eye*," Roman says with a cheeky grin. "What are we going to do when the poor fucker can't pay up? Do we drive him out to a nice lake somewhere and have him look at the ducks?"

"He'll pay."

"You sound so sure."

"One way or another, we're going to get that money back. Either in cash, or we'll find a way to make him work for it."

Roman puts his hands up in mock surrender. "If you say so."

"Why are you still standing there? Don't you have work to do?"

"Are you so eager to get rid of me, brother?" Roman clicks his tongue, a sudden realization twinkling behind that smug face of his. "Oh, I know. You're still trying to hunt down our skimmer?"

I grit my teeth, swallowing my annoyance. My fingers twitch again, eager for a cigarette to hold. I settle for a nearby pen.

For the past three months, I've noticed an anomaly when tabulating the books. It started small at first, a couple of rubles here and there. I chalked it up to minor miscalculations somewhere in our lieutenants' reports. Nothing overly concerning, though it did warrant a long, boring speech about due diligence. Things were perfectly fine after that.

Until two weeks ago—around the middle of November —when I found a series of miscalculations yet again. This time, hundreds of thousands of rubles missing. To say I'm irritated about not realizing sooner is an understatement. Nothing is supposed to get past me, especially something as egregious as this. Someone within our ranks has been helping themselves to my family's money, all while under my nose.

Whoever they are, they're clever enough to only take

small amounts at one time, and always infrequently. There's no pattern to it, no way to predict when it will happen again. And since most of our illicit operation is cash-based and filtered through our taxi company, it's damn near impossible to track. Now I have the wonderful task of picking through every single one of our businesses to find out where our skimmer has been lifting funds from.

At the rate things are going, it looks like they're saving up for one hell of a Christmas celebration. They could buy themselves a brand-new luxury BMW with how much they've managed to steal from us. I guess it's true what they say: there's no honor amongst thieves.

It's a fucking insult is what it is. I refuse to let them get away with it any longer.

"I'm dealing with it," I grumble. "Now, get out so I can concentrate."

"I think we should tell Andrei."

Slowly, I rise from my chair and shake my head. "He doesn't need to know yet."

"But—"

"Andrei and Sandra are enjoying some well-deserved time away with their kids. This happened on my watch, so I'll be the one to deal with it. He does too much for us and asks for little in return. I see no sense in bothering him with something this trivial."

Roman smiles, cocky as ever. "Calm down, Mister Bleeding Heart. I just wanted to know if we should keep him in the loop, that's all."

"I have everything under control."

"You do?" When I glare at him, Roman throws his head back and laughs. "I mean, you do!"

"Nice save," I mutter.

"Oh, don't be such a grump. Christmas is around the

corner. Don't want to end up on Santa's naughty list, do you?"

"Has anyone ever told you how annoying you get around the holidays?"

"I'm annoying all the time," my brother shoots back with a wink.

"That's not something to be proud of."

"It's part of my charm."

"Nothing about you is charming."

"Tell that to the three pretty ladies I'm taking out to dinner tonight." I'm not sure what my face does, but I'm sure it accurately reflects my disgust because Roman then says, "I know, right? They're into sharing or whatever. I bet you're jealous."

I pinch the bridge of my nose and sigh. "I'm not jealous. I'm just worried about my man whore of a brother catching an STD."

"Aww, you *do* care!"

"Get out before I shoot you between the eyes."

Roman chuckles. "I'm going, I'm going. You need to learn to relax, Leo. How about I set you up with one of my dates tonight?"

"Fuck off."

He shrugs as he starts toward the exit. "Suit yourself. I'll leave you here to count your coins, Ebeneezer."

"Knock it off with that shit."

Roman laughs his way out the door. Truth be told, I'm still reeling from Nikita's sweet, wet warmth. Her moans of pleasure and submission still echo in the back of my brain. I went up to that cabin to clear my mind and figure out a way to catch the skimmer. I certainly didn't expect to find a hot damsel stranded on the side of the road, a damsel whose body sang whenever I touched her. I'll stick to counting my coins, thank you, and wondering if our paths will ever cross again.

~

I stay at the taxi depot until the night shift manager, Arman, clocks in. We hired him many years ago, when our taxi company was still learning to walk and our ventures into the criminal underworld were nothing more than an idea. He's not much of a talker, but I think that's one of the things I like most about him. When Arman comes to work, I never have to worry about wasting my breath with pointless small talk.

He's a diligent man. Always shows up on time, never complains about the late nights or long hours. And what's more, he never sticks his nose where it doesn't belong. Arman doesn't ask questions about my brothers' oddly timed comings and goings, nor does he seem particularly interested in finding out. All in all—the perfect employee.

The rest of the night shift shows up not long after. I know each and every one of them by name. There's Vlad whose breath reeks of garlic and onions, but he's never without a smile. Georgi, a kid mid-way through college who works here part-time to earn a little extra on the side. And then there's Kostya. He's the shiftiest son of a bitch I've ever laid my good eye on, but he puts in the hours and never so much as grumbles.

They're a good group, good enough to manage the taxi company while my brothers and I get some well-deserved rest. There have admittedly been a couple of times when I questioned if one of the skimmers could be amongst their ranks, but none of them know about my family's involvement with the Bratva. My brothers and I have been careful to draw the line between our two worlds, cautious not to involve those who have no business knowing. Besides, I doubt any of them have the balls to steal from the likes of me. They're working men, not crooks.

"One of our drivers called out sick," I inform Arman as I pull on my black winter overcoat. "And six of our cars were pulled in for maintenance, so you're working with a smaller fleet tonight. The cold snap this morning shocked the engines."

Arman nods. "Thanks for letting me know, boss."

"Call me if anything unexpected crops up."

"Will do."

And that's that. Nice and painless.

I leave through the back doors of the depot and head to my car. It's nothing special, just the latest model of the Lada Granta in a sleek jet black. As joint heads of the Bratva with his wife, Andrei doesn't particularly approve of us being flashy. Frankly, I agree with him. Showboating is the fastest way to draw the wrong kind of attention. My younger brothers

understand this to varying degrees—Roman being the worst of the bunch with his weakness for parties and arm candy.

The drive home takes less than twenty minutes, most of the day's traffic thinned out into the wee hours of the evening. A thin layer of snow has started to build up on the pavement, a light flurry sweeping over Moscow. Many businesses have taken to putting up colorful twinkling lights ahead of the busy holiday season, little bulbs winking brighter than the stars above.

I'm only a few blocks away from my apartment complex when I spot something up ahead. A familiar face. Erik Belov, standing on the edge of the pavement, looking small and meek under his grey overcoat, his hair still a mess from the earlier feather ruffling in Andrei's office. He's waiting for someone. A yellow taxi pulls over across the street and honks twice. One of the backseat passenger windows slides down, and a woman's hand waves at Erik. I notice the look of surprise on his face, recognizing her. Suddenly, he is illuminated with relief.

I slow down to let him cross, holding back a smile as I wonder if he can even see me at this point. He glances my way and to the right, then bolts straight for the taxi, scuttling across the street like a scared little lemming.

Shaking my head slowly, I drive right by. It's none of my concern. He's free of me until Friday at seven p.m. There's nothing I want more than to go home, kick up my feet, and help myself to a finger of premium vodka until I catch a glimpse of the passenger —merely a fleeting moment that rattles me to the core.

A young woman. Blonde hair pulled up into a messy bun, her locks so light and soft the strands almost look silver.

I've seen her before. I must've. But I'm farther up the road now, and there's enough traffic flowing both ways that I can't turn the car around to have a better look without catching some cop's eye. It's a double continuous line here, and I've already spotted the traffic police stationed on the right side just ahead. These boys need to get their quota of fines on a daily basis, and I have no intention of giving them any more money than what they're skimming off the rest of these fools.

Nikita. She reminded me of Nikita. It couldn't be her though. She lives up north. I left her behind days ago. Damn, she really left a mark on me since I keep seeing her face everywhere I look.

It's best if we never see each other again.

CHAPTER 3

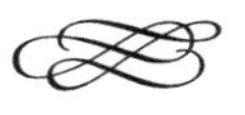

NIKITA

I hope I get to see him again.

Even after the horrendous days that I've had, desperately trying to find my father after I found his apartment door open and his place trashed, I can't stop thinking about Leo, about his brooding presence, the darkness in his expression, the invisible, crushing weight he seemed to carry on his wide shoulders. Everything about him was so *serious*—from his dark black hair, sharp nose, strong jaw and his scarred eye.

Most people might be afraid of a man like Leo. In fact, a sane person probably would have declined his offer of help out of a need for self-preservation. Something in his stance radiated power and danger, but I wasn't afraid. The feeling in my gut told me Leo only wanted to help. He wasn't going to hurt me. And he didn't. Instead, he claimed me for hours on end, consuming me until there was nothing left of me, yet I had plenty more to give him. I still get wet just remembering that night and the first few hours of that following morning. His coat is all I have to remember him by, tucked away in my dresser. More than once, I took it out to smell it, to try to remind myself of our night together.

If Mother ever found out, though, she'd scold me for being so naive. Foolish. But I try not to judge a book by its cover. I'd rather assume the best and be proven wrong, than assume the worst and be proven right.

Leo proved himself to be a knight in shining armor—his rough edges, general gloominess, and stark manner of speaking aside. And I got my father back in one messy piece in the end, though not without me giving him a piece of my mind. I wonder what Mother would say if she found out about Dad's latest blunder. She'd tear him a new one, for sure. All's well that ends well, right? No harm, no foul? I'm sure I can find a few more expressions to hastily describe this past week while I pretend that everything is okay, even when I know it's anything but. My father is in deep trouble, and I'm about to pay the price in order to keep him alive. He may have a complicated relationship with my mother, but I cannot imagine a world without them in it.

"Nikita!" Inessa snaps from the front of the practice room. "Focus! Turn your feet out more. Why are your movements so sloppy this morning?"

I grip the barre tight, forcing a sharp breath in through the nose to help kick start my concentration. I'm horrified to discover that I'm horrendously off-beat, the jovial piano tune and the rest of the ballet company carrying on without me. Instead of racing to catch up, I simply pause, take a deep breath, and then rejoin them with the next warm-up sequence. I'm thankfully back on track, but Inessa's face is still pinched and sour.

There's just no pleasing Mother.

We go through our usual routine. Next comes the guided stretches, then center work, reverence, and then pointe work. By the time we're through, I'm dripping with sweat and red in the face—but I'm having the time of my life. There's nothing more gratifying than the warm hum of my muscles and the light, satisfying burn in my lungs after a morning spent on the tips of my toes.

"Your fouettés are so beautiful," Kseniya says to me after class is done. She's a fellow soloist with gorgeous brunette locks and sparkling green eyes. She's a few years younger than myself—only nineteen—but there are whispers going around that she's likely going to be made a principal dancer after the new year.

I bite down the ugly green feeling of jealousy that rises inside me, forcing the thought away. Kseniya is a wonderful dancer. I try to tell myself I should be happy for her success, that she deserves it. Being happy for others costs nothing, after all. It's just...

It's just that I turned twenty-four the past March and haven't been making any progress. There's nothing more terrifying than the thought of my career at the Bolshoi stagnating. Most ballerinas retire between thirty to forty years of age, which means I'm quickly running out of time. I thought I'd be further along by now. Not to sound boastful, but my skills as a dancer are top tier. I'm good at what I do.

But maybe I'm not good *enough.*

All my classmates at the Vaganova Academy of Russian Ballet have already made their soloist debuts. *Giselle, Swan Lake, Don Quixote...* What I wouldn't give to earn one of my dream roles, to feel the heat of the spotlight on my skin and listen to the thunderous applause of a captivated crowd. It's a terrible feeling—being left behind.

It stings twice as much this year because we're putting on a performance of *The Nutcracker* in December and the role I wanted—the Sugar Plum Fairy—went to Vanya, the

Bolshoi's star soloist. I was relegated to nothing more than her understudy. In all honesty, the announcement didn't come as a surprise, but that didn't mean I wasn't disappointed. I've wanted to be the Sugar Plum Fairy since I was old enough to stand on pointe. I even auditioned for it this year, too. Needless to say, my ego's been crushed into a fine powder.

"Do you want to grab lunch with me today?" Kseniya asks with a sweet smile. "That cute café around the block has the best fruit parfaits."

I reflect her smile. Kseniya is probably one of my closest friends at the company, which is saying something considering we rarely hang out outside of the studio. We eat, breathe, *live* ballet and that usually means very little energy for much else. Which is why my brief trip up to Loza was such an effort, to begin with. Had Leo not found me that night, I don't know if I would've made it back in time for rehearsals. I don't even know if I would've made it safely back home at all.

Professional ballerinas like us—we're obsessive. Dedicated to the craft, the process, the performance. Well-rounded individuals we most certainly are not—and we wouldn't have it any other way.

"Actually," I reply after a moment of mulling things over, "a fruit parfait sounds really nice. Let me just grab some water and—"

"You're not going anywhere, Nikita."

My head snaps up. Approaching quickly and gaining speed is none other than my mother. Inessa and I don't really look alike. I got my blonde hair and blue eyes from Dad. The only thing I inherited from Mother was our shared love of ballet. Back in the day, Inessa was a star. Her face and name were known throughout Russia. The younger dancers in the company talk about her like she's a legend—she *is* a legend—with reverence and awe when she enters the room. Her technique, perfect. Her artistry, unparalleled. Her instruction, invaluable.

I, of course, know the truth.

Inessa Belova is nothing but a tyrant in a sleek bun and wooly leg warmers, chasing after her glory days through her daughter. On some base level, I think everybody knows it. I hear their whispers in the changing rooms, the gossip surrounding me at every turn.

Poor Nikita got yelled at again.

She's just not as good as Inessa once was.

I can't imagine that kind of pressure.

She didn't get a promotion. Again.

"Vanya's going to be here any moment," Mother says. "You need to be here taking notes as her understudy."

I want to protest but think better of it. We're doing the Grigorovich variation, which is as classic as it gets. I've memorized every single move synchronized with every note of the music at this point. Asking me to stay behind would be redundant since I won't actually get the chance

Someone screams. It's a cry of a woman, the sound so chilling it causes the hairs on my arms to stand on end. Panic sweeps through the entire room, whispers and concerned glances passing between the dancers.

"What's going on?" Inessa snaps, rushing toward the door.

I hurry after her, my heart racing in my throat. My hand flies to my mouth, horrified at what I see. Vanya, dressed and prepped for rehearsal, sits on the floor, reaching down to hold her foot. Her face is twisted in agony, tears streaming down her eyes, her mascara a running river of black. When I look down at her shoes, I realize something is terribly wrong.

Her pointe shoes are bloody.

"S-someone put pins inside!" she wails. "Oh my God, who would do this?"

I want to vomit, a wave of disbelief and terror shredding through me. This is too cruel, too vicious. I don't understand who among us would be depraved enough to hurt Vanya—or any fellow dancer, for that matter—in such an awful, potentially career-ending way.

"Someone call the doctor!" I shout, rushing to her side. "Quickly!"

Vanya clutches my hand, trembling hard as she sobs. "It hurts!"

"We need to get her shoes off," I tell my mother.

The damage to Vanya's feet doesn't look too bad, but with our first show only a couple weeks away, there's no way she'll be able to recover in time. This whole thing is incredibly disturbing. No way this was an accident. It was sabotage.

Inessa glares at me. "What are you still doing here? Get back inside and get ready."

I furrow my brows. "What?"

"I'll make sure the doctor takes a look at her. *You* need to start practicing for opening night."

The weight of Inessa's words doesn't truly hit me until I've made my way back into the practice room, dazed and numb. This isn't right. This isn't what I wanted. It's a huge honor to be able to play such an important role in the upcoming ballet, but did I truly earn it?

I stare at my reflection in the floor-to-ceiling mirrors, studying my form. There's no time to waste. I have a lot to prove and everything to lose. Now isn't the time to let my inner doubts win. It's time to introduce this understudy to the limelight.

~

By the time I get home, I'm bone-tired and ready for bed. I can still hear Inessa's shrill voice shouting corrections at me.

Point your feet.

Why aren't you smiling?

Don't flap your arms like that, have a little grace!

All things considered, I thought I managed rather well. Not that my mother had anything encouraging to say.

"Has there been any news about Vanya?" I ask her as we approach our apartment door. We used to live here with Dad until Mother sent him away on account of his gambling issues. She didn't care that he did it for us, for me—in particular. The shame he brought upon us was too much to bear, so he's been living away for a few months now.

Normally, he'd be home from the dealership by now. He works Mondays to Fridays selling cars, though he's always had dreams of becoming a writer—something he's only ever confided in me and not my mother.

"Nothing yet," Inessa grumbles. "But we'll get to the bottom of this one way or another."

"I think I'll buy her some flowers."

"You're probably the last person she wants to see right now."

I frown as Mother jams the keys into the lock. "What do you mean?"

"Really think about it, Nikita. Use that brain of yours. If your understudy got to take over weeks before your performance after a blatant sabotage attempt, would you want to see her?"

My mouth drops open. "You can't possibly think I had anything to do with this. I could never—"

"I know," Mother interrupts. She roughly smooths her hand over my hair—the closest thing to affection she can muster. "You're too sweet to do such a terrible thing. Just be careful, that's all."

"It's just so strange. Vanya doesn't have any enemies. Everybody adores her."

Inessa shrugs. "Don't be foolish. We *all* have enemies. It's just a matter of knowing where to look. Rest assured, the administration is looking into this. They're taking it very seriously."

When we step into the apartment, the lights are off. Unusual, until I remember who's not around anymore. Dad would normally be on the couch watching TV by now or flitting around the kitchen to help with dinner. I've had plans for a while now to move into my own place, but rent isn't cheap on a ballerina's salary, and more often than not, Inessa and I carpool to and from work together so it just makes sense to continue to live with my parents.

I hear a strange shuffling sound coming from my room. Something—*someone*—is rummaging through my stuff. Curious and a bit alarmed, I tiptoe down the hall cautiously, reaching around the edge of my door frame to flick on the light.

"Dad?" I call out.

He whips around, shoving his hands into his pants pockets. He smiles sheepishly, but it doesn't reach his eyes. He's sweaty for some reason, his cheeks flushed and his eyes watery. "Nikita!" he exclaims with an uneasy chuckle. "Welcome home. How was everything today?"

I stare at him, trying to pick through my questions. Where do I even begin? I want to tell him I'm going to be a soloist. I want to tell him about the pins in Vanya's shoes. I want to ask him what the hell he's doing rummaging through my things, but I can't find the words to form proper sentences.

"Dad, what are you doing here?"

He glances over my shoulder with an anxious swallow. "Is your mother here?"

"In the kitchen. Dad, you're not supposed to be here. I thought Mother took your key away."

"I always keep spares," he shoots back with a dry smirk.

"What are you doing here?" I ask again, my voice lower this time. The last thing I want is Mother overhearing us, especially after I had to hail a cab and pick my own father off the side of the road after he called me. I was still looking for him at the time, nearing the edge of madness and about to file a police report. He thinks I'm not aware of his troubles, but I know. I've been pawning stuff just to get money together to save his ass.

He gets up close, shifty and breathless. "I'm sorry, Nikita," he says, barely a whisper. "I'd, uh... I'd appreciate it if you didn't tell your mother."

Concern lances through me. "You're really starting to freak me out. What's going on?"

He rubs the back of his neck. "I... forgot to pay a bill. The rent."

My face falls. "Oh, that's okay. It happens—" Of course, I'm faking it. He wouldn't tell me what happened when I picked him up in the cab. The man's ego is too big, too fragile, and I still don't know how to handle him, sometimes. I keep telling him to get his head screwed back on so he and Mother can make peace, so he can move back here, but I feel as though I've been screaming at the walls lately.

"Things at the dealership... I wasn't able to make very much in commission this month, so I'm a bit behind. "

It's not exactly a lie. What he's earning from the dealership isn't enough to cover his Bratva debt. I keep looking over my shoulder, my ears twitching as I listen to Mother's activities in the kitchen. She can't find him here, like this. Inessa is just as strict at home as she is at the ballet. My whole life has been spent walking on eggshells, afraid to be on the tail end of her disapproval. She's not *all* bad—but she's definitely more prickly than soft.

"How much money do you need?" I ask gently, without a hint of judgment. "I have money saved, you know that. I can just lend it to you and—"

"No, no," he says hurriedly. "That money is for your future."

"But Dad—"

"I'll figure something out." The way he forces his smile even wider makes my heart twist. Maybe I should just confront him and tell him I know everything. I hate seeing the two of us lie to each other like this.

"Can't we just talk to the landlord? I'm sure he'd be willing to work things out with us. We've always been good tenants."

Dad nods, casting his gaze to the floor. "You're right. You're absolutely right. I'm sorry I got so flustered. I should go."

"Don't let her see or hear you," I tell him.

He nods once and shuffles off. I don't hear the front door as he leaves the apartment, which means Inessa didn't hear it, either. Good. I inspect the wooden clothing drawer which is stuffed full of athletic wear—shirts, sweaters, tights, an endless supply of leg warmers. At first glance, I find nothing amiss. I don't know what he was looking for, but I don't think he found it. Hell, I don't know what's going through his head these days or why he does certain things anymore. He is desperate. And whether he likes it or not, I am going to help him. The sooner he's safe and back with us, the better. I remember overhearing Mother when they were arguing, when she flat out told him she knew he was indebted to the Bratva on account of his gambling. I haven't been able to look at him the same since, but he is still my father, and I still owe much of who I am today to this man.

"Nikita!" Inessa snaps from down the hall. "Come eat and then go to bed! We have an early morning tomorrow."

I take a deep breath and try to collect my thoughts. This has been a whirlwind of a day. I sincerely hope I'm not swept off my feet.

CHAPTER 4

LEO

Money is very much like water. It comes and it goes. You can hold onto it tight, but it will still find a way to slip through your fingers.

My goal isn't to hoard every kopeck. It's to spread it out and make it blend in with the hundreds upon thousands of transactions that happen every day. Money laundering is no small feat. It takes a great deal of planning, diversifying our investments and spreading such a large net even if the police are competent enough to follow the trail—which they aren't—it'll take them forever to put together a case against us.

Buying out small businesses, investing in stocks, and occasionally making donations to help keep the Nicolaevich Brothers Taxi Company's public image squeaky clean. It's all a part of a grander plan, one that demands my utmost concentration.

Charlotte barges into my office without so much as a *how do you do*, her red hair swaying from side to side behind her as she walks. "I'm taking the family to see *The*

Nutcracker!" she announces, waving a set of tickets in front of her face like a fan. "Box seats, too. *Very* fancy shindig."

I don't bother looking up from my computer screen. I'm mid-way through a calculation and refuse to break focus. "Don't you know how to knock?"

The only reason I put up with Charlotte is because she's the twin sister of my sister-in-law, Sandra. Charlotte was born the second eldest Antonov by mere minutes, and when our two Bratvas merged, her position of authority transferred along with her. She isn't very hands-on and doesn't play the biggest role in day-to-day operations, but as a ranking lieutenant, she helps out on occasion by checking in on our businesses in the northern districts. I'm only ever forced to tolerate her existence at the rare family function—

And when she shows up unannounced.

"Lighten up, you grouch," she says with a light laugh. She sounds exactly like Sandra, which makes sense since they're identical twins. They're nothing alike personality-wise, though, which is how I'm so easily able to tell them apart.

"I'm not going to watch the stupid ballet."

"Not with that attitude, you're not."

"I have too much work to do."

Charlotte arches a brow. "You're telling me you never take a day off?"

"No."

"Well, this time you're going to make an exception."

"Don't want to."

Charlotte slaps my ticket down on the desk before me. "You're coming."

"Or what?"

"I'll kill you."

I glare up at her. "I'd like to see you try, Cee."

"Will you at least think about it? Even Samuil's going, and you know how much he hates this kind of thing."

I'll admit I'm impressed by this. My brutish enforcer of a brother at the ballet watching pretty women in pink tutus and tights? It's too difficult for me to imagine. She must have forced his hand somehow. What sort of blackmail did Charlotte use to convince him to go? It's terrifying to think about.

"Get out," I grumble. "I have work to do."

Charlotte bats her eyelashes and pouts her lips. "You're not coming to lunch with us? Your brothers and I are going to try that new restaurant, *La Croix*, downtown."

My ears perk up. "Tell Roman to speak with the owner. I want to get the ball rolling and see if we can't get a cut going forward. If that doesn't work, we'll send Samuil and Damien in to convince them."

Charlotte squints at me. "You're an even bigger workaholic than Andrei, you know that?"

"That'll be all, Cee."

"Love you too, jerkface. Don't come whining to me when you get hungry."

"I'm a big boy. I'm sure I can take care of myself."

With a huff, Charlotte slides the ticket forward across my desk before turning on her heel to saunter out. I'm glad to know she likes me as much as I like her—which is barely at all and only because we're technically family.

I'm about to shove the ticket aside and get back to my work, but a sudden idea pops into my head as I study the Bolshoi Theatre's logo printed on the far right. I'm always on the lookout for ways we can filter our illicit funds back into the system. If I ran a significant portion of the Bratva's profits through the taxi company, then through the theater as a sponsor, it would certainly take a massive weight off my shoulders and make it twice as hard for the cops to trace.

I smile to myself, the gears in my head turning in perfect harmony.

Well there's an idea.

Looks like I might owe Charlotte a thank you—though I'd much rather drop dead and die than admit it.

"This is a most generous offer, Mr. Nicolaevich," the director general says, continuing to shake my hand vigorously. He's a stout little man in his late seventies, his ugly brown suit expensive but ill-fitting. He perfectly encapsulates my opinion of the art world—stuffy, elitist, and out-of-touch with reality. "We would be more than happy to have your company as a sponsor. We can talk details in my office, if you'd like—"

"No need. As I've said, my brothers and I are happy to make an annual contribution of one million rubles. In exchange, you'll promote the limousine division of our transportation company through appropriately displayed logos and banners at your functions."

The director general smiles wide. "Of course, of course. I'll have the paperwork—"

"Send it to my office. I'll have it signed and returned."

I check my wristwatch. It's getting late. I wanted to take care of this over the phone, but it's surprisingly difficult to get an appointment. I frankly don't have the patience to sit around waiting for someone to return my calls. The fastest way to get shit done is to show up in person, demand to speak to the person in charge, and get straight to the point. If all else fails, mentioning large sums of money always tends to grab people's attention.

"It's a pleasure to support the arts," I mutter stiffly.

"Won't you at least stay for a tour?" the director asks me. "It's only right that I show such an honorable patron around. I think dance rehearsals are underway, actually."

I'm tempted to say no. I've done what needed to be done. There are a million other things I have to take care of as the Bratva's second-in-command, not to mention the pressing issue of finding the damn rat who's been stealing from us. But I guess I have to lay the groundwork here. A representative from a taxi company showing up out of the blue to offer a sponsorship deal... That'd look suspicious any day of the week. I have to at least *pretend* to be interested in this place in case anyone starts asking questions.

I force a smile. I don't think it translates very well because the director shrinks back a little. Sometimes I wish I had Andrei's confidence or Roman's easy air. "A tour sounds great," I manage to say through gritted teeth.

The building is an architectural marvel and has a rich history that dates back to the late eighteenth century, but I've never been particularly interested in that sort of thing. The humanities are subjective. I'd much prefer the cold hard truths of math and science. There are no surprises—just the way I like it.

He shows me to the main theater, points out where our company logos will be placed on banners. I get to see the props room, the service elevator backstage, the pit where the orchestra sits as the dancers or opera singers perform. I nod along, my interest fleeting.

That is, until we go downstairs to one of the many practice rooms.

We step in quietly. A pianist is tinkering at the keys playing the first familiar notes of Tchaikovsky's *Dance of the Sugar Plum Fairy*. It's bright in here, so much so it kind of hurts my eyes. The air conditioning is on despite the fact that we're in the middle of winter, likely to help the dancers keep cool. A handful of men and women dressed in mismatched athletic wear stand off to the side, some seated against the wall as a ballerina moves across the room in time with the music.

Or more accurately, *floats* across the room.

Everything happens in slow motion. I see her hair first, bright like starlight. Then the shape of her lips, pulled into a wide smile as she twirls in place. She moves like she's made of water, flowing with the elegance and grace of a gentle stream. Even though her brow is covered in sweat, she looks elated to be here. She's mid-spin when our eyes lock. Nikita.

The one who took my breath away.

Maybe I *do* owe Charlotte a thank you, after all.

"You..." She breathes, her chest rising and falling from the exertion of her routine. Her look of momentary surprise transforms into a sweet smile. "Hi."

It takes a lot to leave me speechless, yet she's somehow done it again. I can hardly believe my luck. What is she doing here? Why is she staring at me like that? Well, I'm asking myself a dumb question considering the many hours of frantic lovemaking we burned back at my cabin that night. Clearly, I made a lasting impression.

"Do they know each other?"

"Who is he?"

"*Hey*!" comes the shrill voice of an older woman at the front of the room. She claps her hands together harshly, louder than a gunshot and just as startling. She's the instructor, I assume. The ballet master, or whatever the proper term is supposed to be, dressed from head to toe in black. If I didn't know any better, I'd mistake her for a mourner. "What do you think you're doing? I didn't tell you to stop, Nikita."

Nikita.

Her name echoes around inside my skull. It's beautiful, just like her. Mesmerizing and lovely and delicate. Nikita looks like a princess, her hair up in a bun with a thin white skirt wrapped around her waist. Every inch of her is beautiful. Slender and lean, but incredibly strong. I like the dips of her collar bones, the length of her neck, and the curve of her hips. The sight of her milky skin makes my mouth water. I'd missed every inch of her, more than I thought I would, and I'm only realizing this now upon seeing her again. Clearly, she made a lasting impression on me, too.

The gorgeous ballerina before me chews on the inside of her cheek, addressing the ballet master. "I'm sorry, I—"

"I distracted her," I speak up. "It was my fault."

"And who are *you*?" she hisses, hands bolted to her hips. "This is a closed practice room. If you're with the administration, you're going to have to come back later to investigate the sabotage incident. We're trying to work!"

My ears perk up. Sabotage incident? I decide not to ask further questions. It doesn't concern me.

The director general steps forward and quickly whispers something in the woman's ear. I hear him mention something about *one million*, but that's all I hear. Whatever he says to her results in a quick change of tune. Her entire demeanor suddenly shifts. She smiles, lips curling up with fake enthusiasm.

"Oh, I see! A sponsor. Why didn't you start with that?" She sticks out her bony hand. "I'm Inessa Belova."

My jaw ticks. Belova? Like Erik Belov? Surely it must be a coincidence. After all, Belov is a common name in Moscow.

I shake her hand, if only to keep up appearances. "Leo Nicolaevich."

Inessa grips the dancer by the shoulders and pulls her in. I don't miss the way her nails dig into the poor girl's shoulders. "And this is Nikita, our season's debut soloist. She is also my daughter."

Nikita offers me her hand and I'm far more inclined to take it, carefully grasping her fingers to bring up to my lips. I press a gentle kiss to her knuckles without thinking. My mind is no longer my own. Her presence has entranced me, her beauty hypnotizing as always. The softness of her skin and the faint scent of her floral perfume makes my chest tight. I breathed her in so many times that night, yet her presence still slams into me like a tidal wave.

I'm not a particularly religious man, but the seductive blue of her eyes is nothing short of a holy experience. Otherworldly.

And nothing short of my own personal hell.

My fingers twitch. I bite down on my tongue. I don't know what to say. This woman has me tongue-tied, and that doesn't happen to me. *Ever*. I don't like this feeling. This strange, out-of-control sensation where all I want to do is stare at her pretty face and forget that the rest of the world exists. When I first picked her off the road, we were strangers. I had a feeling I'd never see her again, so I operated with a different sort of confidence. Now that our paths seem intent on crossing again, something has happened. A shift within me that I cannot control.

"I didn't mean to interrupt your practice," I say gruffly. I don't trust my voice right now. Not when she smells so tantalizingly good.

Nikita takes a breath and opens her mouth to speak. "Oh, that's really okay. I was just—"

"She needed a break anyway," Inessa interrupts. I don't

like this woman. Something about her rubs me the wrong way.

"Would you like to take a seat and watch?" the director asks me, gesturing to the rows of elevated seats at the back of the practice room. There's space for at least twenty observers. Some of the chairs are taken up by dancers' belongings—bags and jackets strewn about—but I spot a pair of seats in the very back, hidden beneath the cover of the shadow cast by the angled ceiling above.

My first instinct is to say no. I only came here to make an opportunity for myself and the Bratva. This is supposed to be a financial sleight of hand, nothing more. But one glance at Nikita... The moment her eyes find mine, I'm a goner. Again. Damn, the effect she has on me is undeniable and dangerously powerful.

"I'd love to watch," I murmur.

Inessa turns to the other dancers. "Let's pick up where we left off earlier—"

"No."

She frowns at me. "I beg your pardon?"

I tilt my chin in Nikita's direction. "I want to watch *her*."

CHAPTER 5

NIKITA

I don't get stage fright. A very long time ago, maybe, when I was four or five at my first recital, but not anymore. That is, until Leo Nicolaevich showed up.

I had to pinch myself on the thigh when he first walked into the room because I thought for sure I was hallucinating. What is he doing here? As delighted as I am to see him, the world isn't *that* small. How did he end up here? I told myself we'd never see each other again, yet as soon as our eyes met mere moments ago, my whole body came alive with the memories of our steamy night together. I can almost see the condensation on the inside of his cabin's windows, our legs tangled on the sofa, my skin soft and creamy against his. *Focus, Nikita. He's here, but so are you.*

Moving in time with the music, I try to block the rest of the world out. This dance is an expression of joy, of playfulness and wonder. I must embody the character, turn myself into an actor whilst quite literally keeping on my toes. In theory, I know all the steps—but actually putting everything into practice? Let's just say I'm rustier than I thought.

I've spent the last few months watching Vanya perform

this exact routine, but my movements are stiff with lack of practice. I tell myself it'll get easier. It isn't fair to compare myself to Vanya, who's had triple the amount of time to prepare. I have big shoes to fill, and I'm determined to prove to everyone how worthy I am of this role.

The glissade is easy enough, followed by a strong piqué first arabesque. I'll confess my back is tighter than I want it to be, making it difficult to arch. I can tell in the reflection of the practice room's mirrors that I'm not creating the right shapes with the length of my body, nor am I fast enough when it comes to my turns. I've been at it all morning, which explains the sharp pain in my toes and the building cramp in my calves, but I smile through it. Nobody truly understands that beneath all the effortlessness, ballerinas are under constant and arduous stress.

It's our job to look as light as a feather. It's our job to look beautiful, to follow through with elegant lines and hypnotizing flow. A loud minority of people out there think ballet is girly, that it isn't a real sport, but they couldn't be more wrong. I'd love to see a soccer player or a mixed martial artist jumping around on the tips of their toes all day, doing mid-air splits and bending over backwards just to keep coming back for more.

"Sloppy!" Inessa grumbles, snapping her fingers. "Tighter, Nikita. Your timing is off. Smile more, for God's sake. You're made of magic, remember? The Sugar Plum Fairy isn't trying to cast a curse."

I force my smile even wider even though every muscle in my body is screaming in pain. My cheeks hurt. I want to ask for a break, but one look around the room has me deciding against it. Mother was right when she said people would start to talk. All of my fellow colleagues watch me with intense scrutiny, more than a handful of them whispering to one another under their breaths. Their judgment weighs heavily on my skin, cold and clawing.

"Do you think she did it?" someone murmurs. I try to block out their voices and listen to the music. I need to focus.

"No way. She doesn't seem the type."

"I don't know. She's getting up there. Maybe she got desperate?"

"Stop it, guys," Kseniya tells them. "Nikita's the nicest person here. She'd never do such an awful thing."

Inessa clears her throat loudly. "Quiet! If you want to gossip, do it outside."

"Sorry, ma'am," comes the chorus.

The music ends and I finish well after the final bar. It's embarrassing. Heat pools in my cheeks. That definitely could have gone better, and the perfectionist in me is screaming bloody murder in the back of my head. I have to be so much better than this.

"Again," I say, even though my lungs burn and my muscles are strained to the point of snapping.

Inessa crosses her arms. "No, that's it for today."

"But—"

"We have to move on and you need to rest."

I want to argue, but out of the corner of my eye, I see movement. A large, hulking shadow at the back of the room.

Leo.

I was so focused on practice I almost forgot he was here. My stomach flips at the thought of him seeing all my mistakes. Did he really stay to watch that disaster? And why is he *still* watching me despite the fact that practice is over?

My heart stutters when our eyes lock. He's just so intense, but in an entirely different way than I'm used to. Dealing with Inessa and the rest of the dancers brings with it a certain level of judgment and snobbery. They know all the steps, what the dance is supposed to look like, and if my technique is perfect—which, at this stage, it's not. I don't think Leo understands ballet to quite the same extent. If anything, his gaze is full of intrigue. He's studies me, watching like a hawk.But I do know what to make of the dark hunger in his eyes and the way he shifts out of his chair and starts toward me.

I'm not nervous, per se. More like unsure. He's just so mesmerizing. Even though the other dancers have taken to the floor, there's no question all eyes are on him. He's far more interesting, a stranger to this place, yet he easily commands everyone's attention.

The man is—in a word—magnetic. I'm seeing him in a different light, now, away from the privacy of his cabin. I'm seeing him among other people, and he still dominates the room.

"That was beautiful," he says, his voice far gentler than I would have expected to come from a man of his size and stature. Then again, I've heard this tone before, early that morning, when he asked me if I wanted him to have me for breakfast. I said yes. I'd say yes again in a heartbeat.

For the first time in hours, my smile is bright and genuine. "I could have done better," I confess.

"I was surprised to see you here."

"You, too. I heard something about you being a new sponsor?"

"My company wants to find ways to give back to the community. Being a patron of the arts seemed like the way to do so."

"What kind of company?" I ask, thirsty for any and all facts. We never spoke much about our lives outside of that cabin.

"I'm part-owner with my brothers. The Nicolaevich Brothers Taxi Company."

"Oh, I thought you were an accountant."

"That is my main role with the company, yes."

:I've seen your taxis around the city! You guys are my go-to whenever I need a last-minute lift. Your drivers are always nice and speedy."

"I'm glad to hear it."

"Well, we're always grateful for the support."

I don't miss the way his eyes flit down to my lips and linger there for a few moments too long.

"Dinner," he says, blunt and to the point. "Tonight. Are you free?"

His question takes me by surprise. I'd honestly love to go out to dinner with him, but the moment I open my mouth to tell him yes, Mother Dearest decides that *now* is the time to stomp over.

"I don't think that's a very good idea," she says, her tone saccharine. I don't know who she thinks she's fooling. "Nikita has a very early morning tomorrow. And besides, she needs to watch her figure if she's going to fit into her costume."

Embarrassment floods my veins. I wish I could tell her to leave me alone, but as both my mother *and* technically my boss, I'm in no position to do either. For as long as I can remember, Inessa has policed every single aspect of my life. What I eat. When I go to bed and when I wake up. The kinds of friends I'm allowed to make—which is to say, next to none. I'd say yes to Leo in a heartbeat, but I can decipher Inessa's look of disapproval well enough.

"Sorry," I murmur to him.

Leo shakes his head. He doesn't seem offended, only mildly annoyed—and rightly so—at my mother's interference. "It's no matter. Perhaps another time." With a final dip of his head, he turns and stalks off, the director general following quickly on his tail.

Mother grips my wrist tightly. "Dodged a bullet there."

"What do you mean?"

"Were we even looking at the same person?" Inessa hisses. "What a nasty scar! He looks like trouble."

"You're being mean," I reply tersely. She can't know that we've already met in oh, so many ways. "He seems perfectly nice."

"Don't be foolish, Nikita. A man like that... He's bad news."

I clench my fists and grit my teeth. There she goes again calling me foolish. She says it so often that sometimes I wonder if it's true.

"Go cool down and go home," she tells me, already turning to address the rest of the ballet company. "Make sure to do your stretches. Your flexibility is abysmal."

I bite my tongue hard enough that I taste the bitter metal of iron. "Yes, Mother. Whatever you say."

CHAPTER 6

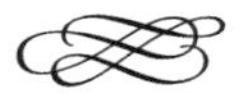

LEO

When I get back to the office later that evening, I bury myself in my work. I drown in the sea of numbers before me as I struggle to keep my head above water. The Bratva is bleeding money. It's not fatal, but we *are* in need of medical attention. The traitor in our midst is getting bolder by the day, more and more of our funds draining away somewhere I can't trace no matter how hard I try. I need to staunch the wound.

I debate whether or not I should be patient or turn over every stone in Moscow to find the rat bastard. Sooner or later, they're going to make a mistake that leads me right to them, but there's no telling when that will be. I don't like the thought of sitting idly by while they steal hundreds of thousands of rubles from us.

Fuck that.

It's a disgrace. It's an insult. And it cannot go unpunished.

I strum my fingers against the desk, uneasy and distracted by thoughts of Nikita. I can still see her, dancing across my mind with such startling beauty it's a struggle to concentrate on anything else.

I shouldn't have asked her out to dinner. That was a bad call on my part. Not because I didn't mean it, but because it wouldn't make sense. We don't match. Nikita is too sweet, too beautiful, and I'm... I'm from the other side of the tracks, from a completely different world. She exists where things are pristine, bright, and safe. I dwell in the criminal underbelly, danger and betrayal lurking around every corner. That night we had was supposed to be a one-off. That's it. That's all it can be. I have no business trying to pursue someone like Nikita.

She's a princess up in her tower.

I'm the troll that lives under the adjacent bridge.

"Knock knock!" Roman announces cheerfully as he enters. Funnily enough, he doesn't actually knock. I'm really going to have to start locking that damn door.

"Did you bring me the ledgers from the businesses in the south?" I ask him, getting straight to it.

"Sort of."

"The hell do you mean, *sort of*?"

Roman reaches into the inner pocket of his suit jacket and pulls out a list of printed names. There are roughly forty to fifty on the page, organized in neat columns and rows. All except one are crossed out.

"Kuznetsov & Sons Butcher Shop?" I read aloud.

"When I asked, they weren't able to pull up their records for me. *Misplaced them*, they said. They asked that I give them until the end of the week to produce them."

I arch a brow. "And you agreed?"

"Do I look like a sucker to you? Of course not. I gave them twenty-four hours."

My fingers twitch, an electric thrill rising in my chest.

This could prove promising. I'm not quite ready to pin the blame, but at least it's a step in the right direction.

"Twenty-four hours is too generous," I tell my brother. "Go back and refuse to leave until they can provide their records. Take Samuil with you. That ought to speed things along."

Roman gives me a soldier's salute, barely containing his smile. "Aye aye, captain. Now, what do you want me to do about the girl?"

"What girl?"

"The pretty blonde waiting out front. She's been asking for you by name."

My face twists in confusion. It couldn't possibly be...

I vacate my chair and stalk past my brother, my feet carrying me forward of their own volition. I recognize her silhouette first. Beautiful long legs and graceful arms. Then I'm hit by the stunning blue of her eyes and the soft wisp of her blonde locks, now free from the tight bun she wore earlier, spilling gently over her delicate shoulders. Nikita hasn't noticed me yet, too busy looking around the garage with innocent wonder and an intrigued smile. I take those few precious seconds to just watch her.

She doesn't belong here. Her light pink sweatshirt and soft white tights stand in stark contrast to the dirt and grime and rust of the taxi depot. Nikita is a bright spot in my field of vision, impossible to ignore. She is a beacon, drawing not only my eyes, but everyone else's. The mechanics, the drivers... They're all looking at her, some with curiosity, some with looks that make my blood boil.

Behind me, Roman whistles. "Pretty."

"Fuck off," I grumble.

"Do you know her?"

I set my jaw. "Go back to the butcher. This is a matter

of urgency." I stomp forward, determined to get to Nikita before any of my employees get to her first.

When she finally spots me, she breaks out into the most brilliant, breathtaking smile I've ever seen. It's like a damn flash-bang, except it's nowhere near as malicious. Her smile is more like a front-row seat at a fireworks show, thrilling beyond measure.

"Mr. Nicolaevich," she greets. "I'm glad I caught you."

"Leo, please."

I must admit, I do like how we pretend we've only just met. The adorable pink of her cheeks sends my heart skittering. She smells so nice, like candied peaches and cherry blossoms combined. I can't tell if I have her perfume or her shampoo to thank. Either way, it's a lovely break from the heavy scent of car exhaust surrounding us.

"Is there something I can help you with?" I ask her, unsure why I soften my tone. I just... don't want to frighten her. If Roman could hear me now, he'd probably tease me about it.

Nikita reaches into the large gym bag strapped over her shoulder, fishing out the overcoat I lent her the morning after the cabin escapade. I'd almost forgotten about it. She's folded it neatly, running her palm over the fabric like it's something precious. "I wanted to return this to you," she says. "I'm glad you showed up at the Bolshoi this morning or else I'd never have found out where you work."

I take my jacket from her with far more care than I've ever been able to muster. My body all but seizes when my fingers accidentally brush against hers. It was a brief, fleeting touch, but her skin is so soft it nearly sends my mind into a feral spin out. I'm suddenly desperate to feel the rest of her all over me again.The taste of her in my mouth.The sound of her moaning while I have her pinned beneath me with her legs wrapped around my hips.

"Leo?" she says, breaking me from my trance. "Are you alright?"

Ah, fuck. I might be in trouble.

"I'm fine."

Nikita sheepishly tucks a strand of her hair behind her ear. "So, listen... If your offer to go out to dinner is still on the table, I'd really love to take you up on it."

"You... really want to go out to dinner with me?"

I cringe internally at my own question. I hope that didn't sound as pathetic as I feel. It's just that... Well, she's out of my fucking league. I know it. The taxi drivers watching from their vehicles know it. I asked her out on a whim, unable to control myself. But this time, she's seeking *me* out, and I frankly don't have the mental capacity to comprehend what's going on. We may have agreed to a one-off, but Nikita doesn't seem content with just that anymore.

"Sure," she says in a chipper tone. "I'm sorry my mother interrupted us before. You seem really sweet despite your surliness, so I figured I'd try again?"

Sweet? Ha. If only she knew who she's really talking to. Then again, I kept most of myself tucked away during our night together. She remembers the dominance, the carnal debauchery, but we never actually sat down to just talk and get to know one another.

"But if you're too busy, I totally understand—"

"Dinner would be great," I say quickly. "I just need to tidy up my office, and then we can go."

Nikita beams. "Alright then."

~

La Croix, that new restaurant downtown Charlotte wanted to drag me to, is one of the most impressive fine dining establishments I've ever set foot in. Classy. Upscale. I'm sure it brings in the kind of clientele that can afford to throw a couple thousand rubles out the window for appetizers alone. That kind of profit margin could be incredibly beneficial to the Bratva.

"Uh, Leo?"

I turn and glance down at Nikita. "Something wrong?"

"Are you sure it's alright for me to come here?"

"Why wouldn't it be?"

She shifts, picking beneath her fingernails. "I'm a little underdressed."

I pause for a moment, baffled at my insensitivity. My name opens a lot of doors, so I'm sure they'll let us in regardless, but I should have taken Nikita's feelings into account.

"Would you prefer to go somewhere else?" I ask gently.

"I just don't want to get us into trouble, that's all."

I almost laugh. *Almost*. My family owns all of Moscow. Getting into trouble is impossible as far as I'm concerned.

"They'll let us in," I say firmly, offering her my elbow. When she slips her slender arm through, I've never been more nervous. She's so small, a little bird clinging to a beast triple her size. I'm not used to handling such fine crystal outside the bedroom, so to speak.

"I trust you," she says.

I almost tell her not to. Only good men are worthy of such a thing. Her trust is misplaced—but for some reason, I'm eager to prove her right.

As expected, the maître' d gives her a judgmental once-over. He turns his nose up. "I'm sorry, but we have a strict policy about—"

"My name is Leo Nicolaevich, and we'd like the table in the back."

The man's face goes white the moment he hears my name. It's a good thing. It means my brothers have already laid the groundwork for me. Knowing Roman, he's probably already spoken to the owners, tested the waters. It's my job to swoop in and start throwing around numbers, except—

I force the thoughts from my mind. Business shouldn't be my top priority. Right now, I want to spend a lovely evening with Nikita and get to know her over a couple glasses of wine and all the food her heart might desire. Normal stuff. A perfectly average date. Surely I can pretend to be an upstanding citizen for a couple of hours.

"That was impressive," Nikita whispers to me when the maître' d hastily grabs a pair of menus and guides us to the back with as charming a smile as he can muster. Where once he was ready to kick us out onto the curb, now he's giving us the royal treatment. I shrug, nonchalant. Best not to say anything more, or it might rouse her suspicions.

I pull her chair out for her like a gentleman. She rewards me with a sweet smile and a light laugh. "Why, thank you."

"May I get you started with something to drink, Mr. Nicolaevich?" the maître' d asks.

"A bottle of your house red."

"Actually," Nikita says quickly. "I can't drink. I mean, I shouldn't. Not with my training schedule."

"What would you like?" I ask. "Anything you want. Just ask."

"Maybe a can of Diet Coke?"

The maître' d once again curls up his nose. "Miss, this is La Croix. We don't serve cans of *Diet Coke*." He says it like it's some kind of a slur, insulting to him in every imaginable way.

I frankly don't appreciate his tone. Reaching into my suit jacket, I pull out my wallet and slap a few bills into his hand. "Get the lady what she wants. Go to a store if you have to. In fact, make it two cans."

"But Mr. Nicolaevich, this is—" I shoot him a hard glare. It shuts him up in an instant. "R-right. Of course. I'll... be right back." He skitters away like a frightened little mouse, nearly ramming into the corner of a neighboring table in his haste.

Nikita blinks up at me. "That was..."

"I'm sorry about that," I mutter, finally taking my seat across from her.

"No, it's fine, I just wasn't expecting you to do that for me." She glances down at her lap. "You must be a pretty important man."

"Not really," I lie. "Money talks, that's all."

"Are you sure you only own a taxi company?" she asks with a light laugh.

To her, it's an innocent, playful question. But to me, it sends all my walls flying up. Nikita can't ever know the truth. I'm sure she'd be horrified if she did.

One-Eye, the Bratva... It's a side of me I need to keep hidden. I live a double life as it is, so I figure keeping up with appearances for her sake can't be that hard. For her, I will lie through my teeth.

CHAPTER 7

NIKITA

"How do you like the food?" he asks me over our meals.

"Delicious. Honestly, it's probably the best meal I've ever had."

He nods, just once, his thoughts indecipherable to me. "How long have you been a dancer?"

I take a sip of my Diet Coke. After that strange interaction, the maître' d went above and beyond and got a chilled two-liter bottle for Leo and I to share. He even got us some fancy highball glasses and decorated them with a fancifully cut lime wheel.

"All my life," I answer with glee. "My parents like to say I was born dancing. I love it more than breathing."

The corners of his lips tick up into a faint smile. I've noticed he doesn't do that a lot—smile. I want to figure out what makes him tick. Can I make him laugh? What makes a man like Leo happy? Does he have hobbies that he enjoys? Right now, he's nothing but a mystery to me, one I want to slowly unravel. The man who had me at the cabin is hidden beneath layers I wish to discover and explore, one at a time.

"How long have you been with the Bolshoi?" he asks

me, sipping his drink. His hand is so large he makes the glass look minuscule. I'm strangely fixated on his hands. Strong and powerful, yet capable of being so tender and kind. His fingers loved digging into my hips.

"I've been with them since I was nineteen. I was part of the corps de ballet for three years, and then I was promoted to principal for two. And now I'm a soloist, but..."

His brows furrow. I like how serious his face is. Leo is a fascinating man to look at. The sharp angles, the dark contours, that heartbreaking scar across his ruined eye. I've wanted to ask him about it from the moment we met, but that wouldn't exactly be polite. I'm sure there will come a time and place, but for now, I'm content just getting to know him.

"But what?" he prods.

I chew on the inside of my cheek. How honest should I be? Would he even care about something like this? It's all internal politicking and derisive gossip amongst the other dancers. Leo probably wouldn't be interested in—

"Someone mentioned sabotage," he points out. I'm surprised he was even paying attention.

"Vanya, the ballerina I'm taking over for... Someone put pins in her shoes. She's not too badly injured, but..." A shaky breath escapes me. "I feel awful for her. She's been working so hard all season. She'll make a full recovery, but not in time for the run."

Leo's face darkens. "Pins?"

I nod slowly. "Terrible, isn't it?"

"Why would someone do that?"

"Honestly? I have no idea. Inessa seems to think someone might not like her very much, but I have a hard time believing it."

"Why?"

I shrug a shoulder, twirling my fork against the plate in front of me. "We're a tight-knit group. I've seen how ballerinas are portrayed in television and movies. People think we're catty. Perfectionists. And maybe we are—perfectionists. But when you spend all day six days a week with a group of people, they become your family. You build trust. We're all here for the love of the craft. It doesn't make sense to me, hurting someone else for your own gain—whatever that gain might be."

I peer at him over the table. I don't think Leo's blinked *once*. My cheeks flush with embarrassment. "Sorry. I'm rambling. You must think it's pretty naive of me, huh?"

He shakes his head. "No."

"No?"

"There's nothing wrong with wanting to see the good in others," he says stoically. The words are stiff rolling off his tongue, almost like he doesn't believe what he's saying. "Did they find who did it?"

"Not yet, unfortunately."

His jaw visibly tenses, the muscles in his face tightening. "Hm."

"It's only a matter of time."

"Do you think they might come after you?"

I swallow a bite of my food. "I hope not. I don't think I've pissed anyone in the company off, so..."

Leo clenches his fist, his whole demeanor suddenly sour. "Be careful."

I can't help but smile. His concern is touching, but unnecessary. Something this grave will be taken care of quickly, not only to bring the culprit to justice, but also to stamp out any rumors from getting out to the public. There's no telling what sort of repercussions could occur if people learned about what happened to Vanya ahead of the show. It could tarnish the Bolshoi's reputation—which is all the more reason for the administration to handle this as quickly and quietly as possible.

"I've been talking about myself all night," I mumble. "Tell me about you."

"What would you like to know?"

"How did you come to own a taxi company?"

Leo sits back, relaxing a little. "My brothers and I founded it together."

"How many brothers do you have?"

"Four. Well, three and a half."

I giggle. We may not be drinking alcohol, but I feel strangely drunk. "What's that supposed to mean?"

"Long story."

"I have time."

Leo presses his lips into a thin line and crosses his arms over his chest. "It's not a fun story. Maybe on our second date."

Giddy excitement rises in my chest. "There's going to be a second date?"

"If you permit it."

I smile at him coyly. His deadpan delivery is hilarious. Who even talks like that? "Yeah," I say. "Yeah, I'd like that very much."

"Mr. Nicolaevich?"

Leo and I both look up at the man standing directly next to our table. He's all sweaty for some reason, his brow shiny, and he's sporting unfortunate pit stains.

"Do you need something?" Leo asks flatly.

"I'm Tym, the owner. I was wondering if I might have a word with you in private?"

I glance between the two of them, concern swirling in the pit of my stomach. Oh God, is this about earlier? Is it because I'm not dressed to the nines and Leo made a tiny scene about not having the drink I wanted?

"Is everything alright?" I ask.

Leo rises from the table, neatly folding and setting aside his cloth napkin. His fingers twitch. "I'll be right back," he promises.

I'm left alone at the table, mildly confused, but at least I have some delicious food to distract me. This place is fancy with a capital F. A crystal chandelier hangs over the main lobby. I'm pretty sure the floors are made from polished marble. Everything from the glassware to the plates to the waiters' uniforms screams *expensive*.

I'll confess I felt embarrassed to walk in here dressed the way I am, but Leo was so confident—so sure—that I seem to have absorbed some of his gusto. I feel safe with him. Able to be myself without a hint of insecurity. But now that he's left the table... I suddenly feel naked.

It seems I've earned myself a couple of snarky side-eyes from the next table over, where a gaggle of older ladies, dressed in fur coats, their ears sparkling with diamonds, sit. I squirm in my seat. I know I'm dressed casually, but I'm not a slob. Except, the longer they glare at me, the more I begin to realize it's not what I'm wearing that they've taken issue with.

It's my lack of wealth.

They sneer down their noses at me. I feel like a cockroach they want nothing more than to stamp out. Their message, though wordless, is loud and clear: I don't belong in their world.

"Bratva whore."

I glance up, startled when the maître' d passes by. "What did you just say?"

He stops, his lip curling up into a sneer. "We don't appreciate your kind here."

Confusion washes over me, cold and vicious. "What on Earth are you talking about?"

"You think you're protected because you're with him? Do yourself a favor and walk away before it's too late. Anyone who gets involved with those assholes ends up with the short stick."

"What—"

"Enough," Leo's low, commanding voice breaks through. It's the first time I've ever seen him truly angry. It's a cold, quiet kind of anger—and I think that's what I find so intimidating. There's a storm brewing inside, held back by a thin sliver of control. "What's your name, boy?"

The maître' d gulps, no longer brave now that Leo has returned. "Alix."

"Well, Alix—you're fired."

My jaw drops. The maître' d looks equally stunned.

"You've got to be joking."

Leo takes a seat at the table, indifferent. Like this is any other Monday evening to him. "I just spoke with the owner of this fine establishment. He sold it to me for a very reasonable price."

"You can't do this."

"I just did."

"You have no reason!"

Leo's eye slides over to me, hard and impossible to read. I wish I knew what he was thinking, but I'm too stunned to even consider figuring it out. "What did you say to her?"

"N-nothing."

"You've upset her. Clearly you said something."

"That's not true at all!"

"Nikita?" Leo says my name so sweetly, so kindly it

almost gives me whiplash. It makes me feel strangely warm. Special. I like this softer side of him. I want it all to myself.

I lick my lips. "He said... He said he doesn't appreciate our kind here." It's a half truth, only a fraction of what was truly said. If Leo learns the man here called me a whore...

"Get out," Leo tells Alix. "Immediately. I have no use for disrespectful employees."

Flustered and shaking, the man leaves. People at other tables are quick to look away, no longer brazen enough to even look in our direction.

My heart hammers loudly in my chest. "Did you really buy this restaurant? I thought you owned taxis."

"I'm a businessman," he says with an air of easy casualty. "I dabble in this and that. Besides, you said you like the food."

"So?"

"You can come here whenever you'd like and eat free of charge."

"Are you serious?"

"Do I look like I'm joking?"

My mouth goes dry, my throat suddenly tight. This is crazy. This is absolutely crazy, and yet...

"I'm coming on a bit strong, aren't I?" he asks, looking a bit perturbed.

"A little, yes, but..." I reach across the table and place my hand over his. "Considering what we did at the cabin and what happened just now, its also the sweetest thing anyone has ever done for me. Thank you for standing up to that awful man."

Leo nods. "He shouldn't have spoken to you that way."

And then, that's that. Leo doesn't bring it up again, nor does he elaborate on his reason or even his means of purchasing La Croix after a brief five-minute talk with the now previous owner. I have a million and one questions, but I'm frankly so flabbergasted I don't even know where to begin. Who *is* he? What sort of man is willing to buy a whole restaurant simply because I like the food, or fire a man without even lifting a finger for so much as looking at me wrong?

We return to our meals, the conversation taking a much lighter, breezier tone. We talk about the weather. Our plans for the weekend. Casual, polite, inoffensive.

But the entire time, a single word echoes around in my skull. Over and over and over again.

Bratva.

It's the Bratva that's got my father stuck between a rock and a hard place.

I try to push it away, try to chalk it up to something spoken out of anger. For all intents and purposes, Leo is a nice man. Business savvy. A patron of the arts. The kind of guy who pulls out your chair and stops in the middle of the street to give your car a boost. He may look outwardly hard, but I can tell he has a good heart.

There's just no way he's a gangster. I refuse to believe it.

CHAPTER 8

NIKITA

"I had a lovely time tonight," I tell him as he walks me to the front door of my apartment building. Leo was courteous enough to drive me home in his car after dinner so I didn't need to call for a ride. When we stepped out of the restaurant, it had gotten significantly darker and colder, prompting Leo to once again drape his overcoat over my shoulders. It's the strangest thing, but I think he likes the way it looks on me.

"I'd invite you up for coffee," I say, "but I live with my mother and... Well."

His smile grows, little by little. It's so strange that such a small expression can feel like such a treat, especially coming from him. "Not to worry. Next time."

I fiddle with my keys. "And when would next time be?"

"Tomorrow," he says. "Are you free?"

I can't help but laugh. Leo is weird in the most endearing way possible. "Two nights in a row? What will my mother think, Mr. Nicolaevich?"

"What your mother thinks is of no concern to me."

"I'm teasing you, Leo. Tomorrow would be great. I should be done with practice around six"

"I'll pick you up."

I nibble on my bottom lip, trying to contain my grin. His eyes flit down to follow the motion, a deep and curious hunger lurking behind his expression. I know he's holding back. So am I. From what I've seen, a man like Leo doesn't need permission. He takes no orders, offers no compromise. This man walks into a room and, on a whim, can choose to own it. I never would have believed it if I hadn't witnessed it happen a few hours ago.

There's something about him that leaves me breathless and amazed. I want to peel the layers back, discover what makes him tick. How has this hurricane of a man not swept me off my feet in the worst possible way? Why do I feel like I'm safe as long as I remain in the eye of his storm?

"May I kiss you?" he asks, his tone flat, his gaze warm.

It's flattering, in a way, that he would ask my consent. Leo has already proven that he's the type to take what he wants. It'd be so easy for him to step forward, wrap his bulky arms around my waist, and drag his lips to mine like he did the first time— yet he *asks*. So courteous and gentle and considerate.

I hop up on my toes and press my hands flat against his chest. He has to dip his head down so I can reach. When our lips slide into place, the rest of the world suddenly fades away and I can't focus on anything else. His hands hover on either side of my waist, like he's afraid to touch me.

"Leo?" I whisper against his lips. "Is something wrong?"

"It's nothing I..."

I reach up to cup his face. "What is it?"

"I'm worried I'll hurt you."

His confession confuses me. "Hurt me? I don't think

that's possible." I reach down and take his hand, pressing it firmly against my hip. "Kiss me."

I see the shift happen, quick and all at once. There's that hungry animal he usually keeps locked up inside, the gates now open so he's free to prowl. To *claim.*

Our kiss goes from something precious to all-consuming. His arms circle my waist and crush me against his body. His tongue slips between my lips to explore my own, searching and tasting and devouring every available inch. Heat pools between my thighs, pleasure making my core throb. I'm blanketed by the heat of his skin, the passion of our embrace, the intoxicating scent of his cologne. It's dizzying. Thrilling in a way I didn't know was possible. If I don't stop this now, Leo will eat me alive. Again.

And I just might let him.

My lips come away swollen. A whimper escapes me when he ends our kiss. The sudden lack of his warmth leaves my mind spinning. I've had another taste of this marvelous drug that is Leo, and now I want more.

"Go inside, Nikita," he mumbles. "Before you catch a cold."

A delightful shiver races down my spine at his concern. "Tomorrow, right?" I breathe. My thoughts are slowly catching up to me, but only just.

"Tomorrow," he says with a nod. "Go inside."

I hesitate, my lips still abuzz. If only I could have a few more moments with him. Ultimately, I know I have no choice. We can't do this the way we did it back at the cabin. It's different, and we both know it. I start toward the doors, giddy and lightheaded. Leo remains planted in place, watching me until I'm safely inside.

~

"Where have you been?" Inessa snaps the moment I step into the apartment. Her eyes snap down at the overcoat hanging over my shoulders. Shit. I forgot to give it back to Leo—*again*. "You went out with him?"

I sigh. "It's not a big deal, Mother."

"I expressly told you—"

"I'm allowed to see who I want," I snap back with ferocity I didn't know I had. It isn't like me to argue with her. For some reason, I'm feeling exceptionally brave. "It was just dinner. He was a perfect gentleman."

"You ungrateful little—"

"Leave her be," Dad says from the kitchen table. He looks worse for wear, but I'm surprised to see him here, to begin with. There are dark circles under his eyes, a general weary slump to his shoulders."Nikita's a smart girl. Not to mention an adult. "

"Dad, you're back?" I ask.

"Your mother agreed to sit down over a glass of wine and talk things through," he says. "I'm hoping we'll reach a better resolution this time. But that aside, you should've at least called to let Inessa know that you would be running late, honey."

I nod, guilty. "Sorry. I'll remember next time."

"Next time?" Inessa seethes. "There's not going to be a next time. Listen to me carefully—you're not to see that man ever again."

I attempt to storm off to my room, but Mother only follows. "I'm twenty-four. You can't keep telling me what to do."

I slam my bedroom door closed and lock it behind me. I'm probably going to pay for that tomorrow morning with an especially gruesome practice, but I don't care. Inessa can't keep breathing down my neck all the time. My whole life, I've been good. Following her instructions, doing as she's told me. Now she's telling me she doesn't want me to see Leo ever again?

Out of the question.

I practically throw myself onto the bed, curling my weary legs up to my chest as I hug Leo's coat. Instinctively, I bring it up to my nose and take a deep, slow breath as I reminisce about our kiss, about everything we did at his cabin.

For some reason, I thought we'd jump right into that animalistic ritual again, that we'd tear the clothes off one another, and he'd have me on my knees, taking all of him in my mouth... But this was different. *Leo* is different from all the men I've come across. He's a walking contradiction I can't seem to get enough of. His presence easily commands attention, power. But when he's with me, he's sweet and shy and treats me like I'm made of glass.

I lick my lips, savoring the remnants of his taste as I drink in the warmth of his coat. I run my hand over the fabric, imagining the hardness of his biceps as I smooth my fingers over the sleeves. I drape his coat over my body, imagining what it would be like to have him bear his weight down on me again. His coat covers me from chin to toes, the memory of our size difference causing pleasure to curl in the pit of my stomach.

A curious hand slips inside my panties, my finger brushing my sensitive clit. I squeeze my eyes shut and try to recall the shape of Leo's hands. What it was like for him to be the one to touch and tease. To lick incessantly until I cried out his name, over and over.

I stifle my moan against the collar of his coat. Heat radiates off my skin like a furnace. I draw tight circles against myself, gathering up my slick arousal to help ease the friction. I'm loving these contradicting sides of Leo... he's a gentleman in the streets—

But an absolute animal in the sheets.

I want him to tease me senseless. I can hear myself begging him to let me come. And just when I can't take it anymore, *that's* when Leo will take me. Hard. Fast. Dirty as sin. And all the while, he'd sing my praises. He'd tell me the filthiest things while calling me his good girl.

I gasp as pleasure seizes my body, my muscles trembling with wave after wave of ecstasy. When I open my eyes, I can't help but smile. I'm *way* too excited to see him again.

Come morning, a sudden bout of nausea hits me. It's strange. It has never happened before. Maybe the dinner from last night didn't agree with me, but that isn't a thing with me, either. I'll eat whatever you put on the table and thank you for it. No, this feels different, and given everything that has been going on lately, it's hard not to put two and two together.

Before I go into practice, I stop by the pharmacy and get one of those rapid pregnancy tests, hiding it inside my coat pocket on my way into the Bolshoi. A rather uncomfortable tinkle later, and I have my answer.

It's not the answer I wanted.

Not the answer I needed, either. But the plus sign on the pregnancy test does not lie. It also matches the timeline. The night at the cabin. The many, many wonderful times that I felt Leo come deep inside me. Of course. It shouldn't come as such a shock. I must've been right in that sweet spot of a fertile window.

But the repercussions of that night... oh, God, I didn't

think any of this through. And I'm going to see him again, too. Do I tell him? What do I tell him? That our one-night-stand got me knocked-up?

"Mother will blow a fuse," I whisper as I discard the test in one of the bathroom bins and thoroughly wash my face with cold water, staring at myself in the mirror. "She will kill me..."

I'm supposed to be the Sugar Plum Fairy all through the winter holidays and well into January if Vanya doesn't recover by then. How long before the bump starts to show? I'll get hungrier and hungrier, what with my show diet, the rough training. Oh, the training. Can I even work myself as hard as I have up to this point?

Dammit, I need to see a doctor. I need to...

I don't even know what I need to do first.

But I do know one thing. Nobody can know about this until I figure it out for myself. Not Leo, not Mother, nobody. It'll be my secret. I seem to be good at keeping secrets since no one suspects that Leo and I have already met—in another life, it feels like...

And in that other life, we conceived a baby.

Nobody can know.

CHAPTER 9

LEO

Only one more hour until I get to see her again. I've been keeping my eye on the clock, the ticking sounds of the second hand an ever-present reminder that I'm stuck here until the night shift arrives.

It's been a relatively unproductive day. Let's just say my heart isn't in it. I'm not only managing the Bratva while Andrei is away, but I'm also managing all of our businesses. It's just another day of wire transfers, spreadsheets, and encrypted emails. Just another day of sending my brothers out to put out fires as they come up—which is often—but I trust their discretion and that they'll get the job done.

I still haven't received word about the butcher's ledger. This could be a problem. I'm giving Roman until the end of the day to provide me with a full report. After that, I'd really rather not get my hands dirty, but that's what happens when I'm in charge.

Arman enters the office and hangs up his jacket. "Good evening," he says politely.

I get up out of my chair faster than I mean to. I swallow my rising excitement. "You're here early."

"My wife wanted to take our kids to see that new Christmas movie with the talking ponies?" he says with a weary smile. "So I lent them the car and they dropped me off. Hope it's alright if I clock in early."

I shrug a shoulder. "Fine by me."

Arman removes his hat, a polite gesture. "Mr. Nicolaevich, I was wondering..."

"What is it?"

"Well, with the holidays coming up, I was wondering if I could discuss the possibility of getting my Christmas bonus in advance?"

There's a tightness to his voice. Anxiety dripping off his every syllable. I can tell this isn't an easy conversation for him to have, and it's taking all his strength to even broach the subject in the first place.

"You see, my children," Arman sighs. "They want these new skateboards. Except they're not skateboards. They're electronic and they only have one wheel that you're supposed to balance on... Unsafe, if you ask me, but they've been begging me and their mother for one to share. And I was hoping... Well, we were *all* hoping—"

"All?" I echo.

"Me and the rest of the night shift boys." Arman clears his throat, obviously uncomfortable. "They're all waiting just outside for their turn to talk to you."

I pinch the bridge of my nose and pray my oncoming headache away. I don't want to spend the next thirty minutes to an hour talking about early Christmas bonuses. What I *want* is to go see Nikita. If I'm lucky, maybe I can catch the tail end of her rehearsal. Getting to see her twirl, that perfect smile on her lips—it's exactly what I need to de-stress right now. I would need more of her, for that matter, but I'll take what I can get outside of my cabin where she's concerned.

"Tell them all to come in," I instruct. "Might as well save myself time."

The night shift shuffles in sheepishly. Vlad smiles at me as usual, but Georgi and Kostya can't bring themselves to look me in the eye. I'm more than aware I have that kind of effect on people.

"Arman has brought forward your request," I tell them, "but it's unfortunately not in the company's policy to give bonuses in advance."

Georgi shifts his weight from foot to foot. "We understand, Mr. Nicolaevich, but we're really hoping you'll make an exception for us. We wouldn't ask you if we didn't each have a very good reason."

I set my jaw, listening on the edge of my patience. "Tell me, then."

"Arman's got his kids to think about. Georgi's kid is going to be back from college and he wants to help him buy next semester's textbooks. Kostya's been working three times as hard than the rest of us, and I... Well, my mother's in the hospital, sir. I'm hoping to use my bonus to pay for her treatment."

I breathe deeply. I'm not an unreasonable man. I can understand that things are always tight around the holiday season. Gift shopping. The feasts. The family gatherings. In the end, everything racks up.

But rules are rules. If I make an exception for these four and word gets out, I run the risk of every single one of our employees asking for their bonuses early. Frankly, that's additional paperwork and a conversation with our payroll department I do *not* have the energy to have.

"Please, Mr. Nicolaevich?" Georgi asks, his voice small

and timid. He's an older gentleman, the strain of his years evident in his vocal chords. "Just this once?"

I glance at my wristwatch. They must have known it would be easier to approach me as a group rather than one on one. Luckily for them, I'm eager to get to the Bolshoi, otherwise I would never have even entertained the thought.

"You keep this between us," I say sternly. "I'll grant you this request, but it's an exception only. I better not have the rest of the company knocking down my door. Got it?"

"Thank you, Mr. Nicolaevich!" Arman says, joy and relief practically rolling off of him. "Thank you so much."

"Don't mention it." I hit them with a hard glare. "Seriously. Don't mention it."

The security guard won't let me into the building. "I'm sorry, sir, but this is a private entrance."

"I'm aware of that. That's why I'm using it."

"Sir—"

"What's it going to take for you to let me in through those doors..." I scan the ID badge clipped to the breast pocket of his shirt uniform. "Pavel," I read.

"Are you trying to bribe me?"

"I didn't say that." I reach into my pocket and pull out my wallet, opening it to flash the cash I'm carrying. His eyes glisten, just as I expected they would. People are so predictable. Money makes the world go round, and I have more than enough to solve all my problems.

The security guard throws a cautious look both ways before taking the money.

"This will be our little secret," I tell him.

"You're not, like, going to murder someone or something, are you?"

"Do I look like a murderer?"

He grimaces. "Well—"

"Don't answer that." I hand him some more money before I put my wallet away. "I'm paying you to not ask questions. You'll get no trouble from me. I'm just... a really big fan of the ballet. Now, if you'd please."

With a hesitant squint, Pavel steps to the side. I don't blame him for his suspicion. He could lose his job if the higher-ups discover what he's done. I suppose I could have sought out the ballet director and asked for another tour as a patron, or really any other excuse I can come up with off the top of my head, but I don't want to go through him every time I come to see Nikita. I'd rather not have someone aware of my constant comings and goings. It's better this way. Discreet.

The practice building is a labyrinth. White walls, white polished floors. It's surprisingly clinical in here, although I don't know what I was expecting. More decorations maybe? Opera and ballet-related posters? It's nothing short of professional, distraction free. I'm grateful there's at least a directory and signs plastered on the walls, or else I never would have found my way to the practice rooms. I know I'm getting close when I hear music—the distinctive opening to the Sugar Plum Fairy's theme.

I step into the room quietly, hugging the walls. It's hard to go unnoticed, given my tall stature and wide frame, but I do my best not to distract the dancers as they move across the floor. Those standing on the sides give me space to walk to the seating area, where I claim a chair in the very back, cloaked in shadows. It's the perfect place to watch them dance. They're midway through, I think. I'm not entirely familiar with the choreography. Lots of jumps and spins.

My eyes lock on to Nikita with ease. She's hard to miss, her smile brighter than the sun, the stars, and the moon combined. I don't know how she does it. She's in white leggings and a tutu with a deep mahogany sports shirt on top. Her hair is pulled up into a tight bun, giving me a clear view of her pretty face. She's a gazelle, twirling and leaping and all those other minute, complex movements executed to perfection—all while on the tips of her toes.

She makes it look so easy that I begin to think even *I* could do it, though I know that's the furthest thing from the truth. This is what years upon years of dedication and training looks like. I remember wondering what she did for a living when I claimed her that night, when I ran my hands, my lips, and my tongue all over that small, taut body of hers. Something related to athletics did come to mind, but not once did ballet cross through. It's a delightful surprise, though. Nikita is captivating, impossible to look away from. The music comes to an end and she holds for the finale. While I think she's the most breathtaking creature I've ever laid my eyes on, her mother seems to think otherwise.

"What the hell was that?" Inessa grumbles. "Your pas de bourree into plie near the end is sloppy. I've never seen such lazy footwork!"

Something protective and fiery rises within me. Who the fuck does this woman think she is? I've only got one good eye, but even I can see that Nikita was nothing short of spectacular. Just when I think about stepping forward, though, Nikita puts her hands on her hips and simply nods.

"I'll do better," she says, resolute and unshaken. I think it's admirable, her determination inspiring. "Just tell me what I need to fix."

"You need to lift up more. They're going to be able to hear you clomping around like a damn elephant. You need to get this right before we move on to the pas de deux."

The doors to the practice room open wide. A group of four police officers step in, the stomping of their hard boots against the floor inconsiderately loud. My first instinct is to look for an alternate exit. Are they here for me? Did Pavel the security guard rat me out and call the cops? Bratva and the law don't mix, so it's only natural that my first thought is to shrink and try to avoid their attention.

Except they're not looking for me. They walk straight to Inessa and Nikita, their expressions as serious as the grave.

"Nikita Belova?" one of the officers says. "Do you have a moment?"

Nikita's about to open her mouth, but Inessa steps in, pushy as usual. "Actually, she doesn't. We're in the middle of rehearsal."

"It has to do with Vanya Karoshka. Concerning what happened the other day."

My ears burn as I listen from afar. I'll admit I've been curious about this supposed sabotage incident I heard about. Nikita didn't go into detail, and I frankly didn't want to push her. But now that I'm here, I'm on the edge of my seat.

"What do you want to ask me?" Nikita pipes up. "I want to help in any way I can."

"We'd rather do this at the station."

I set my jaw, the muscles in the back of my neck growing tight. They want to take her down to the station for a couple of questions? Something isn't right here.

Without a second thought, I rise from my seat and step forward. Were it anyone else, I wouldn't have even considered putting myself in the line of fire. I'm opening a can of worms by staying.

But I can't stand idly by, either.

"She's not going anywhere," I say clearly, firmly. I can feel the heat of everyone's eyes on me.

"Leo?" Nikita breathes. Her smile is both excited and embarrassed. "How did you..."

"And you are?" one of the officers asks.

"Her counsel," I lie through my teeth. If there's one thing I know how to do—it's how to evade *just* enough suspicion to look innocent. Who knew my expertise could prove so useful?

CHAPTER 10

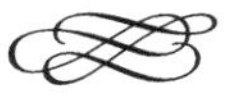

NIKITA

I have a million and one questions, but I don't know where to start.

How did Leo manage to get into the building? Was he watching me during practice? Why did he say he was my counsel? And how the hell is he so calm right now?

By some miracle, Leo managed to convince the officers to interview me in a small spare room right here at the Bolshoi. There's no need to be escorted in the back of a police car down the station. Thank *God*. I can't imagine anything more humiliating. Unfortunately, it might already be too late to stave off the rumors. All my fellow dancers have seen me being led out to be questioned.

I'm seated in a plastic folding chair, wringing my fingers in my lap. At least they gave me the courtesy of letting me change out of my rehearsal clothes. It would have been uncomfortable sitting here in a tutu. Leo sits beside me, arms crossed over his chest, one leg folded over the other. They made Mother wait outside. There's no doubt in my mind Inessa has her ear pressed right up against the door to try and listen in. I bet she's furious.

Nausea is testing my resolve again, but I swallow it back with a gulp of ice-cold water and take deep breaths. I've learned to time these episodes. They never last more than a couple of minutes. Cold water helps. I can do this. I hate lying, I hate not telling the truth—especially about this child I'm carrying, but I don't have any other choice, not with so much on the line here. So I push the truth back to the bottom of my consciousness and pretend I'm fine. I can do this.

"How long have you known Vanya?" the officer asks me, flipping through his notebook.

I glance at Leo, though I'm not sure why. He's not a lawyer. Isn't it illegal for him to say he is? He nods, however, giving me approval to answer. I'm just going to have to ask him for the truth after we get the hell out of here.

"Several years."

"How would you describe your relationship with the victim?"

I gulp. *Victim*? My heart pounds against the inside of my rib cage. This is getting so serious. "Perfectly friendly," I mumble. "We're colleagues. We have a good working relationship."

"She was ranked higher than you, correct?"

My palms are clammy. I'm getting nervous, but I really have no reason to be. "Yes. Technically speaking."

"Did that ever make you feel jealous?"

"Don't answer that," Leo interjects, his words sharp like a knife.

I bite my tongue. We're probably thinking the same thing. I don't know what these officers are playing at, but if they think they're going to get a rise out of me, they're wrong. I have to remain calm, keep cool. If I say something out of anger, there's no telling how it might blow up in my face.

I recognize now how precarious my position is. Mother warned me as much, that there would be eyes on me. Whispers. Isn't it a little too convenient that I should reap all the rewards at the expense of Vanya's downfall? The promotion, the role of a lifetime... I'd be suspicious of me, too, if I weren't the one in the hot seat.

"Where were you the day before the incident?" the officer asks me.

"Here, at the Bolshoi. We have a very strict training schedule."

"Do dancers have lockers here? Some place to keep your things."

"Of course."

"Would you have had access to Vanya's locker?"

Leo bristles. "Don't answer tha—"

I stick my hand out and place it gently on his forearm. I've got this. Calmly, I turn to face the officer. "Yes, I *would*. But I would never think of doing such a thing. I don't know what you're trying to imply, but I'm not the one responsible. You're wasting your time here, and every second you waste is another second the perpetrator remains at large."

"We understand this is a very upsetting time, Ms. Belova, but—"

"If you're so concerned about where I was prior to the incident, you can ask any number of my colleagues. I was already in the practice room for class. You can check the sign-in records since we all have a key card that lets us in and out of the building. And if you're really so concerned, you can ask my mother where I was the night prior because she's a control freak and I have to be home by a certain time or else she loses it." I take a deep breath, for once in my life grateful Inessa is so damn controlling. I have alibis for all hours of the day, making it impossible for me to be the one behind Vanya's awful attack.

Leo rises from his seat first. "You have everything you need."

The police officer sneers at him. "That's for me to determine."

"Is she under arrest?"

"Well, no, but—"

"Then we're done here," Leo states firmly before offering me his hand. I take it, more than a little relieved when he guides me out of the room and down the hall for a moment of privacy.

I can barely catch my breath. I think I handled myself well, but that was nonetheless a terrifying experience. My head is light. The room spins, and the tip of my fingers are buzzing with adrenaline. I've never known that kind of dread before. The way those cops were looking at me... as if they'd already decided I was guilty.

"Are you okay?" Leo asks me, soft and gentle. I adore the tenderness in his eyes, but I'm in no state of mind to enjoy it.

"I'm fine, I think, but the more important question is what are you doing here?"

He cocks his head to the side. "We agreed to meet for dinner, remember?"

Guilt washes over me. After a full day of strenuous rehearsal and then the unexpected grilling from the cops, I'd completely forgotten. "Oh my God, you're right. I'm so sorry, I totally forgot."

"It's alright. Truly."

"No, no, I..." I anxiously rub the back of my neck. This is turning out to be a horrible day. "Why did you say you were my counsel? I mean, I appreciate your help, but won't you get in trouble? Isn't that illegal or something?"

"Not necessarily," he says easily, like it isn't a big deal. "I'm not under oath. I'm perfectly within my rights to offer advice, that's all."

I press my palms against my cheeks. I'm overheating. "Well, thank you. I'm pretty sure I would have been a nervous wreck without you."

"You did great," he assures. "You can breathe easier now, Nikita."

I follow his advice and inhale deeply. The scent of his cologne brings me an immediate sense of peace. Despite my confusion and anxiety, having him here is a great comfort. "Do you still feel like going out to dinner?" I ask him.

"I would love—"

"Nikita!" my mother's shrill voice interjects. I cringe. I should have known she was lurking around the corner somewhere. "How did it go? What did they ask you? And what is *he* doing here?" she pelts me with questions, her syllables so sharp they remind me of a machine gun.

"Everything went fine," I answer. "And Leo is taking me out to dinner."

"I forbid it."

I furrow my brows, swallowing my irritation. "What do you mean you forbid it?"

"I don't want you going out with this man. I've already made myself perfectly clear."

"Mother, you're embarrassing me."

"We'll talk about this more when we get home."

Reaching down quickly, I take Leo's hand. "I'm going out to dinner. Don't wait up."

The vein in my mother's temple pulses. "Listen here, young lady—"

Leo and I are already headed out the door.

"Are you sure this is a good idea?" he asks me.

"Don't you want to grab a bite to eat?"

"Of course, but not at the risk of putting a wedge between you and your mother."

"That's very considerate of you, but don't worry. I promised you tonight."

There's a warmth in his eyes I have a hard time describing. His soft gaze makes me feel tingly all over. Better yet, the corner of his lip curls up into the smallest of smiles. I'm earning it, little by little. One of these days, I'm going to see him beam. I'm going to see that side of him he wouldn't show me on our first night together.

"So," I say the moment we exit the building together, "did you have a place in mind?"

He nods. "I think you're going to love it."

He has his hands over my eyes, obscuring my view. I have no idea where he's taking me, but I like the element of surprise. All I know is we're someplace with high altitude. It's chilly up here; thank goodness for his overcoat. At this point, I'm just going to ask him if I can keep it. It seems he doesn't mind draping it over my shoulders when I have even the slightest of chills.

I can hear the wind whistling past my ears. The air is fresh up here, crisp and cool. The sounds of the city are distant, far below us and almost forgotten. It's a little jarring not being able to see where I am, but I trust Leo not to let me fall. With his chest against my back, he's a sturdy support as he leads me forward.

"Are we there?" I asked him with a giggle.

"Almost. Just one more second."

When he steps away, I finally open my eyes. I gasp at the absolutely breathtaking view.

We're standing on top of one of Moscow's tallest skyscrapers, looking down upon the shimmering lights of the city. Everything looks impossibly small from up here. People and cars appear as nothing more than ants, going about their business while we observe from above. The sun has long since set beyond the horizon, a speckling of stars splashed across the black night sky above.

Most spectacular of all, however, is the single table set up before us. There are two chairs, two place settings, and a single candle at the center. Our food has already been prepared for us, hot and steaming on plates of fine China.

I turn to face Leo, my jaw dropped open in awe. "Did you do all this?"

He nods. "Didn't want anyone bothering us this time."

"When did you even have time to put all this together?"

"I know some people," he says as he pulls out my chair.

I can't help but laugh softly as I take my offered seat. "You're really something else."

"How do you mean?"

I gesture vaguely about the space. "This. Buying that restaurant. Becoming the Bolshoi's top patron. Moonlighting as legal counsel. Owning a whole company..."

Bratva.

I push the thought away.

"I only own a fifth of it," he amends.

His modesty makes me smile. "You're a man of many faces."

Leo shrugs noncommittally, but I catch a glimpse of something almost... *guilty* ghost across his features. It's gone in a flash, though, as he takes his seat and makes for his fork. "Please enjoy."

I dig into my food greedily. We're having spaghetti tonight. A simple dish, but it tastes like heaven. Every noodle is coated in rich Bolognese sauce, and to wash it down, Leo's thoughtfully prepared two glasses of Diet Coke.

"Where did you grow up?" I ask him, eager to finally crack through that thick outer shell of his. Thoughts of Inessa try to weasel their way to the forefront, but I stamp them down into the furthest crevices of my mind. I want to enjoy myself tonight. I can deal with my mother later.

"Born and raised in Moscow," Leo answers. "You?"

"Same."

"Any siblings?"

I shake my head. " An only child."

"I'm envious. My brothers were always such a headache."

A laugh bubbles past my lips. "Are you kidding? I'm the one who's envious. It would have been so nice to have a brother or sister around."

I twirl my pasta onto my fork, thoughts of my lonely childhood playing across my mind's eye. The more I think about it, the more I realize it might have been a blessing. Inessa was always so hard on me. I can't bear the thought of a younger sibling enduring the same constant, suffocating scrutiny she bestowed upon me.

I chew on the inside of my cheek, glancing at him with curiosity. My gaze traces the line of his scar, the grayness of his pupil. "Can I ask you a kind of personal question?"

"Are you going to ask me about my eye?"

"Uh... *no*?"

Leo chuckles. "Go on. I won't be offended."

I take a deep breath. "How did it happen?"

He looks off into the distance thoughtfully, watching the city with quiet contemplation. "My younger brother, Samuil. Always such a troublemaker. The sort of guy who mouths off before his brain ever has a chance to kick in." I'm on the edge of my seat, listening with intent. Leo goes on. "He got into a lot of fights when we were younger. He could handle it most of the time. Until he couldn't."

"What happened?"

"Someone brought a knife to a fistfight. I couldn't let my brother get hurt, so..."

My heart twists in my chest. "You stepped in?"

Leo nods, but there's nothing solemn about it. It's obvious he doesn't regret it one bit, even at the cost of his sight.

Slowly, I reach across the table, my fingers hovering barely an inch away from his cheek. "May I touch it again?"

All through our first night together, I only touched his scar once. He wouldn't let me do it again, insisting I kept my hands anywhere else on his body. There were other places for my fingers to explore, he'd said, and I couldn't exactly disagree.

"You don't think it's scary?" he murmurs, leaning into my touch. I lean forward in my chair to take a good look, running the pad of my thumb gingerly over his scar. A familiar feeling, but never one to fill me with dread.

"I don't think it's scary, Leo," I say softly. "You were protecting your family. If anything, it's a sign of how good a person you are."

Again, that flash of guilt. He looks like he has something to say—but he pulls me onto his lap instead. I instinctively wrap my arms around his thick neck for balance while he circles my waist with his, the combined warmth of our bodies creating the perfect recipe to stave off the evening chill.

His kiss comes more abruptly this time, but I have zero complaints. He commands our movements, devouring my mouth like a man starved. Insatiable. There's nowhere to go with the way he holds me tight, but I frankly can't imagine being anywhere else than right here in the exclusive seat of his lap. A moan rips itself from my lungs as he drags his teeth over my bottom lip, his hands beginning to roam the expanse of my back.

I'm suddenly feverish and aching, a blooming heat stirring in the pit of my core. What I wouldn't give right now to have his hands slip beneath my shirt, down my pants, between my thighs... I'm dizzy and completely at his mercy, barely able to keep up with his demanding tongue.

"L-Leo," I rasp.

There's something strangely comforting in the possessive nature of his kiss. Every brush of his lips against mine is strong and powerful. A statement of claim. This man *wants* me for much more than that one night, and he's channeling every ounce of his energy into each brand-hot kiss. That look in his eye... If I didn't know any better, I'd say Leo is two seconds from bending me over the table and having his way with me.

And I'd wholeheartedly let him, much like before.

"Leo, can we... Can we go somewhere more comfortable? Maybe take this to your place?"

"You're sure?"

I nod, clinging to him like a lifeline. "Yes. I want this."

"Then it's a good thing we're already here."

I frown, a tad confused. "What do you mean?"

His lips curl up into a grin. "I own this building."

CHAPTER 11

LEO

She wraps her legs around my hips, making it that much easier to carry her into the penthouse from the balcony. We don't even bother waiting until we get inside before we're all over each other, clawing at each other's clothes and sliding our tongues into each other's mouths. Nikita combs in her fingers through my hair, nibbles on my bottom lip, grinds her hips against me in a way that drives me certifiably insane.

"Nikita—"

"Kiss me harder," she commands.

I almost laugh. "Bossy little thing. Maybe I should teach you some manners. You seem to have forgotten them since our little training session at my cabin..."

There's something devilish behind her gaze. Dark and mischievous. "I'd like to see you try."

I press her against the nearest wall, mouthing hungrily at the open crook of her neck. "Don't challenge me. I always keep my promises."

"D-don't leave any marks," she says hastily. And then, "At least, not anywhere people can see."

I fight against the growl rising from my chest, my cock straining against the confines of my pants. "You didn't have a problem with that the first time."

"It's different... I'll be wearing slightly more revealing outfits for the Nutcracker. I can't have hickeys on display..."

"Not anywhere people can see? I guess I can do that—"

"*Leo—*"

"But I don't want to."

I dive in despite her little gasp of protest, sucking hard enough to leave a mark on her pearly skin. The sight of it sends me into a feral tailspin. I want all the other dancers to know I was here, touching, kissing, worshiping every inch of her body. I savor her sweet little moans and whimpers, committing them to memory as I gather her wrists and pin them above her head. I slide my free hand beneath the fabric of her shirt, marveling once more at how soft and toned she is.

"Let me hear you, Nikita. I want the whole building to know who's making you feel this way."

She sighs my name as I set her down. The moment her feet touch the floor, I drop to my knees with her waist gripped tight in my hands. I press forward, mouthing ferociously at her, savoring the scent of her need and the warmth of her thighs. Nikita's knees shake, her breath coming out a shudder.

"L-Leo, I—"

"I want to taste you again," I say as I yank her clothes down to expose the soft lace of her underwear. Nikita's hands fly to my hair as I continue to tease her through her clothes.

"Just take it off," she pants, trying to shimmy out of her panties for me. "Here, just—"

I take her hands, forcing her to still. I peer up at her,

adamant and steadfast. "I need you to listen very carefully, Nikita, because I'm only going to say this once."

"W-what is it?"

I lick my lips, happy to drown in her scent of peaches and cherry blossom. "I'm not one to rush. The only way I find true satisfaction is if I make you come. I'm sure you remember how things went the first time. It's how it's going to go this second time around, as well. And the third and the many other times that will follow."

Her cheeks flush an adorable shade of pink. "Then make me come."

"No, you don't get it. Tonight... It's different. It's not just about bringing you pleasure. What I want is to see you unravel. Make you desperate. I'm going to make you come so many times tonight it'll bring you to tears. And just when you can't take it anymore, *then* I'll think about fucking you."

Nikita is quiet for a moment, staring at me with wide eyes. I'm a little worried I might have freaked her out. Lovers in my past have described me as intense. Too much. It's one of the main reasons I've resigned myself to being alone for so long.

But Nikita doesn't look afraid. If anything, she seems intrigued. I guess I've rubbed off on her, already.

" Well, at least I know for a fact that you're not all talk," she says with a soft laugh.

"If it sounds like too much for you..."

Nikita cups my face in her palms, the hallway light overhead casting her in an almost heavenly glow. "Do your worst, handsome."

My mouth waters. I thank my lucky stars I pulled over that night; otherwise I would have passed her by and been none the wiser.

I brush her panties aside and stare at her with unbound

reverence. She's gorgeous, the soft lips of her pussy glistening with want. I grip her hips and hold her steady as I lick and tease, savoring her sweet taste and lick her folds with my tongue. I draw tight circles against her clit, slow and deliberate movements that make her breath hitch and her body tremble with pleasure.

There's nothing more intoxicating than the sound of her languid moans and the way her hips buck and roll against my mouth, seeking more of that sweet friction. Nikita is a sight to behold, especially now that I've sucked hard kisses and left bite marks between her thighs. Perfectly hidden and out of sight, just like she wanted—but not for long. Not if I have anything to say about it.

I can tell she's getting close by the way she grips my hair at the roots and throws her head back, her mouth open to pant and whine. Her moans are a siren's song, luring me to my welcome demise. Nikita screams my name when she comes, her voice ringing out loudly against the walls of the hallway. I lick my lips clean. I'm nowhere near close to done.

Before she has the chance to protest, I throw her over my shoulder and carry her down the hall toward my bedroom, yanking off her panties to abandon them to the floor.

"Leo, where—"

I clap her on the ass, relishing the way she yelps and then giggles. Her heady delirium is contagious. "Just wait and see."

She bundles up the back of my shirt in her fists for stability. "You better not drop me. An injury could ruin my career."

"I wouldn't dream of it. Trust me."

I move with purpose, kneading her ass and biting marks

against her hip as I easily navigate the halls. My penthouse is modestly decorated. Bright during the day thanks to the floor-to-ceiling windows, but plenty cozy once the sun has set.

When we finally get to the bedroom, I place Nikita on the bed with the utmost care, moving quickly to peel off the rest of her clothes. She looks good against my navy-blue bed sheets, her lithe arms and legs contrasting gorgeously. She's a damn work of art.

I stand at the edge of the bed, drinking in every possible detail. I've been thinking about this since the morning I dropped her off at that dingy Abramtsevo train station. She lied about living there, but I can't blame her. Never could. We were complete strangers. We weren't supposed to meet again.

The elegant length of her neck and easy slope of her shoulders. Her pretty, small breasts I'm dying to fill my palms with. I love her muscles, strong and slender, refined from years of dedicated training. I adore the valley of her belly, the dip of her waist, the thickness of her thighs.

She looks at me without fear and with admiration. I can't remember the last time someone looked at me like I was more than some beast. A hideous monster to fear, to run away or cower from. But Nikita isn't like that. From the moment we met, she trusted me. Even when our paths crossed again here in Moscow, she treated me with kindness, spoiling me with her smiles and her bubbly laugh.

I hope she understands what I'm about to do to her... It's to thank her.

And to push her to the brink.

I press one knee against the edge of the mattress and grip her ankles, spreading her legs just so. Her feet, I notice, are covered in a myriad of bandages. It's quite the sight, physical reminders of all the hours she spends on the tips of her toes. Nikita nibbles on her bottom lip, more bashful than I expected her to be given all we've done so far.

"Don't stare," she mumbles sheepishly. "It's the curse of a ballerina. Not very pretty to look at without our pointe shoes on."

I hum, pressing a kiss to the inner corners of her ankles, then her calves, then her knees. "You're beautiful, Nikita. Every inch of you." I release her legs and remove my watch, setting it on the bedside table. "Now, remind me, how flexible are you?"

She squeezes her legs closed, smiling at me coyly. "Very."

I shake my head in disapproval, tapping her knees. "Show me. Like you did before. Pretend it's our first night together. We're starting from scratch."

With a timid little whimper, Nikita does exactly as I ask, spreading her legs into a perfect split, putting herself on full display for me. A feral heat blooms deep within my core, my jaw practically aching as my craving for her flares.

This time when I settle between her thighs, I use my fingers in tandem with my tongue. Not wanting to overwhelm, I start with only one digit, curling my finger back in a beckoning motion to seek out her sweet spot. I know precisely when I've found it. Nikita suddenly gasps, her back arching as pleasure surges through her body, her fingers tightly gripping the sheets.

"*Oh!*"

"Feel good?" I grunt against her, determined to see her fall apart. I press a second finger into her, marveling at how well she takes me. "Come on, Nikita. Let me watch you come on my fingers."

"Leo—"

I bring her to the edge of her climax, tasting her through the first waves of pleasure. Her pussy clenches around my fingers, her hot walls throbbing with earned release. I waste no time in flipping her over.

I wrap my tie around her wrists, binding her. I give her no chance to breathe, practically caging her in with my body as I plunge my fingers back into her. This new angle grants me better access, the tips of my fingers sweeping over her sweet spot again and again until she's practically melting beneath my touch. Nikita groans against the sheets, her hair a mess with sweat dripping down her elegant back.

"More" she pleads with me. "Please, I'm so close."

Who in their right mind could ever deny her?

When she comes on my fingers, she screams into my pillow, her whole body shaking. I am just as breathless as she, drunk on her beauty and high on her ecstasy.

"That's only three. How many more before you finally crack?"

"Leo—"

I flip her over yet again, strapping her wrists over her head to the headboard. She's on full display for me, milky skin practically begging to be marked. Even though I have ensured she's drowning in pleasure, I can still see a challenge in her eyes. I know she won't actually break. There's a fire in Nikita that excites me. That tells me she can handle so much more.

"Take your clothes off," she says to me, panting. "It's only fair."

I shake my head. "You're the one tied up. You're in no position to tell me what to do."

Nikita bucks her hips, her desperation dripping from every pore. "Leo, come on."

But I don't give in. Nobody tells me what to do. I'm in control here, and she's just going to have to deal with it.

I lean forward and suck hard marks against her breasts, her ribs, the flat of her stomach. It's a rush, leaving behind traces of me knowing no one else gets to see them. They're a secret, just for her and me. I lay down on her side and claim her mouth, sliding my tongue over hers as I reach down with a single hand between her legs. I stroke her with my fingers, swallowing every tiny sound she gives me, bringing her to the edge yet again until she can no longer string together a proper sentence.

"Leo, it's—"

"Don't tell me it's too much for you."

"I can't— I just want—"

"Tell me."

"I want you inside me," she begs. "I can't take it anymore."

"That was only four times, sweet thing. Is that really the best you can do?" She lets out a frustrated little huff. I must be going soft because I'm actually starting to feel a little bad. Perhaps another time, I'll make her come five, six, seven times before finally relenting. But the strain of my cock is almost unbearable. I need her, too. "Alright, alright," I lament. "Only because you're such a good girl."

I undressed slowly, deliberately. Nothing is more exciting than the hunger in her eyes. I can tell by the way she squirms that she wants me to hurry, to take her right here and now, but it's as the old saying goes—good things come to those who wait. I enjoy the heat of her gaze roaming over my skin as I shed my shirt, my pants, and then my boxer briefs. I don't miss the way she swallows, licks her lips at the sight of my throbbing cock.

"Like what you see?" I ask her, teasing.

Nikita lets out a frustrated groan. "If you don't get over here right now—"

I chuckle, moving to the bedside table to retrieve a condom. I roll it on before climbing onto the bed, settling between her legs. But again, I don't rush. I run my hands over her legs, her body, give her breasts to squeeze. I want to savor the moment, especially with a woman like Nikita. I don't get to do this often, and when I do, I need to ensure I'm doing it right.

"What are you waiting for?" she asks with a whine.

"What's the magic word?"

"Seriously?"

"Do I look like I'm joking? I know I said we're starting from scratch, but let's not ignore the lessons of the past, either."

Nikita throws her head back in frustration. "*Please*. Leo, please."

A deep growl rises from my lungs. She's so pretty when she's on the verge of tears. I want to put her back together again. Nothing would bring me more joy.

I carefully lay my weight on top of her, aligning myself to her entrance. She may be wet and stretched thanks to my fingers, but I move slowly all the same.

I take my time sliding into her, kissing her tenderly as if to apologize for the discomfort. Her moan vibrates through me, leaves me aching and impatient. She takes me so well, fits me like a glove. And when she cries my name and her walls flutter around my cock, I know she's come undone yet again.

"I'm sorry," she pants. "I didn't mean to—"

I kiss the corner of her mouth, the tip of her nose, both of her cheeks. "It's alright. I've got you. Can I keep going?"

She nods frantically, tugging at her bindings. "Untie me. I want to touch you."

Just this once, I do as she asks, removing my tie from her wrists so she can wrap her arms around me. The first thrust is gentle. Testing the waters. But once I know she can handle it, there's nothing to hold me back.

I snap my hips against her in a rapid, hard rhythm. She feels too good. I can feel myself slipping into a state of pure ecstasy. Something feral rises to the surface, urges me to seek out the most carnal of desires. I want to feel her in every fiber of my being. I need her voice screaming in my ear, her nails racing down my back, her legs wrapped around my hips so I'm free to do as I wish.

A tight, hot coil in the pit of my stomach burns with increasing intensity. Her pussy grips me tightly, the friction so delicious it's almost enough to drive a man insane. Climax hits us both at the same time, a massive wave crashing into us. It's far more brilliant than an explosion, and ten times as powerful. When all is said and done, we are locked in each other's arms, holding on to one another like a lifeline.

I'm quick to scoop her up and press her against my body, tracing my hands over her with the utmost care. I pepper kisses into her hair, looking deeply into her eyes as I wrap her in blankets. She falls asleep on my chest, a smile curling her lips. Never in my life have I been more soothed by another person's presence.

This woman is really something special.

CHAPTER 12

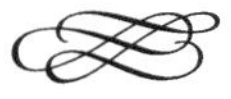

NIKITA

I awake to the smell of crispy bacon, fried eggs, and freshly brewed coffee. It takes me a moment to realize I'm not in my own bed, but once my brain finally connects the dots, all the memories from last night come rushing forward. I give the pregnancy nausea a couple of minutes to do its thing, but once I'm able, I allow myself to fall back into the sweetness of this moment. Everything else is messed up... I might as well enjoy this while it lasts.

Last night was, without a shadow of a doubt, the best night I've ever had. The second best was our first night together.

I've had sex before meeting Leo, but it wasn't very impressive. Sloppy, careless, and I'm pretty sure I didn't even get off. But what I've had with Leo is something else. Practically an out-of-body, otherworldly experience. I'm sore in places I didn't know it was possible to be, but in a good way. My muscles burn like I've just finished a good, rewarding workout. There's a hum in my veins, an echo of adrenaline coursing through me.

Stretching my arms over my head, I throw my legs over

the edge of the bed and take a quick glimpse at myself and the reflection of the bedroom mirror in the corner of the room. I'm covered in marks. Love bites pepper my skin like an arrangement of constellations.

My first instinct is to be mildly perturbed. How am I supposed to cover these before I head into practice? Upon closer inspection, however, I see that Leo was careful to leave them in places normally concealed by my clothing. On my inner thighs, my belly, my breasts. There is one on the crook of my neck, but I'm sure that's nothing a bit of makeup can't help fix.

Amusement rises within me. That sly dog.

I tiptoe around the bedroom and gather my clothes from the floor, dressing in a hurry before venturing out into the hall. The penthouse is far more impressive in the daylight. I almost didn't believe Leo when he said this place was his. He mentioned something about owning the whole building. At first, I thought it was some sort of joke. Maybe a pride thing? But now that I can truly take in my surroundings, I realize he was telling the truth.

I grow more and more fascinated and curious about Leo the more I learn about him. How many businesses is he involved in? Real estate, transportation... It seems he has his hand in a great many pots. Could he be one of those billionaire entrepreneurs I've heard about in the news? The ones who operate with a certain level of discretion. Stealth wealth, or some such. There's no need to brag when you have it all, and I don't get the sense Leo is the type to do such a thing.

Bratva.

That damn word again. No, he can't be. I push it out of my head.

I find him in the kitchen. It's massive, almost the size of

my family's entire shared apartment. He's dressed in a suit, prepared and ready for the day as he fixes us breakfast. He must have heard me coming because he speaks without turning.

"Take a seat."

"You know how to cook, too?" I tease him. "You're a man of many hidden talents."

"All men should know how to cook," he says, sounding mildly perturbed. "It's important to be self-sufficient."

I can't help but giggle. "Are you always so serious first thing in the morning?"

"Usually." He tosses his chin toward the coffee maker on the counter. It's a fancy thing with so many knobs and buttons I'm worried I could accidentally set off a self-destruct setting. "Would you like some?"

No sooner do I nod does Leo walk over and pour me a fresh cup. I don't think I've ever felt more spoiled, more taken care of.

"How do you feel?" he asks me, his tone tender and sweet. I like getting to see the side of him. It's a part I fear he hides most of the time. Getting to see him like this makes me feel special.

"I'm good," I reply softly. "Last night was amazing."

His smile grows, the widest I've ever seen. I knew Leo was handsome, but getting to see him truly smile feels like a treat. His whole face lights up, taking away all the heavy stress he always seems to carry with him. It's enough to make the butterflies in my stomach flutter, and it makes my heart skip a beat. I wish I could see him do it more often. I almost want to make it my life's mission to figure out all the little things that can make them happen.

"Last night *was* amazing," he murmurs. "I can't help but

appreciate how resilient you are. I wasn't too hard on you, was I?"

"A little bit," I confess. "But I liked it. It wasn't exactly my first tour de force, either, was it?"

He chuckles. "Good."

"I wish I could stay and eat all this food, but I'm running late for rehearsal."

"That's okay. I can pack it up for you to take it for the road. Would you like me to drop you off?"

I shake my head, grinning gleefully. "I can just walk. It's not that far."

He frowns at this. "Out of the question. I'll give you a ride."

"When do you think I'll get to see you next?" I nibble on my bottom lip, recognizing that I might be a *tad* too eager. "Tonight?"

The corners of his eyes crinkle as he smiles even wider. "Not tonight, I'm afraid. I have some business to take care of."

As disappointed as I am to hear it, I also totally understand. "Let me give you my number. Text me when you're free next?"

"Gladly."

I'll confess I'm more than a little distracted during rehearsal. I'm supposed to be perfecting the pas de deux with my dance partner, Ilya, who plays the prince, but all I can really think about is Leo.

Whenever Ilya takes my hand, I imagine it's him instead. I imagine Leo lifting me, spinning me, supporting me while I'm up on pointe. I imagine Leo when I'm trying to find a spot on the opposite wall to keep from getting dizzy.

My fantasies are always short-lived, however, because my mother is dead set on yelling at me for even the slightest of mistakes.

"Keep your spins tighter," Inessa instructs. "Pull up more. Your posture is atrocious today, Nikita."

All morning it's been a non-stop barrage of criticism and judgmental side eyes. I'm normally pretty good at keeping my frustration in check, but I can't go five seconds without my mother pointing out something I'm doing wrong. I swear I'm not that bad. I'm a skilled dancer, a professional. But with the way she's coming after me, I'm starting to wonder if I'm delusional. Her harsh words have begun to chip away at my thick skin, allowing for the doubts to creep in and take root in my mind.

When the music finally comes to a stop, Inessa claps her hands twice. Sharp like the crack of lightning. "Enough," she says with an irritable sigh. "Just stop. Nikita, come here."

I am more than a little aware of all the stares and whispering from my fellow dancers. I try not to pay them any mind, ignoring the cold lump lodged at the back of my throat. They're talking about me. I know they are. Will I make everything ten times worse if I try to address it?

"Where were you last night?" my mother asks me under her breath. "You didn't come home. I had half a mind to call the police and report you missing."

"I was just—"

"You were out with *him*, weren't you?"

The accusatory nature of her tone unsettles me. "So what if I was?"

Inessa hits me with a hard glare. "Nikita, how many times do I have to tell you? That man is—"

"Stop it," I snap. "I don't know what your problem with Leo is, but he's been nothing but kind to me. You're judging a book by its cover."

"He's not a book. With people, you can always tell."

"I'm not talking about this with you. I'm an adult, Mother. I'm allowed to see who I want to see. I'm allowed a fucking life!"

I stomp off to a different corner of the practice room where I placed my gym bag aside, refusing to listen to another word. It's time for the other dancers to practice, and I frankly need a well-deserved break. I'm probably going to pay for that little outburst later.

Kseniya is the only person to join me, helpfully handing me a water bottle and a protein bar to snack on. She wears a bright, sweet smile. "That was gorgeous."

I let out a deep, weary exhale. "Thanks. It seems like you might be the only one who thinks so."

"Are you kidding? That was nothing short of perfect. You're a huge inspiration to me. Hopefully I can dance as well as you one day."

Her words make me feel warm and tingly. After an entire session of being berated by my mother, her kindness is exactly what I need. Unfortunately, the feeling is short-lived when I notice all the people staring at me like I have a second head.

"Do you think she did it?" someone whispers.

"She couldn't earn the promotion on her own, so she had to resort to dirty tactics. It just makes sense."

"She doesn't strike me as someone who could stoop that low."

"Shhh... Quiet, she'll hear you."

Kseniya pats me on the shoulder. "Ignore them. They just like to talk."

It's hard for me to not feel vulnerable, to ignore all the gossip. It's frankly enough to make me feel a little crazy. I would never hurt Vanya, or anyone else, for that matter.

"You don't believe it, do you?" I ask her.

"Of course not! Don't you pay attention to them. Just stay focused and in your lane. They can talk until they're blue in the face. It doesn't change the fact that you're a brilliant dancer."

I breathe a little easier. "Thanks, Ksenyia."

"So, um... can I ask you kind of a strange question?"

"Sure."

"Who's that guy who's been coming around? You know, the big one with the scar?" There's an excited glint in her eye, like it's Christmas morning and she's preparing to rip into her pile of presents. "Is he your *boyfriend*?"

A shy little giggle bubbles past my lips. "I don't know that I'd label him my boyfriend per se..."

"But you're seeing each other?"

"Uh, yeah, I guess so."

"I'm *so* jealous." She pouts her lips. "I wish I had time for a boyfriend, but I'm stuck here most of the time. How did you two even meet?"

"I was having some car trouble," I tell her honestly as I begin sifting through my bag for a new pair of pointe shoes. I've been using the pair on my feet all morning, and now they're close to dead—no longer capable of supporting my weight properly. Most ballerinas go through three or four pairs a day. It's a good thing the Bolshoi provides us new pairs for free; otherwise it'd be one massive bill.

I stop rifling through my bag, however, when my hand brushes up against a piece of paper. It's small, torn out by hand with wonky edges. Something has been written on the front in sloppy handwriting. Carefully, I pick it up between my thumb and forefinger, staring at the words with growing horror.

Retire, bitch.
you better watch your back.

My mouth suddenly goes dry. My heart plummets to the pit of my stomach. Who could have done this? Gossip is one thing, but leaving threatening notes in my gym bag is something else entirely. I look around at my fellow dancers. It could have been any one of them since I left my bag unattended. Someone here is out to get me, and I have a sneaking suspicion they might be the same person who sabotaged Vanya.

Now they have a new target in mind: me.

CHAPTER 13

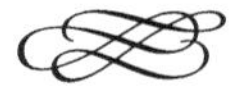

LEO

Another day, another dollar.

I once again find Erik in my office, bumbling like a moron about to wet himself on the carpet. My brother, Samuil, stands in front of the door, blocking any potential for a hasty exit.

"Do you have the money?" I ask tersely.

"Sort of..." he stutters pathetically.

I lean back in my office chair, swallowing my irritation. I could be watching Nikita dance right now, but instead, I have to deal with this slimy little idiot. "What do you mean *sort of?*"

Eric reaches into his shoulder bag and produces several pieces of fine jewelry. He sets them on the desk before me, as if for inspection. I'll be the first to admit I don't understand the first thing about gems or precious metals. For all I know, these could be fake, made of cheap plastic. Worthless.

"What the hell am I supposed to do with this?"

"I just thought... Look, I don't have the cash on hand, but these pieces are worth plenty. This one here? Real diamonds. A whole chain of them."

"Erik, I was more than kind when I accepted your cash payment for ten percent of what you owe two Fridays ago, even though I instructed you to deliver the full payment. And now, you still don't have the rest of my money. Instead, you're bringing me jewels? Make it make sense."

"Like I said, real diamonds... I'll get more money soon enough and pay it all off. Please, accept this as a gesture of good will."

"You expect me to hock these?"

"I tried finding a pawn shop that would give me the money for it, but they kept underselling me. I figured out of everyone, you might have the proper connections to give you a fair price."

I pick up one of the jewelry pieces and inspect it carefully under the light. A bracelet. A thin silver circlet with fine engravings etched into the metal. Credit where credit is due, it *is* pretty. Small diamonds lay inset, creating a sort of polka dot pattern. It could be worth several hundred thousand rubles, but that's just an estimate. I'm going to have to rely on a consultant to determine its full value.

But the longer I stare at the bracelet, the more I can picture it around Nikita's slim wrist. She doesn't wear a great deal of jewelry from what I've seen, but this might look nice on her. A perfect fit, as a matter of fact.

There are other pieces here, too. Necklaces, a few pairs of earrings, a pearl brooch. I have half a mind to ask Erik where he got all of this. What poor woman did he steal from? Did he swipe these things from his wife? Maybe from a daughter or sister? I have a hard time believing he held a jewelry store up at gunpoint, so it's really the only reasonable explanation.

Waiting around for an appraiser would take too long, but I know for a fact Roman knows his way around jewels.

He's pretty good at figuring out price points, especially considering how he wastes his money on buying fancy presents for his flavors of the week.

"Fists," I say, "call the Negotiator in."

All it takes is for Samuil to stick his head out the door and bark a quick *get the fuck in here*. Roman arrives not thirty seconds later, smoothing the lapels of a suit jacket.

"You called?" he says with an overly chipper grin. "Did you get lonely in here?"

I ignore his joke and gesture to the jewelry on the table. "How much would you say this is worth?"

My younger brother saunters over, ignoring Erik outright. He whistles as he inspects the pieces. "These are pretty. How old would you say they are?"

"A couple of them have been in my family for generations," Erik explains. "Keepsakes."

Roman hums. "Dude, this one here is an antique. I'm talking Romanov era."

I drum my fingers against the desk. "How much do you think we could get for it?"

"In total, probably eight-hundred thousand rubles."

I click my tongue. "Looks like you're a hundred thousand short, Belov."

Erik's eyes widen. "Please, this is all I have left. A hundred thousand rubles is nothing to you people."

"Money is money," I state coldly. "Count your lucky stars I haven't left you out in a ditch somewhere. You're just going to have to figure it out."

"I've already given you everything I have."

"Then you shouldn't have been gambling at one of our dens."

"The game was rigged," Erik grumbles.

I will neither confirm nor deny his accusation. There's a

reason our gambling dens are underground and well-hidden. The house is guaranteed to make bank off suckers like him. It's obviously not meant to be fair, but they should know that going in. Eric tested his luck and came out a loser. It's not my fault he didn't have the good sense to walk away.

"What are we going to do?" I ask, putting the ball in his court. "Would you prefer it if I take you out back and shoot you between the eyes? Or are you going to pay me back what you owe? I've already given you plenty of time."

Eric puts his hands up, like he's gesturing for me to slow down or stop. "I'll come up with something. I'm sure there has to be a bill or two I could push. I'll get you your money, I swear."

"That's what you said last time. Why should I believe you?"

The poor man looks like he's about to be sick. I decide not to push him any further. It's not like the Bratva is hurting for a measly hundred thousand rubles. Besides, the sooner I clean up this business, the sooner I can go and watch my favorite ballerina.

"Mark my words, this is your last chance. Do you understand?"

"Y-yes, I understand. Thank you."

I gesture to Samuil. "Get him the hell out of my face."

We go through the usual rigmarole. Bag over head, escorted out roughly. At this point, I feel like I'm going through the motions. My days are dragging out longer, slower. There will never be a shortage of people who owe us. There used to be a thrill in the chase, a sick, twisted satisfaction that came with a full repayment.

Now? Not so much.

Roman turns toward me and laughs "It could have been

worse. Remember that guy who offered to pay us in fruit baskets?"

I roll my eyes. "Don't remind me. We had to break his kneecaps to get the point across."

"I'm assuming you want me to sell these off somewhere?"

"Yes and be discreet."

"When am I ever not discreet?"

"I'm not going to dignify that with the response. Just get it done." My brother reaches for the jewelry, but I pick up the bracelet I had my eye on earlier before he can get his hands on it.

"Something caught your eye?" he asks me wryly.

"I'm keeping this. Sell the rest. Make sure the buyer doesn't rip you off."

Roman huffs. "You're talking to the Negotiator here. Getting a good deal is what I do."

"Good, then go do it."

"You know, you've been kind of absent these last few days. Where have you been sneaking off to?"

I shrug. "I don't know what you're talking about."

"Come on, man. Since when did you start keeping secrets?"

"I'm not keeping secrets."

Roman puts his hands up in mock surrender. "Fine, don't tell me. And definitely don't tell me about that secret girlfriend you've got hidden away."

I bristle, the muscles in my shoulders tensing. I don't want him or the rest of my family to know about Nikita. I've always believed in having a hard separation between personal life and work life. She's a little slice of Heaven I plan on keeping all to myself. "There's no secret girlfriend," I grumble.

"Then who's the bracelet for?" Roman urges, too keen for his own good. "I know for a fact you're not the type to play dress up. Your wrists are too fat."

"Would you get the hell out of here? I gave you a job. Any updates from the butcher?"

"None. I'm going to pay him a visit very shortly."

"When you do, I want to come with. I want this whole thing sorted before Andrei comes back from his vacation."

Roman gives me a mock soldier's salute. "You've got it, One-Eye."

Once the coast is clear, I run the pads of my thumbs over the bracelet. I can picture Nikita's face when I give it to her. I hope it will make her happy. Nothing would bring me more joy than to see her face light up with that gorgeous smile of hers. Of course, if she asks where I got it, I'll just have to spin the truth.

It's the thought that counts, after all.

CHAPTER 14

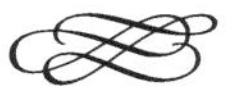

NIKITA

I get home from the Bolshoi well before Mother does. I'm thankful for it. I frankly need a break from her breathing down my neck at all hours of the day. I get no peace when I go to work, and I find no peace when I go home. Silence, at this point, is paradise to me.

Unfortunately, Dad didn't get the memo.

By the time I get back to the apartment, the lights are all on. It looks like a tornado tore the place apart. Books have been removed from shelves, all the cupboards have been opened, their contents dumped. I find Dad rummaging through the hallway closet, a collection of silverware and a few small crystal decorations gathered in a garbage bag. I have no idea what he's looking for. All I know is he looks frantic, sweaty, and pale in the face with small trinkets of varying value resting by his feet.

Dammit. Mother just allowed him to move back in, and now he's doing this again. My heart aches. The taste of disappointment lingers in my mouth.

"What's going on?" I ask, calm but embittered by an unpleasantly familiar sight .

"Nikita," he rasps. "Nikita, I'm so sorry. I thought I could handle it. I thought I could pay him back."

I drop my things on the floor and rush to my father. "What are you talking about? No more secrets, Dad. Tell me what's going on."

Dad takes a deep breath, his hands shaking with fear. "I made a mistake. The car dealership let me go."

For a moment, my mind blanks. "Wait... They fired you? When?"

Crap. It's way worse than I thought.

"A few weeks ago."

"A few *weeks*?" I exclaim. "Why didn't you say anything sooner?"

His eyes drop to the floor, unable to look at me. "I was ashamed," my father confesses. "I'm the man of the house. I should be able to provide. That job was all I had to support you through your lessons. To keep a roof over our heads."

My stomach ties itself in knots. "You said something about paying someone back?"

"I was desperate," he continues. "A friend of a friend told me about the place. A gambling den downtown. It's not easy to find. The type of place where you need a password to get in."

A sharp chill stabs through my chest. "This can't be happening. Please tell me it isn't true."

"I wasn't thinking. I took what little I had in our savings account and thought I'd try my luck. There's no limit in these places. I thought maybe I could make just enough to keep us going for a little while longer. And in the beginning, I was doing really well! I made a hundred thousand and then two hundred thousand. It kept going and going. I was on a hot streak!"

Dad doesn't even have to finish his sentence for me to understand what's happening. I think I might vomit.

"Then what happened?" I ask, forcing myself to stomach listening to the rest.

"Fortune is a fickle lady," he says cryptically. "One thing led to another, and suddenly I was out so much money it would make your eyes roll into the back of your head."

I worry my bottom lip with my teeth. "And who exactly do you owe this money to?"

Dad dares to look at me, the corners of his eyes red rimmed and glossy. "Oh, Nikita."

"Tell me, Dad. Just say it. I already know but I need to hear you say it."

I have never known my father to be a weak man. All my life, he has been a steady fixture within our family. I love him with all my heart. When my mother was angry or disappointed in me, I could always trust that my father had a hug and kind words to share. I went to him when I had nightmares. I trusted him to tuck me in at night. I have always admired and respected him.

But right now, standing before me, he seems like nothing but a stranger.

"The Bratva," he says gravely. "I owe the Bratva."

I'm not sure which happens first. Does the room start spinning before the floor falls out from under me? Or is it the other way around? I suppose it doesn't matter. What *does* matter is the fact that my father owes money to the worst possible people to owe money to. We're in a world of trouble. I'm torn between being disappointed and downright angry. But I knew all this. I've known for a while since it's why I went to Loza in the first place. I've known, but knowing and hearing the words aloud are still two very different things.

"How much do you still owe?"

"Only a hundred thousand."

"*Only*," I scoff. "How much did you originally owe?"

"That's not important."

"Dad," I state firmly. "You better tell me right now before I lose it."

"It really doesn't matter," he says in a small, almost defeated voice. "I gave them almost all of your and your mother's jewelry to pay for everything."

My jaw drops. *Now* I'm mad. Now, finding him rummaging through my things that evening makes more sense. I should've checked my jewelry box right then and there. I would've found it empty. "You *what*? How could you do that? Dad, what were you thinking?"

For the first time in my life, I see my father cry. He sobs into his palms, shoulders shaking, his face twisted with shame and grief. "I'm so sorry," he says over and over. "I'm so sorry. I keep making mistake after mistake. I'm trying to fix this. I *will* fix this. I just need more—"

I shake my head, turn on my heels, and take the duffel bag out of my room. This day was bound to come. At least I was prepared for it. "This is what's going to happen, Dad," I say as I hand the wads of cash over to him. This is more than enough to cover the remainder of what you owe, and it should keep you out of trouble. You're going straight to whoever you're supposed to pay. You're going to wipe your hands clean of this nonsense, and we're going to forget it ever happened."

He is understandably baffled. "Where did you get this much money, Nikita?"

"I pawned some of my things and Grandma's silverware

from Loza," I say, my tone flat. "I have known about your financial misery for a while. I just thought you'd have the wisdom to resolve this yourself and in an honorable manner after Mother threw you out the first time. Clearly, that wasn't the case. Here you are, rummaging through our drawers again..."

"You're not going to tell her?"

I chew on the inside of my cheek. On one hand, I know I should. Inessa may be getting on my nerves right now, but she deserves to be kept in the loop. Shouldn't her husband be honest with her? But on the other hand, I understand my father's hesitance. She is a frightening woman on a good day. I can only imagine what it would be like to deliver this awful news, especially after how horribly she blew up when she first caught him looking for things to pawn around the house.

"You need to get going. Fix this, once and for all," I say to him.

Dad nods slowly, gloomy defeat set into the dark features of his face. There are heavy circles beneath his eyes, his lips are chapped, his nose is runny. He's a shadow of the man who raised me.

He takes the money and leaves first. Ten minutes pass in heavy silence as I blink the tears away and decide I need some fresh air. As I head toward the door, I can't help but wonder if there was something I could have done differently. What would have happened if I had noticed something was wrong sooner? He has been suffering with this guilt the entire time.The thoughts rattle around inside my skull as I exit the building, pulling my winter jacket closed over my chest. What a nightmare this has been.

I barely make it two blocks before my phone dings with a text message.

. . .

I hope you had a good day.

Leo's text immediately lifts some of the stress off my shoulders. I have half a mind to tell him what's happened, but maybe that isn't the sort of thing you drop on a person you've just started seeing. Well, I'm also pregnant with his child, but that's a whole other can of worms that's waiting to be opened at some point. Instead, I text him back.

It was good. I'm thinking of you.

I'm thinking of you too.
When can I see you again?

I'll be practicing late tomorrow.
I trust you have a way in?

I'll see you then.

CHAPTER 15

LEO

I bring flowers, a massive bouquet of white and red roses, their thorns already removed. I don't want Nikita pricking herself.

My dear friend Pavel, the security guard, lets me in after I slip him a couple hundred. He turns a blind eye as I step into the building, pretending to be incredibly interested in whatever non-existent dirt is beneath his fingernails.

Finding her is easy. Since it's after hours, the lights of the vacant practice rooms are all off, making it easy to spot her from down the hall. Musical notes float into my ear, melodies mixing with harmonies, sweeping and cinematic.

I stand in the doorway and watch her through the glass, admiring the beautiful lines she creates with her body. I've never been a fan of ballet— until now. I can see its appeal. The beauty and innate charm, the discipline that goes into creating a living work of art.

I especially love how Nikita loses herself in the music. It's like she's on an entirely different plane of existence when she dances, moving about a space only she can see and feel. Her emotions come alive with every delicate swoop of her arm and the intricate footwork carrying her around. I thoroughly believe she is a fairy, spreading magic and love and cheer. She transports me through her storytelling. I can only imagine how wonderful it will be to see her in full costume.

But the longer I watch her, the more I begin to realize something is wrong. She makes mistakes from time to time, which I frankly don't see anything wrong with. It's just that she grows increasingly more frustrated. There's a weight to her today, like something is bearing down on her thoughts and body. She doesn't float as easily as she normally does, her smile seems a bit more forced than usual. When she makes an abrupt stop, places her hands on her hips, and grumbles something under her breath as she glares at the floor, I realize I need to intervene.

Something isn't right.

I need to *make* it right.

She notices me the second I step into the practice room, her eyes sparkling with recognition. She hurries to the small stereo where her iPhone is plugged in to play the music, pressing a button to pause it mid-note.

"I was wondering when you were going to show up," she says lightly, whatever trace of irritation I saw earlier is gone in an instant.

I approach, flowers in hand. "I had to make a pit stop."

"These are beautiful, Leo, thank you so much."

"Is something bothering you?" I ask, not one to let sleeping dogs lie.

"I'm fine," she says a little too easily. I can tell she's lying, though, because of the stiffness of her words and her inability to look directly at me.

"Nikita, did something happen?"

The sound of her name breaks her from her trance. She shakes her head profusely, forces a smile. "Nothing happened. I just practiced a little too hard. It's been a long day and I think I need a break."

"Fair. Do you need help stretching?"

She giggles. "Are you volunteering?"

"Depends on your answer."

Nikita sets her bouquet of flowers next to her gym bag. I notice a small, crumpled up piece of paper sticking out of the corner. Curious, I bend down and pick it up before she has a chance to protest. What I see greatly disturbs me.

"Who wrote this?" I ask, trying to keep my voice level and my rage in check. "Is someone threatening you?"

"It was a joke," she says. I don't believe her. Nikita takes the note back and squeezes it tight in her fist before tossing it away into a trash bin near the door.

"I'm not well-versed in comedy, but that doesn't look like a joke."

"It's nothing, Leo. Come on, come help me stretch."

I want to press the issue. I never did find out what happened with the saboteur. If there's even a chance they could be going after Nikita, I want to take matters into my own hands. What if they take things too far? One day, it's threatening notes. The next day, someone's taking a bat to her knee to take her out of the running. Even though it's all hypothetical scenarios made up in my head, they nonetheless make my blood boil and my heart pound. I can't stand the thought of Nikita getting hurt.

The moment she takes my hand, all my stress suddenly melts away. Nikita guides me to the barre and places my palm over the wood railing.

"You could use a stretch, too," she says, teasing. "You're all bunched up in the shoulders. Here, do as I do."

"I didn't realize I'd be joining the class. Not exactly dressed for it."

"Take your coat off and stay awhile," she says easily before hinging at the hips and exposing her tight little ass through her light pink tights. I have a sneaking suspicion she is doing this on purpose, because within an instant, my mind goes blank and I can no longer focus on anything but her long legs and supple behind.

I step forward, crowding behind her, hands on either side of her hips as a low moan escapes me.

"You look pretty in pink," I mutter.

"You're not stretching, Leo."

"No, I most certainly am not."

Nikita rises, pressing her back against my chest. I watch her in the reflection of the mirror, engrossed by our size difference. I like how much shorter she is, how much smaller. I could wrap her in my arms for days, keep her safe in my embrace.

Unable to help myself, I dip down and kiss her shoulder. Once, twice, working my way up to the crook of her neck. She sighs contentedly, reaching up with one hand to comb her fingers through my hair and caress my cheek.

"You really *are* a bad influence," she mumbles, giggling to herself.

"We're the only ones here, right?" I ask her, a sudden hunger latching on to my hind-brain. I want her. I *need* her.

Her cheeks turn a bright pink. "Here?"

"Not if you don't want to." Except I really, *really* hope she wants to. I don't think I can survive the trip back to my place, the wait too excruciating to bear.

Nikita licks her lips, her eyes full of lust. "Go on, then. Show me exactly what you want to do."

My hands have a mind of their own, reaching up to

cover her breasts and give her nipples a light pinch. I bury my nose in her hair, breathing her in. I'm an addict, unable to get my fix. All I know is I need more.

"Are you particularly fond of these tights?" I ask her.

"No, why do you as—"

Before she even has a chance to finish, I reach down, press her shoulders forward so she bends, and grab a fistful of the delicate fabric, tearing it apart in one swift motion. The sound of the rip is delicious, enticing, as is her soft, delighted gasp. I'm already rock hard and aching to have her, but like always, I want to make sure her pleasure comes before mine.

I slide a finger between her legs. It comes away soaked with her arousal. I let her watch in the mirror's reflection as I suck my finger clean, savoring the sweetness on my tongue.

"Already so wet for me," I mutter. "Do you want me, Nikita?"

"Yes," she breathes, her pupils blown wide.

I drop to my knees and lick her pussy, teasing her entrance and circling her clit with my fingers. She grips the bars, her knuckles white, all while her heated breath fogs up the mirror in front of her. I like the way her knees shake, how she's at my mercy and already dripping for me.

"Feel that," I tell her, taking one of her hands to press against my erection. "Feel what you do to me, Nikita. You're going to have to fix that."

"Tell me how," she says around a moan. "Tell me what you want, Leo."

"I want you on your knees, pretty girl. I want to see your mouth on me."

With a nod, Nikita turns and hastily begins to work on my belt. The metal rip of my zipper rings loudly in my ear.

She's quick to yank the waistband of my underwear down, freeing my throbbing cock.

All I can do is stare as she wraps her lips around the head, her tongue darting out to lap at the bead of cum collecting there. She takes me into her mouth, inch by careful inch, the wet heat of her tongue nothing short of nirvana.

It feels good. Maybe a little too good.

She bobs her head up and down the length of my shaft, her fingers wrapping around the base to stroke me in tandem. I barely have a grip on reality at this point, each sweet pass of her tongue whiting out my mind.

I smooth my palm over her hair, gripping her neat little bun for purchase. "Ease up," I tell her. But she doesn't. Nikita's enjoying herself a little too much to bother listening to me. That won't do at all. I slip my fingers beneath her chin and tilt her face up. "Come here."

No sooner do I help her to her feet do I spin her around and bend her forward against the mirror. She grips the barre for support as I shove the scraps of her tights and underwear aside, sliding the head of my cock over her folds. I can't take it any longer, and judging by her lustful gaze, neither can she.

I press into her, relishing the heat of her body. My pace is brisk and unrelenting, but I know she can take it. Nikita is so much stronger, so much more resilient than she looks. I know this deep down, because on some level, she and I are the same. Our burdens may look different, but they weigh heavily on our shoulders all the same. We're both dedicated to our crafts. We both know what it's like to put the hours in, often thankless. Even though she doesn't know what I do, I feel like Nikita is the only one in the world who truly understands me.

She finds her pleasure with a breathy shout, her knees shaking as climax grips her tight. I'm not far behind her, the hot coil in the pit of my stomach burning brightly, until all of a sudden, it explodes like a fireworks show. Brilliant, hypnotizing, and unfortunately over all too fast.

I sweep her hair aside and kiss the nape of her neck, breathing in peaches and cherry blossoms. I wrap my arms around her middle and hold her against me. We may be sated for now, but I'm personally nowhere near through with her. I have all night, and I intend to use every minute to its fullest.

"Let me take you home," I murmur in her ear.

She nods, watching me in the mirror's reflection. "Please," she says, so soft and sweet.

CHAPTER 16

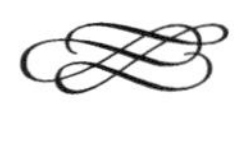

NIKITA

Mother's probably going to have a fit again when she realizes I'm not coming home tonight, but I don't care. When I'm with Leo, it's like I have blinders on. All I can see, all I can hear, all I can even think about—is him.

The drive to his place is spent in quiet anticipation. My core throbs, eager for his touch as we make our way through the late-night streets. There's next to no traffic, making for a smooth ride. When he offers me his hand over the center console, I take it. Leo is so tender when he wants to be, brushing the pad of his thumb over my knuckles. His touch is intimate, thoughtful. I think about what my mother said about judging a book by its cover, how with people you supposedly can always tell. She's wrong. Especially about him.

He puts his hand on my knee, and I close my eyes to focus on the feeling of his calloused palm sliding up my thigh. I suck in a sharp breath through clenched teeth when he brazenly slips his hand down my pants and underwear to roll his fingers over my clit.

His attention is split between me and the road as he growls. "Still so wet for me. I can't wait to get you home."

"Drive faster," I whimper, gripping the door handle as pleasure builds. Am I about to come in his passenger seat? *God*, I really hope so.

"Not yet, naughty girl," he says with an easy chuckle. "Just wait until we get back to my place. I've got a treat for you."

My face feels warm, flushed with arousal and excitement. "What kind of treat?"

"You seem to really enjoy being tied up the other night. Am I wrong?"

"No, you're not wrong. I really liked it."

"Thought so."

I lick my lips, letting a hand slide between my legs to keep his fingers pressed against me. "Just tell me."

"I don't think I will. It'll be better as a surprise."

My heart skips a beat when I hear the genuine delight in his tone. My curiosity burns hot. What on Earth could he be talking about?

By the time we finally get to his penthouse, I'm practically buzzing with barely contained excitement. The trip from the car to the elevator feels like it takes forever. I can hardly stand it. Neither can he. The moment the elevator doors close, he's on me, corralling me against the wall and caging me in with his massive body. He kisses me with urgency, like the world's about to end and he'd rather spend his last few seconds breathing me in.

The elevator ride up takes an eternity, but I don't mind so much. Not if it means I can have Leo all to myself. I can't stop touching him. I want my fingers in his hair, stroking his jaw, rolling over his shoulders and chest and arms and abs. I want to feel the weight of his body on me at all hours of the day, a shield against the rest of the world.

His arms bring me a sense of safety, his warm glances a sense of calm. Is this what love feels like? To feel so wholly connected with another soul that the thought of not having him in my life leaves an awful sting in my chest?

When the elevator doors ding and slide open, Leo is quick to scoop me off my feet. I wrap my legs around his hips and my arms around his neck so he can carry me more easily down the familiar hall to his bedroom.

He sets me on the edge of the bed, grinning.

My heart stutters. I have never seen a man more beautiful.

"Where's the surprise you wanted to show me?" I ask him with a giggle.

"Here," he replies, starting toward his bedside table. He opens the drawer and pulls something out. Something red and silky. Upon further inspection, I realize what it is.

Rope. *Shibari* rope.

I'll confess I'm not overly familiar with Shibari, though I have seen it in passing on the rare occasion I decide to spoil myself with a quick peruse through a porn site. Women have needs too, after all. Before tonight, it never really occurred to me how enticing it could be. Maybe because I never had anyone in my life I trusted enough to tie me up and mold me the way they see fit.

"You can say no," Leo says. "It's not for everyone, but I figured maybe..."

"Yes," I say quickly.

"Are you sure?"

"I trust you. Whatever you want—yes."

The look in his eyes is both vulnerable and hopeful. He kneels before me, rope in hand, tilting his head up to kiss me sweetly. "I'll take such good care of you," he says, like *I'm* the one doing *him* a favor.

I caress his cheek, running my thumb over his scar with the utmost care. I don't think there's anything in the world I wouldn't give him. This is a man who has only known control, but for the first time, I sense his hesitation. His nerves. Like the simple act of expressing his interest, something so niche and perhaps misunderstood, has exposed him like a nerve. He'll find no judgment in me, no repulsion. I am here, open and willing.

"I know," I whisper with a smile. "I know you'll take care of me. How do we start?"

"By establishing some ground rules."

I throw my head back and laugh. "Seriously?"

Leo hits me with a hard look. "Seriously. If at any point you become uncomfortable, or you decide you don't want to do this, you have to let me know, Nikita. I have to trust you'll tell me."

I nod, moved by his concern. "I will, I promise."

"Okay," he murmurs. "Now what I want you to do is to undress."

I do as he asks, rising to my feet as I slowly slip out of my clothes. I let them fall to the floor, forgotten. The entire time, our eye contact is not broken. He remains clothed, seated on the edge of the bed. He watches me like a hawk, savoring every moment like it's a holy experience.

"Come here," he says.

I step forward obediently, waiting on bated breath as he begins his intricate work. The rope is soft against my skin, dragging with next to no resistance. I don't know why I thought it would be rougher, so it's a pleasant surprise when he sweeps the end over my chest and crisscrosses it. Leo works diligently, his concentration never wavering. He's really good at this. Twisting the rope here and crossing the ends over one another, knotting everything behind me neatly so my wrists are bound behind my back.

He's created a sort of harness, one that cups the shape of my small breasts and accentuates the dip of my waist. The pattern is tight, the rope flush against my skin, but I don't feel constricted or claustrophobic in any way. He's made sure of that. The gentle sweep of his fingers over my skin makes me want to melt, his attention to detail rendering me a puddle in his hands. When he's done, he carefully turns me so I can review my reflection in the bedroom mirror.

It's beautiful. I feel beautiful.

I feel desirable.

"How is it? he asks me, checking in. "Not too bad?"

"It's great."

"I'm going to fuck you now," he growls in my ear, his voice vibrating through my chest.

"Stop talking about it and do it." I challenge him, every fiber of my being on edge and ready for whatever comes next.

He guides me to the bed, presses my belly to the mattress. I can't move, but that's sort of the point. I have complete faith in him, that he won't take things too far. It's that trust, that deep, inexplicable understanding in one another that's so appealing to me. My arms can be bound, his weight bearing down on me, but I know in the end, he'll keep me safe.

He spreads my legs and settles between my thighs, kissing hard marks against my skin before teasing me with his tongue. He prods my entrance with the tip, uses his fingers to drive me to the point of madness. I lose track of how many times he makes me come. I'm lost to my pleasure, drowning in ecstasy, and I still crave more.

"Please," I beg him. "Please, I want you inside me. I can't take it anymore!"

"You want my cock, Nikita? Do you want me to fuck you until you scream?"

"Yes!" I exclaim, writhing beneath him. I moan his name, again and again, a prayer I can never get enough of. I'm desperate, unhinged. I need this man like I need air.

The sound of his zipper and the jingle of his belt is music to my ears. It means I'm getting close. It's the reward I've been waiting for, the finish line.

I gasp when he plunges into me, pistoning in and out at a rapid pace. The friction is delicious, the burn is otherworldly. The head of his cock sweeps over my sweet spot over and over, almost like he's aiming for it. Even in the throes of passion, he's thinking of me. He wants me to come undone first, like it's his mission in life. How did I get so lucky as to have such a selfless lover?

I don't last very long. My senses are alight. My skin is on fire, the intoxicating moans and grunts of our lovemaking ringing loudly in my ear. I can smell the scent of his pine cologne, can smell him on the richness of his sheets. I can taste his tongue on mine, see a blur of color as the room spins around us. The tips of my fingers and toes tingle, a warm hum following the aftermath. Exhaustion is quick to follow, but it's a good kind of tired that leaves me thoroughly satisfied.

He comes inside me, his seed filling me up. My pussy throbs around him, clenching around his thick shaft. I try to catch my breath, try to recollect my thoughts. I whine when I feel his weight leave me, but it's only momentary. His hands roam my body, quickly undoing the knots of his rope. It goes slack, freeing my arms from behind me.

Leo pulls me into his embrace, lovingly pressing kisses

to my hair, my cheeks, the tip of my nose. He spoils me with sweet nothings, murmuring how beautiful I am, how good I did, how wonderful I make him feel.

It's hard to keep my eyes open, but I don't think Leo cares. He combs his fingers through my hair and speaks in hushed whispers. My heavy eyelids flutter shut and sleep finally claims me.

CHAPTER 17

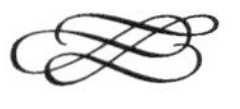

NIKITA

I wake up first. The golden light of morning streams in through the curtains of Leo's bedroom, painting his sleeping face in a calm, soothing light. I try not to rouse him, instead taking the opportunity to study his features.

He looks younger when he's asleep, less troubled. The permanent scowl he wears is nowhere to be found, his easy breathing rhythmic and calm. A part of me wants to stay here forever, locked in this moment for all eternity. We don't have to think about our troubles or the world outside these walls.

I've found a lovely little escape here with Leo. I don't have to think about the endless hours of practice, the frankly hostile environment I have to go to work in every day, or the fact that my father has been hiding money problems from us for weeks. The more I dwell on it, the more anxious and tight my chest becomes.

There's nothing else in the world I love more than ballet, but my mother has really ruined any joy I once found in the art form. Nothing is good enough. *I'm* not good enough. It's all the more reason I want to stay with Leo. To him, I can do no wrong. I'm beautiful and perfect and who wouldn't want to bask in his compliments and attention?

I dip down and kiss his forehead, studying his scarred eye with great interest. It doesn't scare me in the slightest. If anything, I almost feel sad. It must have hurt. The fact that he so selflessly put himself in harm's way to protect his brother is just a testament of his character.

"See something you like?" he mumbles sleepily.

I pull back a little and giggle. "Sorry, did I wake you?"

He hums.

"I have to get going. I need to grab some fresh clothes from home and then go to rehearsal."

"Do they ever give you a day off?"

"Nope. Not this close to the show's opening."

Leo grumpily wraps his arms around my middle and hugs me tight. "Don't go."

I laugh. "Are you pouting?"

"*No*."

"You totally are."

Leo yawns, his eyes cracking open. "Maybe a little. At least let me make you breakfast?"

I smile so wide my cheeks start to hurt. "How can I possibly say no to that?"

I'm just about to throw my legs over the bed and get started for the day, when Leo says, "Wait, I have something for you."

"For me? Is this another one of your surprises?"

Leo sits up in bed and reaches to his side, pulling something small from the bedside drawer. A square box that fits in the palm of his hand. At first, I think it might be a ring which sends my heart into a tizzy. It's a little early to be thinking about such things, isn't it? But then I realize the box is much bigger, the size of a notepad. I tell my racing mind to calm down.

He hands it to me. "Saw this and thought of you."

Nibbling on my bottom lip I lift the lid and peer inside excitedly. My face falls when I see it. A bracelet. Silver with intricate etchings, small inset diamonds in the metal. It looks familiar. *Too* familiar.

I gave them almost all of your and your mother's jewelry to pay for everything.

Dad's words scream loudly in my ear.

This has to be some sort of coincidence. Surely more than one version was made and sold. I'm sure there's a logical explanation here.

The Bratva. I owe the Bratva.

That ugly fucking word again.

"Is something wrong?" Leo asks, his brows furrowing.

"No," I say quickly. "It's just so beautiful. It just took me—"

"By surprise?"

I laugh weakly. I hope he doesn't notice. "Yeah, exactly."

Leo takes the bracelet from me and slips it onto my wrist. A perfect fit. Almost like I knew it would be. "It looks good on you."

"Where did you even get this?" I ask as casually as possible. I have no reason to be suspicious of him, but my guts are tying themselves into knots. There's no denying this is incredibly strange.

"A pawn shop," he says smoothly. "I was passing by. Saw it in a window. I thought you might like it."

I can feel the tips of my ears burning. He saw it in a

pawn shop? Dad *did* say he sold our jewelry because of the money he owed. Leo wouldn't lie to me, would he? What reason would he have?

Bratva.

"Come on," he says, offering me his hand. "I'll make you breakfast."

The moment I slip my palm into his, my worries wash away. How ridiculous am I being? Leo, a member of the Bratva? How silly. There's simply no way. Wouldn't he have guards or something? Everything I've heard about the Bratva is terrifying; Leo is far from terrifying.

I throw on one of his large shirts because I frankly can't be bothered to pick up all my clothes right now, and I like the way he smells. He throws on a pair of sweatpants before wrapping his arm over my shoulder, our hips bumping as we make our way down the hall side by side, laughing softly.

Everything is normal until we round the corner. I stop short, swallowing a yelp when I see a group of people standing in his kitchen. Four men, two women—the latter of whom are identical twins. They're dressed rather well for so early in the morning, business casual with discrete pieces that hint at their wealth. The men have their silver Rolex watches, the women have understated diamond stud earrings. If I didn't know any better, I'd say they were just about ready to start some sort of conference.

"Leo?" I say, looking up to him. "Who are they and what are they doing in your breakfast nook?"

"Sorry," one of the women says. She has vibrant red hair and dazzling blue eyes. "We didn't realize Leo had company; otherwise we would have called first."

Leo sighs, running a hand through his hair. "You should call regardless, Charlotte."

"It's a bit of an emergency," one of the men says. I think I've seen him before, at the taxi Depot. Roman, I think he said his name was.

I give Leo's hand a squeeze. "Emergency? Is everything okay?"

I notice a shift in his demeanor almost instantaneously. Where a moment ago he was completely relaxed and content, now everything about him is hard, cold, and tense. There's a tightness in his shoulders, a rigid set to his jaw. His frown has come back, deep and intimidating.

He dips down quickly to press his lips to my temple.

"Go get dressed, Nikita."

"But—"

"*Now.*"

He's never been short with me, which tells me something serious is going down. Who are these people? Family? It's the only explanation I can think of that would explain how they gained access to his penthouse so easily. The men sure do look like him. Brothers. The women I have no idea about. Friends maybe? Either way, I don't stick around long enough to find out. Leo gives me a firm nudge in the direction of the bedroom. They don't start talking until I'm well out of sight.

I pick up my clothes and get dressed, straining to hear down the hall. I pick up bits and pieces, but not enough to get a whole picture.

"You're back early, Andrei," Leo grumbles.

"One of the twins came down with a cold. We decided to come back so they can get some proper rest."

"I didn't know you had a girlfriend," someone else says.

"What's this about?" Leo snaps, ignoring the comment.

"We got a report in. A lead on the butcher. Someone said they closed up shop. They're in the wind."

"I want this dealt with, Leo." It's a woman who speaks this time. One of the twins.

"I'm handling it, Sandra."

"Are you? Seems you have a pretty little distraction taking up all your time."

"Leave her out of it."

"Does she know?" someone else asks. Roman, I think.

The rest of the conversation is too quiet for my ears to pick up. My heart beats rapidly in my chest. I know it's rude to eavesdrop, but my curiosity is piqued. What are they talking about? What butcher? I thought they owned a taxi company?

They all hush up when I return, properly dressed with my hair pulled back in a loose ponytail. Not sure what else to do and feeling incredibly awkward, I dare to give a little wave.

"Hi, everyone. I'm Nikita."

Both women are quick to greet me, sauntering over with big smiles. They have a breathtaking presence, impossible to ignore.

"I'm Sandra," the first one says, offering her hand to shake. "And this is my sister, Charlotte. It's very nice to meet you."

"Likewise," I say.

"So," Charlotte starts with a mischievous tone. "How long have you and Leo been a thing?"

From the other side of the kitchen island, Leo clenches his fists. "Cee." It's a warning. I'm not sure why he's so irritated.

"Not very long," I admit.

"You two serious?"

I wouldn't be surprised if my whole face is red. It *feels*

serious, but I'm not sure if I'm ready to have this conversation. Especially not with so many people in the room. "I should really get going," I say with a nervous giggle. "I have to get to practice."

"Practice?" Sandra inquires.

"I'm a ballerina with the Bolshoi."

Charlotte turns and pumps her brows at Leo. "The ballet, you say? Goodness, and here I thought Leo didn't enjoy the arts."

"Quite the contrary," I reply. "He made a massive sponsorship donation only a few weeks ago. He's one of our biggest patrons."

Leo clears his throat, uncomfortable about something. He makes his way to me and places his hand on the small of my back to guide me towards the elevator. "You don't want to be late," he mutters, his words unusually tight.

"It was nice to meet you all."

He presses the button, calls for the car. "Sorry about them. It's just business."

"It sounds serious."

"I have to deal with it. Otherwise, I'd drop you off myself."

I press my hand to his chest and smile. "It's okay. I understand. Truly."

"Can I text you later?"

"Of course." I hop up on my toes and press a kiss to his lips. "I'll see you later, handsome."

Leo places his hands on my hips and kisses me once before the elevator finally arrives. I get the idea he doesn't want me to go, and I frankly don't want to go either. But time isn't on our side, and we both have pressing matters to attend to.

I get into the elevator and wave goodbye as the doors slide closed. When I catch a glint off the bracelet he gifted me, my smile falls. Something isn't adding up, but I don't even know where to begin to look for answers. There's more to Leo than meets the eye. More than he's letting on.

And if I'm being honest, it's starting to worry me.

CHAPTER 18

LEO

"Cute," Andrei says as he takes a seat at my kitchen table, steepling his fingers together and resting his elbows on the surface. "She doesn't exactly fit your type."

"Let's cut to the chase here," I interject. "You said the butcher's on the run?"

Roman nods. "Samuil and I followed up in person like you asked. When we arrived, the whole place was shuttered."

A flicker of annoyance licks at the nape of my neck. Not good. "Any sign of them?"

Samuil crosses his arms. "If we knew where they were, we would have dealt with them."

Sandra sighs as she takes a seat across her husband's lap. Outside, the two of them are fierce pakhans. They rule Moscow together with an iron fist and unwavering loyalty to one another. But inside, they're lovey dovey as hell and it's frankly too much for me to stomach so early in the morning.

"You did a good job of running things while we were away," she says, "but now that we're back, we need to tighten our leash on Moscow. It's not your fault, of course.

Andrei and I expected people to get a little brave in our absence. But it's time to crack down on this misbehavior. If the butcher is skimming off the top, we need to make an example of them."

I nod. "I agree."

"The three of you will go and investigate," Andrei says without missing a beat. He and Sandra are always so in tune, always on the same wavelength. It's no wonder they make one hell of a team. "Charlotte, put some feelers out. There will be a monetary reward for any information provided that will lead to their capture. Although I'd ideally like to handle this as quietly as possible. We don't need our enemies knowing we've got trouble within our ranks."

"I'll get dressed," I say. "This could have been a phone call, you know."

Roman laughs. "Oh, we're sorry. We just figured you'd have breakfast ready by now."

I sneer. "Who said I'd feed you?"

"You're, like, the designated family cook," Charlotte says. "Come on. We can't go cracking heads on an empty stomach."

With a weary grumble, I start toward the stove. "Fine. God, you're all insufferable."

"We're *family*," Roman corrects.

Kuznetsov & Sons Butcher Shop is a real hole in the wall, wedged between a dry cleaner, and what I'm pretty sure is a condemned apartment building judging by its boarded up windows and the massive lock on the front door. The awning that provides shade for the display window is covered in moss and leaves, practically rotting. The inside is completely dark, but even without power, the place looks so unwelcoming it's frankly a surprise it's managed to stay in business for this long.

Samuil tries the door. He shakes his head. "Locked."

I tilt my head in Damien's direction. "Check the back."

He nods. "On it."

Roman and I wait on the curb, looking around at our surroundings. It's relatively quiet this morning. Not a lot of foot traffic. This is a sleepy neighborhood. Unassuming. Even if we wanted to ask around, there aren't enough people out and about to ask questions. Tracking down our missing butcher might be a far more difficult task than I first anticipated.

"How much has this guy stolen from us?" Roman asks.

"If he's the one skimming, enough to retire to Fiji."

"We can't let him get away with it."

"Tell me something I don't know."

I'm growing impatient, my fingers twitching. I haven't craved a smoke in a long time. In fact, I haven't thought about a cigarette once since meeting Nikita. Maybe there's something to this whole stress theory. Now that Andrei and Sandra are back to take the helm, maybe it will take some of the burden off my shoulders. Still, being in the field isn't ideal. I'd much prefer to work behind the scenes, not chase after money that's rightfully ours.

Damian returns. "The back door's locked from the inside."

Irritated, I step forward, using the momentum to drive my heel into the front door's lock. It swings open violently, bits of the wooden frame splintering off. I don't have time or patience for this.

"Do a sweep," I order. "Anything that might be a clue as to where they went."

My brothers move quickly, efficiently. Unfortunately,

this isn't our first rodeo. Back when we were nothing more than common street thugs, we had to chase our fair share of debtors. We searched the premises, looking for anything and everything that might have resale value.

The butcher shop has been pretty much trashed beyond recognition. Kuznetsov might have expected us to come a-knocking, so he salted the earth before our arrival. There's still meat in the refrigerator, left to spoil. There's no cash to be found in the register, gutted for every kopek. The processing machines in the back could fetch us a decent sum, but upon closer inspection, I realize they've all been dismantled. Parts are missing or destroyed. The butcher was thorough.

I force my way into the tiny little office in the back. It's no bigger than a broom closet, a tight squeeze. Documents and receipts lie shredded on the floor, an impossible jigsaw left for me to sort through. Even if I could put everything back together, it'd take too long. I doubt I'll find anything of use here with regards to their finances.

A bitter taste coats my tongue. This isn't turning out the way I'd hoped. I can't help but shoulder the blame. If only we had acted faster, maybe we could have caught our man before he escaped into the night. I'm going to have to report back to Andrei about this, and that's never a conversation anyone wants to have. He may be my brother, but he's still the ruthless leader of the Bratva. I can only hope he'll be lenient with me for old time's sake.

"Anything?" Roman calls from the front.

I'm about to yell back when something catches my attention out of the corner of my eye. A picture frame, lying flat on its face on the small administrative desk. I pick it up, exposing the photograph within. It's a picture of Kuznetsov and his sons, after which this butcher shop was named.

Kuznetsov himself is easy to identify given the bloody apron he wears. His sons, four of them, are also surprisingly recognizable.

Staring me in the face are Arman, Vlad, Georgi, and Kostya.

The night shift.

The motherfucking night shift.

This whole time, they've been right under my nose. How could I have been such an idiot? Not only have they been skimming off the top, but they even got my approval for a Christmas bonus. Those assholes took advantage of my rare—and rightfully so, it would seem—kindness, and I've never been more pissed. They have made a fool out of me. They've made a fool of the Bratva. I have no choice but to go to extreme measures, something I was desperately hoping to avoid.

They'll find no pity from me. If they really were that desperate for the cash, I'm sure we could have come to agreeable terms. But they still stole from us, stole from *me*. I don't always like what I have to do, but now they've given me no choice in the matter.

I present the picture to my brothers who have now gathered in the front of the shop. With a glance, they understand the severity of the situation.

Roman reaches for his phone. "I'll call Andrei. We'll bring them in."

"What if they're gone already?" Damien asks.

"They couldn't have gotten far," Samuil points out. "At least now we know who we're dealing with."

"Put a reward out," I say. "No need to go into details. Just circulate this picture amongst our network. Whoever brings these men to us will be paid substantially—"

Before I can get another word out, the angry screech of

tires breaks the tension in the air. Through the shop's front display window, I see a dark SUV racing into our line of sight. The windows are lowered, several guns pointed in our direction.

Shit.

It's an ambush.

"Get down!" I shout at my brothers just in time for a hail of bullets to burst through the windows.

My brothers and I drop to the floor. Glass shatters all around us, the walls shaking with the violent attack. Dust rises into the air, mixing with pulverized drywall. We're pinned down, unable to return fire. They don't give us a chance. I can barely move without being nicked by a stray bullet, shards of glass, broken metal.

It cuts my skin, rings in my eardrums. It doesn't take a genius to know who our attackers are.

By stealing from us, they've guaranteed our ire.

By firing on us, they've guaranteed their death sentence.

It feels like a miracle when it finally comes to an end. They've either run out of bullets, or they've run out of time. In the distance, the pathetic squeal of incoming police sirens. Our attackers drive away in a hurry, leaving skid marks on the pavement outside. The air smells of burning rubber. A quick glance around confirms that my brothers are alright. Understandably rattled, but none of us are hurt.

Fucking amateurs. They should have made sure to finish the job.

Now they face their reckoning.

"Move it," I snap at my brothers. "We need to tell Andrei and Sandra. It's open season on Kuznetsov and his sons."

CHAPTER 19

NIKITA

I anxiously spin my bracelet around my wrist, thinking about Leo's answer.

A pawn shop. I was passing by. Saw it in a window. I thought you might like it.

I turn his words over in my mind. What are the chances Dad would hock our jewelry at the same pawn shop Leo just happened to be strolling by? That's one hell of a coincidence, but I'm not sure what else to believe. The odds are too astronomical, but the thought of Leo being a bold-faced liar doesn't make sense to me, either. He's been nothing but courteous and kind. What reason would he have to lie to me? Then I think about the impromptu meeting in his apartment. All of those people in expensive suits and his abrupt dismissal of me. I don't know what to think, so I try not to think anything.

"Are you okay?" Kseniya asks me. "You look a little pale."

I snap back to reality, blinking away my confusion. Kseniya and I are seated at the side of the room, preparing for our daily warm up. My mother, as expected, is downright pissed with me. How can I tell? It's simple, really. She hasn't bothered to look at me once, nor has she spoken a word. When Inessa gets like this, she freezes me out and makes her disappointment glaringly obvious.

I decide not to let it bother me. I'm not sure which is worse, putting up with her constant criticism or her silence. I guess I can't have it both ways. It's unfortunate there doesn't seem to be a middle ground with her, so for now, I'll stay in my lane and keep my head down. I have too much on my mind, anyway.

I rifle through my bag, looking for the spare bandages I keep at the bottom to wrap my toes. Every inch of my body is sore from over practice. My feet are in a sorry state of disrepair. I've got blisters, my arches ache like you wouldn't believe and now, to make everything so much worse, I can't find my things.

"Here," Kseniya says, handing me a roll of her spare athletic tape, as if reading my mind. "That's what you need, isn't it?"

I breathe the sigh of relief. "Thank you. I could have sworn I packed it. My warm-up jacket is missing from my locker, too." Concern suddenly swirls within me when I connect the dots. Could somebody be stealing my things?

First the threatening notes in my bag. Now my missing things. We never did find out who was behind putting pins and Vanya's shoes. I can't fathom their motivations. I've never done anything to warrant such treatment. But what if they're after me now? What if I've become their new fixation?

"Alright," Inessa says clearly to the room. "Everyone, line up. It's time to practice our jumps."

Dancers move about the space, getting into position in a

hurry. I still have to put on my pointe shoes. I pull them from my gym bag and slip them on—

Only to stop short, something cold flooding my veins.

Something sharp is poking into the base of my foot. Thank goodness I have good reaction time, because when I pull a shoe off and look inside.

Razors.

Someone has sewn razors into the sides of my pointe shoes.

I think I'm going to be sick.

Not knowing what else to do, I rush to my mother, presenting them to her with wide-eyed horror. The realization that someone has sabotaged my shoes snaps her out of her mood.

"Are you hurt?" she asks, concerned. It's the sweetest she's been to me in ages, suddenly snapping from her ballet master persona into that of a caring maternal figure. I don't know whether or not that should make me cry.

"I'm fine. I noticed them before it was too late."

"Stop," she yells at the room. "Everyone, stop what you're doing and come here." Dancers gather around, whispering to themselves as Inessa shows everyone the insides of my shoes. "Who did this?" she demands. "Who would do such a terrible thing?"

Understandably, nobody steps forward to claim responsibility. Why would they? It's nothing but intense silence and scrutiny, a few looks of pity sprinkled in. There's something else, too. As I look around the room and scan people's faces, I see *doubt*.

"She probably did it herself," someone in the back grumbles, just loud enough to get a rise out of the crowd.

My heart sinks into the pit of my stomach. "Why would I do that?"

"Probably to shift the blame?" someone up front, one of the corps de ballet ballerinas, says without apology. "We all know it was you who sabotaged Vanya."

My jaw drops open. "No. No, that's absolutely ridiculous."

"You had the most to gain," someone else comments, volleying their accusation at me without remorse. "You were jealous of Vanya's role, so you put pins in her shoes to take her out of the running."

My stomach clenches. "I would never do that. That's awful!"

"We all know you've been trying for that promotion for years. You probably just had enough and snapped."

"Yeah, and you probably put razors in your own shoes to make yourself look innocent."

"No one's buying this goody two shoes act of yours."

"You should apologize to Vanya. You could have ruined her career!"

"Prissy bitch."

The comments become more heated, more vitriolic. Suddenly the whole room erupts into accusations, name calling, and downright nastiness. When I try to protest, my voice is easily drowned out by the chaos. No one is willing to listen to me. No one is giving me a shadow of a doubt. The other dancers only feel more emboldened the more people speak. It's a growing hate train, a bandwagon designed to punch down.

"Inessa probably had something to do with it too," someone comments from the crowd.

Mother's face turns red. "Who said that? Show yourself."

"Oh, please. Nikita never would have gotten the role of the Sugar Plum Fairy all by herself without your help."

"Do you think they planned it together?"

"Could be. They both have access to the change rooms."

The room spins. My legs have turned to jelly. My stomach cramps and my lungs burn.

For once in my life, I'm thankful Inessa is such a domineering presence. She claps her hands twice, so loud and so sudden it deafens the room. I've never seen her so pissed.

"I will take this matter to the director at once," she says. "Practice is canceled. If you know what's good for you, you'll stop this unwarranted slander."

"See?" someone in the back grumbles. "She's trying to silence us. Intimidation won't work anymore."

"Enough!" my mother roars.

I've stopped listening at this point. I think the other dancers want to be mad for the sake of being mad. No matter what I say, they're not going to listen. They'll either talk over me or call me a liar. I know deep down I would never do such a thing, but the truth doesn't seem to have much weight in the court of public opinion.

My eyes burn with the threat of tears, my nose stuffy and my throat raw. I'm reaching a boiling point. If I have to endure another second of this, I think I might genuinely have a mental breakdown.

I can feel the first few tears slipping down my cheeks. I turn away from the crowd, unwilling to give them any more ammunition than they already have. I quickly gather my things, bare feet padding over the floor, before hastily making for the exit. The room has finally gone quiet at my mother's order. What I really need right now is fresh air. Some space. A shoulder to cry on.

And the only shoulder I want is Leo's.

After getting dressed in a hurry in the change rooms, I leave through the back exit of the training hall and pull out my phone. I dial his number, waiting with bated breath. I feel a little bad about interrupting his workday, but I don't have anyone else to talk to. I don't trust anyone else after the way my fellow dancers turned on me.

He doesn't answer.

My heart twists. I tell myself he's probably busy. But I desperately need to hear his voice right now. If anyone can comfort me through this awful mess, it's him. I try again, and then one more time for good measure. Each time, the call goes to voicemail.

Feeling alone and afraid, I decide to text him instead.

I'm sorry to bother you.

I'm going through a really hard time right now.

Can I come see you?

I wait for a few minutes. Leo is normally very quick to respond. Unfortunately, today seems to be the exception. Cold and shivering, I pull my winter coat closed over my chest. I want to go home, curl up in bed, forget all this even happened. I'm sure Inessa will take care of the rest. This is the second incident in under a month. The director has to get to the bottom of it before something tragic happens.

I take the subway home, a foggy haze clouding my mind. Can this day get any worse?

When I get back to the apartment, I realize it can.

Dad is nowhere in sight. The lights are off, the air is still. At first, I'm hit with a wave of confusion, immediately followed up by a sickening sense of worry. I gave him the money to pay off his debt collectors, but I haven't heard from him since. Just when I feel myself about to go into a full blown panic, I see an envelope on the kitchen table, Dad's neat handwriting gracing the surface.

It's addressed to Mom and me.

With shaky hands, I tear it open and pull out the letter from inside.

I'm sorry.

I should have been honest and upfront from the very beginning. I owe some very bad people a lot of money, and while Nikita—my darling daughter—you have given me the money to square my debts away, I feel an overwhelming sense of guilt and shame.

I've made yet another mistake. I have a problem. A gambling addiction. I took the money you gave me, Nikita, and I went back to the gambling den to try and make enough to at least pay you back.

I'm pathetic. I lost it all. I'll make this right, I swear. Until then, I need to lie low. I'll come back once I have paid them. They shouldn't give you any trouble.

I'm so sorry. I love you so much.

My hands are shaking with unchecked rage and disappointment by the time I finish the letter. I thought I was helping him by giving him the money to pay off his debt. And what did he do? He squandered that chance. I don't know where he's gone, I don't know if I'll ever see him again. Does he not realize the danger he's put us in by owing the Bratva? What's to stop them from coming after Mom or me when they realize he skipped town?

My stomach twists. I'm suddenly nauseous, barely able to keep down my lunch. This can't be happening. Maybe I was too trusting, too naive. I thought my father would do the right thing, and now he's proven me wrong, and has taken advantage of my kindness.

I'm bitter, frightened, and fed up. I'm scared to bring this up to Inessa, but I have no choice. We're in hot water, and I only just realized I'm boiling alive. It's clear that I need to take matters into my own hands. I need to pay off my father's debt —for real this time— as well as get to the bottom of whoever the saboteur is.

The dancers were right about one thing. It was only a matter of time before I snapped.

CHAPTER 20

NIKITA

I grip the envelope full of money tightly, my heart racing in my throat. This is the last of my savings, but at least it's enough to square some of my father's outstanding debt away.

I've heard about the Bratva in passing and always on the news. They're a criminal organization that basically runs all of Moscow, and probably the entirety of Russia. They can get up to some pretty terrible things, but I have to swallow my fear. I need to get this over with. The sooner I do, the sooner Dad can come home.

I'll confess I'm not entirely sure where to start. It's not like people openly advertise their illegal gambling dens. There's no big flashing sign to point me in the right direction. The only thing I can think to do is head to arguably the roughest part of the neighborhood, a small district in the south that's seen better days. There's a low police presence here, high levels of graffiti. I wouldn't normally come here by myself, but desperate times call for desperate measures.

Moscow at night is an entirely different beast. It's alive

with the sounds of sirens, the smell of rubbish. People are out and about, unsavory characters. The types I would normally cross the street to avoid. Tonight, though, I decide to face them head on.

A group of rough and tumble men approach, eyeing me up and down like a piece of meat. I've got a small canister of mace in my pocket, my thumb hovering over the trigger button, but I take a deep breath and find my resolve. I'm pregnant with Leo's child—he may not know about it, but the thought alone is enough to get me going, to push me forward with my chin up. Worst-case scenario, I will pull the baby card if I run out of options to keep myself alive in this place. Good grief, I'm carrying a Bratva child. What would he say if I told him about this? What does it matter if it's a Bratva child? It's still a child. An innocent baby. *Get a grip, Nikita.*

"What's a pretty little thing like you doing in a place like this?" one of them asks me. His face is covered in tattoos. A few of his teeth are missing. Even a mother couldn't love a face like that.

"I'm wondering if you can help me," I say, speaking as calmly as possible even though I feel like I'm seconds from rattling out of my own skin.

"Oh?" he says. "What do I get in return?"

His buddies chuckle. It makes my skin crawl. I know exactly what he's trying to imply, but I don't give him an inch.

"Look, I'm just trying to pay back a debt."

"To who, girly? You can give the money to me. I'll deliver it for you."

I lick my lips, steel my spine. "I owe the Bratva."

There's no denying the sudden shift in the air, a subtle

imbalance. Their obvious unease tells me I've struck a chord.

"Who runs this place?" I ask. "This territory." I don't know if I'm talking out of my ass, but I'm pretty sure an organization as large and intricate as the Russian mafia needs to have a chain of command. Surely there's a lieutenant or a captain I can talk to who'd be more than happy to point me in the right direction.

Or stab me and take my money, but I'll get there when I get there. Hopefully, I won't get there. I can just scream that I'm carrying Leo's baby. I bet that'll turn some heads. Dammit, Nikita, what did you get yourself into? I was scolding my father for getting involved with the Bratva, but haven't I been doing the same? Not knowingly. Would it have mattered? If I'd known who Leo was from the beginning? Would I have stayed on that road in the middle of a snowstorm? I doubt it.

"We answer to Samuil," the thug says. "We can just take the money for you."

I stiffen. There's no way in hell I'm going to fall for that. What if they take the money and run? "I don't think so. Just tell me where to find him."

"What's wrong, girly? You don't trust me?"

"Tell me what I want to know. This payment... It's urgent. You don't want me to tell Samuil you slowed me down, do you?"

The man visibly blanches. I've struck another nerve. "Samuil isn't here right now, but you can probably find him at the depot."

"What depot?"

"The taxi depot. You didn't hear it from me, but they operate out of the Nicolaevich Brothers Taxi Company headquarters."

Hearing the name is more painful than a slap to the face. This has to be some sort of mistake. Maybe the stress of the day has finally caught up to me and I'm hearing things.

No. No, that's too many coincidences in a row. The dots aren't connecting, my logic isn't lining up. I don't understand how it keeps circling back to Leo, but I'm realizing with growing horror that he might be the answer to everything.

I've been to the taxi depot once before when I tried to return his coat. It had been busy then, but even more so now. Something big is happening. There's an almost frantic electricity in the air. I suppose it works to my advantage, because I'm able to slip in without being noticed. I make my way down the hall toward the office, startled to find a large group gathered out in the hall.

The men I saw earlier this morning at Leo's apartment. His brothers. I cling to the shadows. None of them have spotted me yet.

"I want a full sweep," Leo's voice rumbles like thunder. "Leave no stone unturned. They couldn't have gotten very far. Do we have our men posted at all the exits to the city?"

"Yes," someone answers. A woman. Sandra or Charlotte. They sound exactly the same so I have no idea. "They won't be able to slip past us. Provided they haven't already left."

"I want them brought in alive," someone else speaks. He sounds like the one in charge. "I know you're angry, Leo, but we can't risk a gunfight on the streets. We're going to take care of this quietly."

"My reputation's at stake here," Leo hisses. He doesn't sound like the same person I've come to care for. I hear the anger dripping off every syllable, can feel his rage radiating from the room. "Those bastards made a fool of me. Justice needs to be swift."

"I don't disagree, but we need to handle this carefully. You've left us in a vulnerable position. You've proven that people can steal from the Bratva and potentially get away with it."

The air knocks itself from my lungs. That's it. The proof I needed.

Leo is with the Bratva. This entire time, I thought I was crazy. I thought he was just some super successful business entrepreneur. That's why he could afford to be a patron of the Bolshoi, buy a restaurant on a whim, own a building with a penthouse. How could I have been so stupid, so naive? I have never felt more humiliated and blindsided in my life.

I have half a mind to run, but I'm done being nice. I'm done being played the fool.

I stomp forward, emerging from my hiding place around the corner, elbowing my way into the room so I look him dead in the eye.

He stares at me. The silence between us is excruciating. Heavy and thick enough to carve with a knife. He seems just as surprised as I feel.

"Nikita? Nikita, what are you—"

"Is it true?"

He shakes his head, tries to deny it. "I don't know what you're talking about."

"I heard you. I heard all of you."

"Nikita—"

My heart can't take it. I turn on my heels and leave the

way I came. I pray this is some sort of nightmare, because if this is reality, it's far too cruel. How could I have let myself care for a man who isn't honest with me? He has lied to my face time and time again, and like an idiot, I believed him.

I've barely had the chance to make it outside before he catches up to me.

"Nikita, wait." He takes my hand gently, with all the tenderness I've come to be familiar with. But I rip away. I can't even look at him. "Nikita, what you heard, it's all a big misunderstanding."

"Is it? Don't you dare lie to me, Leo."

"Look, can we talk about this somewhere private?"

"Is there a point?"

"You heard a conversation out of context."

I dig my heels in and stare him down. "Do you smell that?"

"Smell what?"

"*Bullshit.*" I shove the envelope of money harshly against his chest. "There. Erik Belov, paid in full."

The look he gives me can only be described as a mix of confusion and heartbreak. "Erik Belov?"

"My father," I bite out, angry tears welling up in my eyes. "Was this all a part of your plan? Seduce me to somehow use as collateral against my father?"

"Nikita, I would never do that. I had no idea he was your father. Belov is an incredibly common name."

"How am I supposed to believe you?"

"You trust me, don't you?"

I stare at him in disbelief. "I *did.*"

"I'll admit I haven't been very forthcoming, but you can see why I wouldn't want to tell you the truth. I was worried how you might react."

"Leo, you're a *criminal.*"

He looks like he has a million and one things to say, but when his mouth opens, no sound comes out. I can tell he wants to reach out. But whatever I thought we had between us, I'm not sure it can ever be repaired.

I almost gave my heart to a gangster. I loved too hard and fell too freely.

"Give me a chance to explain myself," he says, firm and resolute. "Come to my place tonight. I have to wrap up this meeting, but I swear to you, I'll tell you absolutely everything. No more lies."

The logical side of my brain tells me to just leave. What's there to explain? Leo breaks the law for a living. Am I supposed to give him a second chance? Not only that, but he put my father through hell the last few weeks. I can only imagine the countless hundreds, maybe even thousands of other people he's collected debts from. Is that even the extent of his work? What other horrible things is he capable of?

I shift uncomfortably from foot to foot. It's cold out. I want to go home. Leo looks at me without a hint of anger, only anguish.

"Please," he says. "Please, give me a chance."

My mouth is dry. I don't know what to believe anymore. The last twenty-four hours have been a whirlwind, and I'm frankly holding on for dear life. Everything is crashing down around me, and I'm so exhausted I have half a mind to let it bury me. I'm a raw nerve scrubbed within an inch of its life, barely keeping it together.

For a brief moment, I wonder if this is some sort of trap. What if Leo is trying to lure me somewhere private where he can take me out? I'm a risk, aren't I, knowing all that I know? Aren't I a liability to someone like him?

My gut tells me it's not possible. I don't sense an ounce

of maliciousness. Not when he's looking at me like I'm holding his heart in the palm of my hands.

"Fine," I grumble.

He gives me a spare key from his key ring. "I'll meet you there."

CHAPTER 21

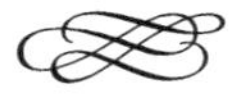

LEO

I can't remember the last time I was this stressed. The elevator ride up to the penthouse has a completely different vibe than it did last time. Before, I was excited to see Nikita, knowing the night we had ahead. Now I'm excited to see Nikita for an entirely different reason, because if she did in fact show up, it means she's giving me a chance to explain myself.

The only problem is I don't know where to start.

If only I had known Erik Belov was her father–I actually don't know what I would have done. I probably would have thought how incredibly unfair it was that a mousy little thing wound up with such a beauty of a daughter. She deserves better than a father with a gambling addiction and no impulse control. She deserves better than to bail him out. The envelope she gave me, the one with enough money to cover his remaining debt, burns a hole in my pocket. Did she have to cough that up to cover his sorry ass?

Does this mean the jewelry he gave me the other day belonged to her? Suddenly everything makes sense. The strange look she gave me when I presented her with the bracelet... It occurs to me now how messed up that was, to gift her something that was originally hers to start with.

I find her seated at the kitchen table, positioning herself in such a way that she can keep an eye on the elevator. Everything about her body language screams defensive, tense. She reminds me of a scared little rabbit, ready to dash off the moment she senses danger. My chest tightens knowing I am the cause of her worry.

Nikita doesn't say anything as I approach. I move slowly, afraid one wrong move will send her running. I don't want to scare her. That's the last thing I want. But right now, with her wide eyes and lips pressed into a thin line, I feel like I'm walking on eggshells. I screwed up by not telling her the truth. I know that. But what on Earth was I supposed to do?

I take a seat opposite her, ensuring she has enough space to feel comfortable. The silence that follows is thick and heavy. I can't remember the last time I was this nervous. I can't remember the last time I *cared* about someone else's opinion as much as I do Nikita's. What does she think of me? What will she say? How can we ever hope to move forward from here?

"I want the truth," she says, her voice steady and clear. "Start from the beginning. Leave nothing out. And in return, I promise to sit here and listen. If I sense one ounce of bullshit, I will get up and leave and you will never see me again."

In the grand scheme of things, that's as generous an offer as I'm going to get. I clench my fists, chewing on the inside of my cheek as I search for the right words. She wants me to start from the beginning? That's a long story, even for me, but I want to give Nikita everything she wants—the truth included.

"My father was a mechanic. My mother was a schoolteacher. We didn't grow up with a lot of money. I think we were always destined for this kind of life. My father drank a lot. He had a temper. Our mother shielded us from most of it, but I'm sure you can imagine the kind of influence that has on a kid.

"We lost our mother pretty young. She got sick, and because our father preferred to piss all our money away on alcohol, we couldn't afford to get her the proper treatment. To add salt to the wound, he started seeing a mistress on the side. Wound up getting her pregnant. That's how we ended up with our half-brother, Damien. We lost our mom not too long after, and things at home only deteriorated from there.

"As you can imagine, nobody really believed we'd accomplish much. Our teachers had given up on us. We didn't have the resources for counseling. It was easy, falling into a life of petty crime. Started off small. Boosting cars, shoplifting and the like. But my brother, Andrei, he's always been a visionary. If the world was going to deal us a shitty hand, then the least we could do is make sure we wouldn't die two-bit thugs.

"So we worked our way up, made a name for ourselves. Long story short, we wound up leading the Bratva. Andrei leads it with his wife, Sandra, who you met. One of the twins. She comes from Bratva royalty. I won't get into the details, but the point is that through ambition and tenacity—as well as an opportune marriage—my brothers and I now rule Moscow."

When I finish, I let out a heavy sigh. I'm not sure how detailed she wants me to be, but I think I've captured the gist of the situation. It's strange, summarizing my family's rise to power so casually.

"I have done things I'm not proud of," I continue, "but

that comes with the territory. I'm not going to fool myself into believing I'm a righteous man doing the wrong things for the right reasons. I have pride in my work. This is what I do, who I am."

Nikita visibly squirms in her seat, her brows knitted into a steep frown as she laces her fingers together and places them on the surface of the table. She looks off into the distance, eyes cloudy. I can't get a read on her. She's completely still, an impassable wall separating the two of us. I'm so used to her smiles, to her carefree laughter that this version of her, angry and understandably bitter, puts me on edge.

"What exactly do you do within the Bratva?" she asks softly.

"I'm the numbers man." I try to swallow the sticky lump in the back of my throat. It doesn't budge. "The accountant. I handle any matters related to money. I never lied to you about that."

"Including collecting debts?"

My heart twists in my chest. "If I have to."

I can see the tears glossing her eyes, the edges turning red. She works her jaw. "How did my father come to owe you money?"

"We have a number of establishments scattered throughout Moscow. Gambling dens. From what I understand, he was on a losing streak."

"How much?"

I hate the way her voice trembles. I want nothing more than to reach across the table and take her hand in mine, to brush her tears away.

"It doesn't matter how much."

"It does to me."

"Nine-hundred thousand rubles."

Nikita, understandably, looks like she's about to be sick. "My dad lost his job recently. Did you know that?"

"I didn't know."

"But if you had, would you have gone easier on him?"

"Nikita—"

"Answer me."

I grind my teeth. "It's not a question of whether I'm hard or easy on Erik. The fact of the matter was, and continues to be, that he owes my family money. He must pay it back."

"Can't you make an exception?"

It's a simple question, but the answer is complicated. Far too complicated for me to try and explain.

"If I make an exception, it'll make me look lenient. And if I look lenient, our enemies will have no trouble leveraging that against us."

"So you have to hound a man for what I'm sure you consider pocket money just to save face? Tell me, Leo, how much money do you make in a month? A week? A *day*? What my father owes you is chump change."

"That's not the point. He owes what he owes. Tell me, if one of your dancer friends owed you a handful of rubles, would you not ask for them to pay you back?"

"That's different."

"Is it?"

Nikita glances away. "Have you ever hurt people? When they don't pay you back."

I think very carefully before I speak. I know she wants the truth, but it would only terrify her. If I'm being perfectly honest, yes. Yes, I have had to twist an arm here and there. A little *motivation* is what we call it.

Do I particularly enjoy that aspect of debt collecting? No.

But do I feel bad about it? Also no.

To me, this is all part of the job. It's a part of my expectations.

I must be silent for a little too long, because Nikita looks at me sharply. She's never looked at me like that before—and I hate it. I don't want her to be upset with me, but in the same breath, I also completely understand.

"So when you picked me up from the side of that road, did you know who I was?"

"No."

"And when you came to the Bolshoi," she says carefully, "did you really have no idea who I was?"

I shake my head. "None."

"But what if you had? What if you realized Erik was my father? Would you have pursued me anyway?"

"I don't know how to answer that, Nikita. I don't like hypotheticals. All I know is the moment I saw you at the Bolshoi again, I knew I couldn't let you go."

"Why?"

"Because I —" I cut myself off. What am I going to say?

I care for Nikita deeply. Maybe more than I ever thought possible. How do I even begin to explain she's the first thing I think about when I wake, and the last person I think about when I go to bed? How do I explain to her that getting to see her dance fills me with a lightness I haven't experienced in ages? How am I supposed to tell her the reason I kept my identity a secret was so that maybe, just maybe, I could have a chance to be with her for real?

I have never felt this way about anyone in my life. I want to curse my rotten luck that I'm about to lose it all anyway.

"I wanted to tell you," I say gently. "I would have. But I was afraid of *this*. What would you have thought if I told you I'm a gangster? That I basically threaten people for a living to make sure they cough up their cash? What would you have said or done? Can you understand why I didn't want to tell you? You wouldn't have looked at me twice."

"You don't know that," she snaps.

"Look at me, Nikita. No, you wouldn't have." My throat is tight. My lungs burn. "You're too good for me, Nikita Belova. I knew that the second I saw you. I think that's why I was so desperate to keep the truth from you. Because I knew you'd never be able to look at me the same way. You'd never give me a shot."

Her bottom lip trembles, tears slipping down her cheeks. Her mouth opens only to close again, whatever she had to say dying on her tongue.

"I asked you once before," I say grimly, "but I'll ask you again. Are you scared of me, Nikita?"

"No, I..." She lets out a shaky breath. "Should I be?"

I can't stand the way she's looking at me. I can't stand the cold twist in my chest threatening to shred me into ribbons. Things are different now. There's no going back—no matter how hard I wish for it.

"What do we do now?" I ask.

Slowly, Nikita rises from her chair. "I'm going to go home now," she says. "I am allowed to go home, right?"

The fact that she would even ask hurts more than a slap to the face. "Of course, I would never keep you against your will," I murmur. "You know I would never hurt you, right?"

She doesn't answer. Instead, she turns and starts toward the elevator. "I need some time to think."

I'm quick to vacate my seat, catching up to her just in time to gingerly take her hand. "Nikita, wait."

I consider it no small miracle when Nikita doesn't pull away. She lingers, her fingers limp in mine, and she refuses to look at me. I dare to take a step forward, placing myself in her space if only to breathe her in for a moment longer. I don't want her to leave like this, but at this point, I don't know what else I can say to make this right.

"Please don't go," I whisper. "Stay with me, Nikita."

It takes all my willpower not to dip down and kiss her. What I wouldn't give to press my lips to hers.

"Give me some time," she pleads before finally slipping from my grasp. All I can do is watch her go.

I'm numb. That could have gone better, but I'm glad it wasn't any worse. Did I expect her to come running to me, hugging and kissing me like nothing's wrong? Of course not. I wrack my brain, struggling to figure out a way to make things right. I'm half tempted to chase after her, to try and convince her to stay. To hold her, to kiss her, to make her mine. But I understand why she would want space.

I wouldn't want to stay in the same room as a monster, either.

CHAPTER 22

NIKITA

When I wake up the next morning, I'm greeted with a sudden, overpowering wave of nausea. Ugh, it's getting worse. I barely manage to scramble out of bed, my feet tangled up in my sheets, before racing to the bathroom out in the hall. I get sick in the toilet, retching so hard I see black spots blooming across my vision. I feel my own forehead, noting how my skin feels sweaty, but cold.

I can't let the pregnancy symptoms get out of control like this. Not with opening day mere days away. But given how shitty things have been going, I wish I could say I was surprised. It was only a matter of time. Maybe some vitamins will help take some of the edge off.

"What do you mean?" my mother shrieks. "What do you mean you owe the Bratva?"

My ears perk up. Is Dad home? Did he finally return? I've been worried sick.

I pull myself to my feet and hastily sprint down the hall to find my parents in the living room. Dad sits on the couch, hunched over with his head in his hands while Mother stands over him, a looming sentry. It's almost six in the morning, but I can smell the alcohol wafting off my father from here.

"What's going on?" I ask.

"Your father told me everything. Well, everything about his more recent gambling exploits, since this fool refused to learn his lesson," Inessa says, glaring a hole into my forehead. "He says you knew all about this. How could you have kept this from me? Do you have any idea the damage you could have done to our family? He's already hurt us so badly, and now you, too?"

Dad looks up at me, his complexion blotchy and oily. There are dark circles beneath his eyes, his lips chapped like the cracked surface of the desert. I have never seen my father more pathetic. I have half a mind to cuss him out, to tell him how unbelievably selfish he's been, but from the sound of it, Inessa might have beat me to it.

It's then and only then that I see the thick yellow envelope sitting on his lap. The top has been ripped open haphazardly, exposing the wads of cash inside. It's more money than I've ever seen.

"What is that?" I ask, concern lancing through me. "Did you steal it? Or were you gambling again?"

Dad shakes his head, shame dripping off him in waves. "Neither. One-Eye tracked me down and gave the money back."

One-Eye. I've never heard the name used, but I automatically know who Dad is referring to. I think it's a cruel, awful nickname.

"Wait he... he gave the money back? Why would he—"

A shiver races down my spine. Is this Leo's way of making things right? It has to be. There's no other explanation. I doubt Dad is resourceful enough to find this kind of money just lying around. After I left his apartment, did Leo go looking for my father to cancel out what was owed?

My mind is in shambles. I don't know how to feel. Relief, at first, knowing my father no longer owes the Bratva is a massive weight off my chest. It means they won't come knocking down our door demanding funds we no longer have. On the other hand, though, I'm torn up inside. This doesn't excuse the fact that Leo is a criminal.

I still can't believe it. All this time, I was so blinded by his brilliance that I didn't see the red flags. I should have known better, maybe even from the start. Leo isn't just mixed up with the wrong crowd, he *is* the wrong crowd. There's no telling what other horrible things he's done in this past, what horrible things he will continue to do. The way he was talking about his family, the Bratva... I doubt there's anything I could say that could convince him to leave. There's no walking away from that sort of life, not when it's so deeply entrenched in his being.

I didn't want to leave him last night. If anything, I appreciated his honesty. I felt like I was finally getting to see the real man. No pomp, no circumstance, no lies. Sitting before me was none other than Leo Nicolaevich. A gangster, sure, but also the man who makes me feel special.

Loved.

Leo has been nothing but kind to me.

But that doesn't excuse the fact that he does bad things for a living.

With a deep breath, I step forward and pick up the envelope, peering inside. There looks to be a note stuffed in there as well. I slip it out and read it. I'm only a little disappointed to see that it isn't a message from Leo, but a brochure for Gamblers Anonymous. They apparently host meetings once a week at a local bookshop after close. It might be helpful for Dad to check it out.

In many ways, this feels like Leo extending an olive branch. The first attempt at making amends. I'd be lying if I said it didn't make my heart flutter, but it does nothing to remedy the cold pit in my stomach.

There's a small bag on the couch beside Dad, too. I reach for it, opening it to reveal all the jewelry he tried to sell in order to pay back his debt. Every single piece is here and accounted for. Earrings, necklaces, broaches, bracelets... Did Leo go to the trouble of buying back every single one?

"You sniveling piece of shit," mother hisses. "I knew I should have been the one in charge of our finances. The only reason I asked you to manage the books is because I've been so busy at the ballet. You're useless, Erik. I asked one thing of you. How could you do this to us? How could you rope your daughter into it?"

"Mom, please calm down," I say cautiously. "Yelling isn't going to solve anything. Can't you see he feels horrible enough as it is?"

Inessa jabs an accusatory finger in my direction. "Not a word out of you. I'll chew you out later. Keeping secrets from me? This family is falling apart!"

I don't condone what my father did, but even a blind man can see how sorrowful he is. He has been beaten down so many times I swear his body has shrunk. He wears his remorse on his skin, so sad and full of regret it almost breaks my heart. I pity him, but that doesn't mean he needs to endure a tongue-lashing on top of it all. He's probably spent the last little while beating himself up all on his own.

"Leave him alone, Mom. We have the money back. Everything can go back the way it was."

She snatches the envelope of cash from me, leaving a wake of paper cuts on my palms. "I'm going to the bank right away to deposit this. In a separate account where this idiot can't touch a kopek. When I get back, we'll talk divorce."

Divorce?

My blood runs cold. I feel helpless, like I'm drowning and there's no lifeline in sight. Dad looks equally heartbroken.

"Inessa, let's talk about this," he says, voice weak and thin. "Let's not do anything drastic."

"*Drastic*?" Mother hisses, her lips curling up into a sneer. "I'll tell you what's drastic—not divorcing your sorry ass sooner. You're nothing but dead weight. I only married you because I got pregnant. I didn't even *want* her, but you convinced me otherwise!"

I swear I can feel my heart shatter, the hard truth hitting me like a runaway train. "You didn't want me?" I ask, throat squeezing closed.

"I had a whole life before I had you," she seethes unapologetically. "My entire career was ahead of me. And then I made the stupid mistake of getting knocked up by this loser. I was a star, do you understand? A *star*. The whole world of ballet knew my name and now look at me, barely making ends meet with a deadbeat husband and a disgrace of a daughter. Sometimes I wish you'd never been born!"

I stop listening at that point, deafened by my own anguish and disbelief. This wasn't what I was expecting to hear first thing in the morning, but now I have no choice but to face it. I always knew my mother was a piece of work. Ever since I was a little girl, she's been nothing but harsh to me. Cold and bitter and demanding. All I've ever wanted was to make her proud, which is why I try so hard during practice, why I strive for perfection—hoping she'll finally approve of me.

Now I see even perfection isn't good enough for her—because she didn't want me in the first place.

All of her resentment, her regrets, I can see now that they have been festering for years, resulting in this unmitigated disaster of an explosion. What's been said cannot be unsaid. I have never felt more unwelcome in my own home.

I can't tell which is stronger, my anger or my sorrow. Either way, they result in ugly tears. My cheeks are red, my nose is stuffed up, and to make matters even worse, my nausea has returned in full force. I cannot fathom being able to tell a person you wish they never existed, let alone telling your own daughter.

I think about yelling at her, calling her out on her bullshit and cruelty, but I decide not to waste my breath. She doesn't want me? Fine. Why bother sticking around, then? It's high time I found a place of my own, anyway. I won't be able to avoid her at work, but at least I won't have to deal with her at home. I have no real game plan, but I sure as hell am not going to stay here.

"One hundred thousand rubles of that money is mine. Leave it on the table before you go."

Without another word, I turn on my heel and head to my room, slamming the door while my parents proceed to yell at each other. Dad expects me to keep his secrets, Mom expects me to fall in line. I'll have none of it. Neither of them is worth my energy. All I have ever tried to do was be kind, supportive, and understanding. Now I see there's no point.

There's no room for kindness in this world. People like me—we're taken advantage of. A sucker's born every minute, as the old saying goes, and I regret to admit I was one of them.

Not anymore.

I work in a hurry, flitting around my room to grab the essentials. Clothes, important documents, extra workout gear. I stuff it all into my duffel bag, cramming it so full the zipper almost doesn't shut. I have to get out of here. I can't stand another moment of this toxicity. I'll just have to figure out how I'm going to deal with Inessa at work later. Right now, removing myself from this environment is my top priority. I'll have to think on my feet.

"Where do you think you're going?" Inessa snaps at me. I ignore her as I grab my money off the table.

"Sweetheart, come back," Dad calls out to me. I ignore him, too.

Mom tries to grab me as I open the door, but I shove her back. "Don't touch me! Don't you ever fucking touch me again!"

I leave in a hurry, practically sprinting down the stairs to the main lobby. I shiver against the cold winter air, my jacket too light for this kind of weather.

Aimlessly, I begin walking. I make it two blocks before I pull out my phone. Who should I call? One of my colleagues? No, they all hate me. They think that I sabotaged Vanya. I sincerely doubt any of them would let me crash on their couch if I asked. Maybe I could go to a cheap motel somewhere and stay there until I figure out something more permanent, but I don't want to spend any of the money I've saved to find my own, permanent place.

The most natural thought that occurs to me is to reach out to Leo. There isn't a doubt in my mind that he'd be willing to give me a spare room for a little while. I know for a fact he has at least six in that penthouse of his, but...

Things between us right now are uncertain. Now that I know he's a criminal, it colors my decisions differently. Would I feel comfortable temporarily living under the same roof with him? The world isn't black and white, but I don't think I'm adept enough to navigate the gray area.

I glance at the time. I need to get to the Bolshoi for dress rehearsal. Knowing I'm going to have to deal with my mother is already draining enough. Maybe if I dance it out a bit, work up a sweat, I'm sure a solution will present itself.

Otherwise, I don't know what I'll do.

CHAPTER 23

NIKITA

By the time I arrive, there's some sort of commotion. A large group of dancers has gathered around someone. The director, I realize. Standing beside him is Kseniya, all dressed up in her gear, her pointe shoes tied together by their ribbons slung over her shoulder.

"It's such an honor," she says, her cheeks rosy as she beams with pride. "I promise to do my best. I know we're really close to opening day, but I've been studying very closely and practicing in private."

The director pats her on the back. "I'm sure you'll make a wonderful Sugar Plum Fairy."

A small, sharp gasp escapes. Surely, I didn't hear that right. "What's going on?" I ask.

All eyes are on me. I can feel the weight of their hateful gazes burning the surface of my skin. My heart thuds loudly against my rib cage. I think I'm going to be sick. Again. Not now, baby, not now...

The director glances at me with a hard frown. "Nikita. With me, please." The cold, almost robotic delivery sends me into a tailspin.

"Am I in trouble or something?"

The director ushers me out of the room, but it's hard for me to miss the whispers and the jeers.

"Told you she did it."

"Do you think she'll go to jail?"

"I hope so. It's basically assault."

I have never been more terrified in my life than in this moment, nor as confused. The director doesn't speak until we reach the women's change rooms. He knocks on the door, calling out to make sure we're the only ones there. To my utter horror, he walks straight to my assigned locker.

"It seems you must have left the lock undone," he says. "One of the cleaners found this this morning."

He opens it to reveal its contents. Sitting at the very bottom of the locker is a toolbox, the lid propped open to expose nails, bits of glass, and razors. I shake my head adamantly.

"This has to be some sort of mistake. It isn't mine. I've never seen it before in my life."

"We're taking this act of sabotage very seriously," the director says. "You were the only one to gain anything from Vanya's displacement."

For a brief moment, I wonder if I was some sort of tyrant in a previous life and I'm just now receiving my karmic justice.

"I'm being set up," I insist. "I would never do—"

"We're getting the police involved," the director cuts me off. "They'll be here shortly to ask you a few questions. They'll be fingerprinting the tools in your locker, as well. Unless you would like to save us all the time and confess."

Rage boils inside me unlike anything I've ever experienced. This has to be some sort of cruel prank. Why is this happening to me? What did I do to deserve any of this? I'm at my breaking point, seconds away from shattering. But I'm not done yet. I'm not going to let them kick me while I'm down.

"I didn't do anything," I state firmly.

The director sighs. "Very well. Until we get to the bottom of things, we're suspending you."

"But the show—"

"You have already been replaced. Don't worry. Kseniya will do a marvelous job. No one will even notice it isn't you on stage. Now wait here until the cops—"

But I don't wait. I'm not going to sit around and let them pin the blame on me for something I didn't do. Panic grips me by the throat. I need to get out of here. Apparently, if I want something done right, I'll have to do it myself. I need to get to the bottom of this, but I can't very well do that if I'm cooped up at the police station. What I need is someone with resources. Someone who's willing to take big risks for even bigger rewards.

Before the director has a chance to stop me, I whip around and make a break for the exit. He has no legal recourse to keep me here. If the police want to question me, they'll have to come pick me up, because there's no way in hell I'm going to let them embarrass me here. I leave in such a hurry I nearly ram into Pavel, the security guard.

"Whoa!" he says. "Where's the fire?"

I don't answer him. There's no time to talk. I'm out of a home and out of a job. I see now there's only one person left in the world I can talk to. I don't trust my family, nor do I trust my friends.

So who do I turn to?

CHAPTER 24

LEO

Any updates? I text Roman.

Not yet. We're still looking.

Hurry up.

Yes, your highness.

I'm quietly praying Roman's connections across Moscow will turn up something fruitful. He's always been a people person. Where I specialize in collecting debts, Roman collects all manner of favors. I'm sure he'll be able to pry information concerning our missing night shift sooner or later.

Right now, though, patience isn't exactly one of my virtues.

I check in personally with a handful of potential leads. Most people, upon seeing me, stumble through their eyewitness accounts. I'm more than aware I have that effect on people—which is unfortunate because it's starting to get in the way of our investigation.

A few folks claim they saw Arman packing his things in a hurry, leaving with his family in the dead of night. Others say they saw him packing weeks in advance, which I believe is the more believable possibility. These sons of bitches had this whole thing planned out, so I wouldn't put it past them to have the foresight to move their loved ones and their lives in advance, too.

I tried tracking phone numbers, credit card records, and even social media posts. Sometimes criminals are stupid enough to post pictures of their spoils. No such luck, however. The night shift has been surprisingly thorough. If I weren't so pissed off right now, I would be impressed. It takes a lot of organization and coordination to pull this kind of stunt on the Bratva.

After chasing yet another dead end, it's safe to say my irritation is mounting. The pressure is on, but I'm thankful I've always been relatively cool when under the gun. I'm confident we will be able to track those assholes down, but the more time that elapses, the more distance they will likely put between themselves and Moscow. The Bratva has significant reach outside of the city, but our chances are much better within city limits. We need to catch them before they get too far.

I get into my car with a huff. Everything is cold. These winter nights are becoming unbearable. From the frigid steering wheel to the cold leather under my ass, I've basically walked into a fridge box. It reminds me a great deal of the night I first ran into Nikita. The world around me was frigid and dark, maybe even more so now than it was then. Until I saw her.

I haven't been able to stop thinking about her. About how we left things. A small part of me always expected to have this blow up in my face. What did I think was going to happen? Nikita is inquisitive. I'm sure she would have found out who I am and what I do sooner or later.

I can't convince her to feel okay about what I do for a living. But I can't abandon my brothers and this way of life, either. I don't want to. I'm unapologetic in that fact. I was always meant to be the Bratva's number man, the same way Nikita was always meant to be a prima ballerina. It's in our blood. It's what we do. And maybe it's that innate stubbornness that was going to do me in from the start.

I twist the keys in the ignition and peel away from the curb. I've done as much as I can tonight. My brothers are still scouring the city, investigating their sections as delineated on a map. I've already checked every nook and cranny in the section assigned to me. I've exhausted my options. The night shift isn't here. All I can do now is go home and wait for one of my brothers to turn something up.

What a shame I hate fucking waiting.

As I drive, I lose myself to my thoughts, the meditative act of being behind the wheel the perfect opportunity for me to reflect. If I were a rat bastard who dared to steal from one of the most powerful crime families in the world, where would I hide? Where would I go? I try to put myself in their shoes. Try to think like them. I turn up nothing. Credit where credit is due, they have a lot of balls to pull something like this off.

I'm still several blocks away from my apartment building when I spot someone walking on the sidewalk. I recognize the light blonde of her hair first, her locks catching the golden light of the streetlamps overhead. Then

I recognize her silhouette, slender and graceful and the perfect fit for my arms.

Confusion washes over me. What the hell is Nikita doing out here so late? Why does she have a huge bag of things slung over her small shoulders? Doesn't she understand this is a dangerous part of town? Something innately protective rises in me. It's dark, it's cold, and she's all alone. Things between us may be dicey right now, but I'm sure as hell not going to let her walk by herself.

I pull up to the curb and roll down my window. "Nikita?"

She startles, turning to face me while hurriedly wiping her hands over her eyes. Concern stabs me in the chest. Her face is puffy and red from crying, her lips chapped from the cold. The tip of her nose is bright as well, both from a combination of her distress and the chill.

"Leo?" she croaks. Sounds like she might have been crying for a while. "What are you doing here?"

"I'm on my way home." It's the truth, but I realize maybe it seems like too much of a coincidence. "I wasn't following you, if that's what you're thinking."

Nikita chews on the inside of her cheek. "Well that's what I'm thinking *now*."

"What are *you* doing here?"

"I..." She glances down at the sidewalk, her bottom lip trembling. "Where do I even begin?"

I have half a mind to tell her to get in the car so I can take her home. She shouldn't be out here. "There's a cafe up ahead," I tell her. "Hungry?" I can see her hesitation as clear as day. I don't blame her. I take a deep breath and speak as calmly as possible. "I'm not going to try anything. You just look like you could use a hot meal and someone to talk to."

Nikita smiles appreciatively. I wish it reached her eyes. "Okay," she murmurs before reaching for the door handle.

~

The cafe in question is a real hole in the wall. Nothing to write home about. Peeling wallpaper, worn down, salt-stained floors, with rickety furniture that looks too precarious for me to sit in. I'm genuinely concerned that the wooden chair beneath me is about to collapse at any moment under my weight. I count my blessings they're even open this late. The small hot chocolate Nikita is nursing seems to be brightening her spirits.

We sit in silence for a long time, but it's not as uncomfortable as I would have expected it to be after a huge blowout. Nikita is shifty, wringing her paper napkin only to tear it to shreds, anxiously spreading out the pieces only to collect them into one giant pile again on the table. Whatever happened to her must be weighing on her mind heavily. I don't push, however. I don't ever want to push. When she's ready to talk, I'll be here to listen.

"My parents are getting divorced," she says in a small, mousy voice. "My mother found out about my father's debts. About how he owed the Bratva. How he owed *you*. She didn't take it very well."

I set my jaw. I don't know what to say. Apologizing doesn't feel like enough, but I also don't feel like an apology is needed. It's as I said: Erik Belov owed us money. I'm not in the business of forgiving debts just to make someone feel better.

This one exception aside.

"Thank you for giving the money back," she whispers.

"And our jewelry." Nikita peeks up at me through her long, curling lashes. "Why did you? Was it for my sake?"

I take a deep breath. "You know it was."

Nikita taps her fingers against the ceramic mug in front of her. "I appreciate it. Thank you."

"There's no need to thank me. I just..."

"What?"

Again, I don't know what to say. I want to tell her there are very few people in this world who I care enough for to make exceptions. And the short time I've known her, she's become one of those people. I know it's crazy. Probably insane. But the way I feel about her is so undeniably strong it makes me want to break every single one of my rules.

A man like me can't afford to care. But I *want* to care about Nikita. It comes easy to me, like breathing.

"What else happened?" I ask, because I know her well enough to know there's more. "And don't try to deny it. What's with the bag?"

"Oh, that... Things with my parents got really heated. My mother said some things she won't ever be able to take back. She might have never said it straight to my face if I hadn't tried to defend my father, but she..." Her voice tightens to the point of breaking.

She wipes at her eyes before her tears can streak down her cheeks. "She said she wished I'd never been born. That she had a whole life before she had me. And to make matters even worse, I've been replaced at the ballet. Apparently, they found a toolbox full of nails and glass and razors in my locker. I swear I've never seen that stuff in my life. And it's so strange because I always make sure to lock up when I leave. The point is that even the director thinks I'm the saboteur. Someone *framed* me. I lost my job, my role, the roof over my head, and my parents all in the span of twenty-four hours and I think I'm going insane." She sighs, controlling her tears.

"I don't know what to do anymore, Leo. I don't understand why this is happening to me. I feel like I'm everyone's punching bag and all I want to do is..." Nikita clenches her fists, sets her jaw. "I want to get to the bottom of this. I'm done being the butt of everyone's joke. I'm tired of people stepping all over me. They mistake my kindness for weakness and try to take advantage of that fact. But I'm done. I want to be the one on top. I want to be the one punching down. I want—"

She sobs into her palms, her red-hot fury contagious. That was a lot of information to take in, but now that I've had a chance to process everything, I share in her rage. Things have reached the boiling point, and Nikita has been scalded by no fault of her own. I'm not sure what I need to do, only that I have to be the one to protect her. Justice must be served, though that may look a little different from where I'm standing. But first...

"You need a place to stay?" I ask her.

"I was thinking about going to a hotel or something. Just until I can figure something out."

"Stay with me." The offer comes without thought, without hesitation.

She nibbles on her bottom lip. "Are you sure that's a good idea?"

"I won't try anything. You need a place to crash, and I have plenty of space. What do you say? You can have the entire west wing of the penthouse."

Her eyes widen. "You're serious?"

"When it comes to you, I always am."

She pauses for only a moment. I think she understands as well as I do that she doesn't have very many places to turn. I mean what I said, though; I'm not going to try anything. My only concern is making sure she feels absolutely comfortable, even if I have to put my feelings for her momentarily to the side.

"Come stay with me," I say, "and together, we'll get to the bottom of your sabotage problem."

"How? I don't even know where to start."

"It's time to play dirty, Nikita. Whoever's doing this to you clearly doesn't have any qualms about stooping low. I need to know you're willing to let me do the same."

Nikita studies me carefully, her brilliant blue eyes piercing through the gloom. I know she's a good person, and my tricks might seem distasteful if I ever went into detail about them. The fire in her eyes tells me she's already reached her limit. She has nothing left to lose now.

I'm not at all surprised when she says, "I want to help, too."

CHAPTER 25

NIKITA

My nausea still hasn't subsided, but the prenatal vitamins have been helping just a little bit. I take them when nobody's watching and pray to all the gods and the stars that I can keep this up for a while longer. At least until we figure out what is going on. Until things find some sense and my life doesn't feel so scrambled anymore.

I'm developing quite the appetite, though. It's good for the baby, but it may hinder my practice efforts. Then again, what do I need practice for since I just got wrongfully accused of assault and suspended from the frickin' Bolshoi, huh? Dad has tried to call me several times, and he's also sent me a myriad of texts asking if I'm okay.

My mother hasn't sent me a thing.

When we get back to his place, Leo is nothing short of a gentleman. He's once again reverted back to the soft version of himself, the one I so adore. He opens the car door for me, offers me his hand, and even carries my things up without so much as asking. Leo shows me to one of the many rooms in the west side of the penthouse. It boggles my mind that he has so much space, but on a sadder note, has so little to actually fill it.

I choose the guest bedroom in the corner because of its wrap around windows that offer a gorgeous view of Moscow at night. The city lights twinkle far brighter than the stars above, the red glow of brake lights a ribbon of crimson weaving in and out of the streets.

Emotionally, I'm exhausted. It's frankly a miracle that I have the energy to stand on my own. Physically, though, I'm restless. "When do we start?" I ask. "Do you have contacts with the police? Or are you going to hire a private investigator?"

Leo chuckles. "You should rest for now. We'll start in the morning."

"I'm anxious," I confess.

"I know you are. But these sorts of things take time to put together. If we rush and make a mistake, the perpetrator could get away with it. We need to cover our bases. Make sure they don't see us coming."

I bite my tongue. I suppose he's right. Still, it does nothing to settle the butterflies fluttering in my stomach. Anxiety twists in my guts. I think about Kseniya standing at the front of the practice room, smiling brightly. I think about the director, and how he didn't even give me a chance to explain myself. He refused to listen. Until now, I've unknowingly been saddled to a runaway horse, and I didn't see the danger until it threw me off. Now all I want to do is pull on the reins.

"There's a bathroom through there," he tells me. "If you need anything... you know where to find me."

I'm blown away by his endless compassion. I don't think he expects anything in return, yet he's doing all this for me without complaint. It's a struggle sometimes to consolidate these two sides of him. The criminal and the saint. Now I'm starting to see that maybe I'm looking at this whole thing all wrong, trying to understand him from a one-sided point of view.

A man can be more than one thing. Do I like the fact that he's done some less than legal things in his lifetime? Of course not. But the more I think about it, the more I'm starting to realize it's wrong to judge him solely on his crimes. He explained everything perfectly to me.

He is who he is today out of necessity.

And that has made him the man I love. The man whose child I'm carrying. I will have to tell him, eventually. But when? Given our circumstances, is there even a right time to do it?

"How much is my portion of the rent?" I ask.

"I'm not charging you to stay here."

"How long can I stay?"

"As long as you want."

"I promise when things calm down I'll start looking for my own place."

Leo's face hardens. I can tell he has something to say by the way his fingers twitch, but he doesn't utter a word.

"I have some business to take care of," he says. "Get some rest. We'll get started in the morning."

"Leo?"

"Yes, Nikita?"

Fuck it. I can't fight this feeling anymore. When I'm without him, I'm miserable. I would much rather accept him for who he is and be at his side than endure another day without him. I want to be his and I want him to be mine, damn the consequences. The people I thought I could trust all turned their backs on me. He's the only one on Earth I would trust with my life.

I rush toward him and practically fling myself into his arms. Always at the ready and prepared to catch me, Leo lifts me up off the floor so I can wrap my arms around his neck and my legs around his hips. Our lips crash together, desperate tongues tangling as we soak in each other's warmth.

"I'm not scared of you," I tell him earnestly. "I could never be scared of you."

The warm glint in his eye speaks volumes. There's no need for long-winded speeches or heartfelt words. We can feel it instead, the connection between us burning brighter than the sun.

Our kisses become heated, every touch feverish to the point where I feel like I might fall apart without him near. Leo carries me down the hall to his bedroom without even breaking a sweat. I wonder if I'm as light as a feather to him.

He helps me out of my clothes, I help him out of his. I feel his rough palms everywhere, touching and exploring like he's determined to map out every curve, line, and dip. I drown in the scent of him lifting off his sheets, his skin. I get drunk off the taste of his tongue, high off the sound of his voice murmuring in my ear.

"Should I break out the rope?" he asks me with a light laugh.

I smile at him. "Actually, can I give it a try?"

He arches a brow. "Feeling adventurous are we?" he asks, but he nonetheless walks over to his bedside table to retrieve the red silk rope. He hands it to me, delicately placing it in his hands.

"Do you trust me?" I ask him.

He nods, not a hint of worry to be found in his ruggedly handsome features. "I trust you, Nikita."

I lick my lips, my mind racing at the endless opportunities before me. "This might be a bit messy. I'm no Boy Scout."

"Anything you want, Nikita."

"Get on the bed and put your wrists together for me."

Leo does exactly as I ask, settling against his headboard with a few pillows propped up behind him to support his back. He holds his hands out, wrists together, awaiting further instruction. There's something strangely euphoric about being able to tell someone like Leo what to do. He's giving me that control, that power. I realize now that this rope is so much more than just something to spice things up in the bedroom. It requires a bond and unshakable faith in one another.

My knots are unfortunately sloppy, and there may be a little too much slack because I'm still too inexperienced to trust I won't cut off his circulation.

"Let me know if it gets uncomfortable," I tell him.

Instead of brushing off my concerns and telling me he'll be fine, he says instead, "I promise. Now, show me what you want to do, Nikita. Take what's yours."

A warm shiver snakes down my spine, sending goose-bumps crawling down my arms.

I straddle his thighs, reaching between us to give his cock a few languid strokes. He's thick and hard against my palm, my fingers curling around his shaft with unhurried admiration. I like the way he groans, low and hungry, his gaze nothing short of ravenous. I take my sweet time, teasing him to the point of unraveling. I know he must be getting close because his breathing becomes strained, the rapid rise and fall of his chest a clear indication I'm pushing him closer and closer to the edge.

"Nikita," he rasps. "Nikita, stop teasing."

The corner of my lip turns up into a smirk. "What are

you going to do about it? Your hands are tied. Wow, this *is* fun."

Leo throws his head back with the huff. "I'm regretting this already," he grumbles.

A bubbly anticipation builds in my rib cage, the air in my lungs burning like soft fire. This is thrilling, just as heart-pounding as it is in the wings of the theater waiting for my cue to dance. I want to give a show. I want to leave him in complete awe and begging for an encore.

I carefully shimmy down so I can hinge at the hips and bend toward his cock. I wrap my lips around the head, teasing him with the tip of my tongue. The sound he makes is to die for, a cross between a moan and a growl. His hips buck involuntarily, shoving his cock a few inches further into my mouth. I pull away and click my tongue.

"Now, now," I chide. "Lie back and relax while I do all the work."

"Your mouth feels so good, please just—"

I giggle. "Begging already?"

I ignore his irritated little grunt and continue my work at a leisurely pace. I savor the taste of his cock, thick and heavy on the pad of my tongue. A little salty, but also undeniably *him*. I want more. I might get addicted to this.

Little by little I take him further into my mouth, hollowing my cheeks so I can make room for him. I swirl my tongue around, stroking him in tandem with the up and down motion of my head. He almost loses his mind when I dare to give his balls a little squeeze.

"*Fuck*, Nikita!"

He tries to reach for me, but with his hands bound behind his head he can do no such thing. He strains against the ropes, his body arching with pleasure as I continue to suck him off. A part of me really wants to get him there, to see if I can get him to come down my throat… I want to be naughty. I want to make an absolute mess of him, but the unbearable throbbing heat between my legs needs to be addressed sooner rather than later.

My mouth pulls off his cock with a soft popping sound. I look him directly in the eye as I lick my lips clean, spurred on by his erotic moan. Moving slowly, I run my hand over my breasts, down my belly, until I can finally brush my fingers over my aching clit. I can tell how badly he wants to be the one to touch me. But not tonight. Tonight he can be a good little audience member and let me perform.

"Do you like what you see?" I ask him as I draw a tight circle against myself. Pleasure balloons deep within me, growing with an intense, fiery heat.

"Yes," he pants. "You're so beautiful, Nikita. I want—"

"What do you want? Tell me."

"I want to see you ride my cock like the dirty girl I know you are."

Encouraged by his words, I move into position, straddling his thick thighs. I spread my legs, reaching down to guide the head of his cock to my entrance. "You want to see me ride you? Is that what you want?"

"I want to see you take control."

I lower myself slowly, relishing the stretch of the burn. Leo is so big it's frankly a miracle I managed to take him all the way down to the base. With my hands on his chest, I begin to move, rolling my hips against him to take my own pleasure. Now that I have control, I give myself permission to let it all go.

My pace is fast and breathtaking. I chase more of that sweet friction, the head of his cock hitting my sweet spot again and again. It isn't long before sparks fly across my vision and liquid fire spreads through my veins. My walls clench around him, throbbing with ecstasy. The thing about being a professional athlete, though, is that I have a lot more stamina than meets the eye.

I continue to ride him, grinding against him like a woman on a mission. I tease my clit, and I'm flying within a matter of seconds. I come again, this time with a breathy scream. All Leo can do is look at me with reverence and awe. His eyes are the only spotlight I crave now.

"I'm getting close," he grunts. "Nikita, I'm—"

"Come inside me," I moan desperately. "Come inside me, Leo. I want you to fill me up."

Something feral overtakes Leo's expression like he wants to claim me as his own. "Let me put a baby in you, Nikita."

A whimper escapes me. He's already done that... At least I know now that he wants one. God, I've never desired this man more. "Please," I whine, "Fill me up."

"Untie me," he orders.

The moment I untie his hands, Leo grabs me by the waist and flips us over so he has me pinned against the mattress. He's an animal, fucking me like he owns me. The snap of his hips and the harshness of his kisses overwhelm me in the best of ways.

"I'm going to make you the mother of my child," he groans against my ear, his hot against my cheek.

I already am, is all I want to scream from the bottom of my lungs. But I push the thought back down so I can revel in this moment.

He comes inside me with a roar in the exact same moment I once again fly off the edge.

He holds me like he never wants to let go.

"Be my woman," he says, his tone stern but his gaze

gentle. "Be my woman, Nikita, and I will make sure you want for nothing."

His offer makes my heart flutter. After all the shit I've been through, who could blame me for wanting someone so strong, so generous to take care of me? All I've ever wanted was for someone to love me. My mother never cared for me; my father has only ever been capable of his own selfishness. But when Leo says it, it feels like a vow. An unbreakable promise. He will make good on his word.

I want that. I want that more than words could ever describe. At this point, I don't care what he does for a living as long as he never hurts *me*. He's frankly treated me better than everyone else in my life. Better than my parents, than my coworkers and friends.

"I'm all yours," I tell him, and I mean every word.

I just need to work up the courage to tell him about the baby, too.

Soon. Eventually.

CHAPTER 26

LEO

"Follow my lead," I tell her as we approach the practice building.

My good old friend Pavel stands just outside the door, looking as serious as ever. He crosses his arms when he sees me, then scowls the moment he spots Nikita to my right. He immediately holds a hand up and shakes his head.

"Ms. Belova, I have been given specific instructions not to let you into the building."

Nikita doesn't shy away. Instead, she takes a step forward and meets Pavel head on. "I'm only going to ask you once for old time's sake—let us in and don't let anyone know we were here. We just need to check on something."

"I really can't do that. I've been making too many exceptions lately as it is. You could get me in a world of trouble if you're caught."

I frown. "Too many exceptions? Who else have you been letting in here?"

Pavel presses his lips into a thin line, the color from his face momentarily draining. "Uh... No one?"

Nikita and I exchange a look, a silent conversation

passing between us. I think she has the same idea as I do because she crosses her arms and mirrors Pavel's stance. "You know, Christmas is just around the corner. Tell me, was your holiday bonus particularly large this year?"

Over the years, I've become incredibly skilled at reading people's faces. There's a minute shift in his expression, barely perceptible, but I can tell it's there. It's sleazy. Greasy. Leaves a bitter taste on my tongue. I can tell we've finally captured his attention. Money talks, after all. It always has and it always will.

"How much are you going to give me?" he asks, cutting straight to the chase. Typical sleazeball. No point in trying to be delicate about it. We all know what he wants.

Begrudgingly, I reach into my pocket and pull out my wallet, flipping it open to pull out the small stack of bills I have tucked away. I give him all my money. It's peanuts to me in the grand scheme of things, but the sum total is probably more than he makes in an entire month.

Pavel makes a great show of counting each and every bill, relishing his victory. I don't much care for it, mainly because he's wasting our time. "Fine," he says after a moment. "Go on inside. I won't say anything."

"Actually, we need you to tell us who you let in," Nikita says hurriedly. "Have you seen anyone strange coming and going?"

"Strange? No, no one strange. Though, the director and that dancer Kseniya have been here after hours often."

"The director and Kseniya?" Nikita echoes. "That doesn't mean much. They both work here."

"You misunderstand me," Pavel says. "I mean they've been showing up *together*."

I place my hand on the small of Nikita's back. "Let's get

inside before someone spots us. Tell me, are there security cameras in this place?"

"Of course."

"Do they feed in through a central system? Or is the feed outsourced?"

Pavel squishes up his face like I just asked him to calculate the speed of light. "How should I know?"

"Do you genuinely not know the answer to my question, or are you being dense on purpose?"

He glances down at the imaginary dirt beneath his fingernails. "I don't know. How much is that information worth to you?"

I clench my fists. I can't remember the last time I had to deal with someone so insufferable. Roman, perhaps, but he's my little brother so that doesn't really count. Pavel is really starting to push my buttons. I'm half-tempted to grab him up by the collar and give him a good shake—maybe that'll knock some sense into that thick skull of his—but not with Nikita here. I don't want her to see that side of me. Especially not now that she has given me the chance. I can solve this without the need for violence. I can toe the line of criminality without crossing it.

"How much do you want?" I ask him.

"How much you got?"

"Don't push it." With no other option, I reach for my checkbook. It's not under my name, but the taxi company's. I'm going to have to write this off as a networking expense. Thankfully, as the Bratva's accountant, I'm in the position to do just that. I write what I consider a reasonable amount and sign my name. "Merry Christmas. Now, tell me what we want to know."

Pavel folds the check neatly in half and tucks it away into his pocket. "It's a closed circuit. Everything records internally. The only way to access the footage is by logging into the director's computer."

Nikita tugs on my sleeve. "Come on. I have a feeling all our answers are in there."

"You're going to need a key," Pavel points out, not so casually gesturing to the ring of keys hooked through one of his belt loops.

"Let me guess," Nikita grumbles. "It's going to cost us, isn't it?"

He shrugs. "Maybe."

I fight the urge to punch him in the face. At the rate things are going, this son of a bitch is going to bleed me dry. Hell, I wouldn't be surprised if he ends up leveraging just as much as the night shift has stolen from us. But I have to deal with one problem at a time, and right now, I'm willing to throw every ruble I have at him if it means getting Nikita some well-deserved answers.

I write him another check. "Lead the way, and don't try anything funny."

We're forced to work in the dark, feeling around the office space with an air of unease. It may be late, but there's no telling if the director might feel the need to pop in for an unexpected visit.

A series of posters decorates one wall, all of them framed in mahogany and covered in polished glass. The posters are of ballets past, used in city-wide advertisements. I can tell which ones are newer, because the older ones have faded in color from years of exposure to the sun. To the far right, the newest addition. It's a poster for this season's production of *The Nutcracker*. A handful of the dancers have been photographed in position, an ensemble brought together by magic and whimsy. In the back of the composition, a picture of the Sugar Plum Fairy.

It's not Nikita.

She stares at the poster, her obvious irritation manifesting in the form of tight shoulders and heavy breathing. "That's supposed to be me," she says weakly. I can hear the hurt in her voice by the way her words come out a bitter croak.

I give her shoulder a light squeeze. "We'll make everything right. I promise."

"I don't know. This whole thing has really dashed my spirits." Her smile is small and fragile. "All I've ever wanted to do is dance, but I don't know if I have the heart to keep going if this is the environment I find myself in. I'm going to have to give my future some serious thought, that's all."

I nod reassuringly. "I'll admit that I love watching you dance, but I want whatever you want."

"What I want right now is to figure out who the real saboteur is."

"Then let's get to work."

I take a seat in the director's chair. The base is lumpy and the lumbar support—or lack thereof—is so terrible the lower muscles in my back want to scream in agony.

It takes a second for his computer to boot up. It's big and clunky, something from the early 2000's that whirs to life with the force of a freaking jet engine. I consider it nothing short of a miracle when the screen actually manages to load, revealing a simple log-in screen. By the look of things, the director uses a four-digit passcode.

I grit my teeth. "This could take a while."

Nikita hovers beside me, one hand on my shoulder as she leans forward to investigate. "Don't you have... I don't know, connections? Do you work with any hackers or something like that?"

"We used to, but he retired a while ago from the business. One of Sandra's uncles. We're just going to have to brute force it."

"That could take all night."

"We don't have very many options."

Nikita looks around the office space. I can practically hear the gears in her head grinding as she attempts to formulate a plan. "He's an older man," she mutters aloud. "I'm sure he's the type to pick a PIN that's easy to remember, like a birthday or something."

"Do you know his birthday?"

"No."

She wanders over to a glass display shelf behind us, browsing through the numerous plaques and awards. She zeroes in on a frame image of the Bolshoi Theatre itself, framed and kept at eye-level—an obvious beloved peace.

"Maybe it's not *his* birthday," she mumbles. "Try 1825. The year this place was built."

I type the numbers in and press *ENTER*. A little gray circle rotates in the center of the screen, but five seconds later, I'm greeted by the blindingly bright background of rolling pastures on the director's desktop.

"Good guess," I say.

Nikita beams. "I honestly didn't think that would work. Now, where are we supposed to find the footage?"

It's a great question. The director, in typical old man fashion, has a desktop littered with a hundred different icons. It's a disorganized mess that causes the knots in my shoulders to tighten.

"Good God, how does anyone *live* like this?" I grumble.

Nikita taps the screen gently, her vision far sharper than mine for a singular, obvious reason. "Here. I think this is it."

I click on the folder and it, too, is just as much of a mess as the director's shitstorm of a home screen. No wonder his computer is already overheating despite being on for less than five minutes. There are thousands of hours of surveillance footage backed up to this single folder, dating as far back as five years ago. Why in the ever-loving hell would someone keep this much video on a single hard drive? I can chalk it up to his advanced age and general ignorance—but *holy shit* it's a miracle his computer hasn't caught fire.

I click on one video, a recording from earlier this morning, scrubbing through and pausing when I spot even a blur of movement. It always ends up being nothing, though.

"This is going to take forever," Nikita grumbles, understandably irritated.

I frown when I spot something inconsistent in the folder. "A few dates are missing."

"What?"

"November second, November fifteenth, and yesterday."

Nikita's eyes widen. "Oh my God."

"What?"

"November second is the day Vanya's shoes were tampered with. November fifteenth was when I found razors in my shoes—"

Alarm lances through me. "Fucking *what* in your shoes?"

"Oh, I might have forgotten to tell you."

"Nikita—"

She shakes her head, gesturing back toward the screen.

"Not important right now. And yesterday... That was when the director confronted me about the toolbox in my locker."

"Are you suggesting the director knew exactly what was going on and deleted the footage to cover his tracks?"

Nikita nods. "Too much of a coincidence, don't you think? The director is one hundred percent in on whatever's going on. Is there a way to recover the footage?"

My brain goes into overdrive. "Maybe we don't need it."

"I don't follow."

"We have the dates. We know who's involved. I think we have enough to confront that so-called friend of yours."

"But without any proof—"

"It's called a bluff. Do you know where she lives?"

Nikita gives me a worried glance. "We're not going to whack her or something, right?"

"Not unless you want me to."

"Not funny."

I take her hand and lightly squeeze her fingers. "We're not going to do anything to her, Nikita. We're just... going to apply a bit of pressure. Get her talking."

"Are you sure?"

I flash a grin. "Trust me. I'm a professional."

CHAPTER 27

NIKITA

The only reason I know where Kseniya lives is because she once invited me over for a movie night with a bunch of her friends. Not ballerinas, but a troop of improvisational jazz dancers. They were nice, from what I remember, but they were a rowdy bunch and I don't remember staying for very long. I'm pretty sure Inessa was blowing up my phone asking me where the hell I was so late, so I made up an excuse to leave and ducked out.

The outside of the building is nothing to write home about. Just your standard gray concrete with neatly lined windows, stacked row upon row for about ten floors into the sky. The neighborhood is unassuming, complete with a little deli around the corner and a small kiddie park just across the street. Easily forgettable. Easily forgotten. Kind of like Kseniya herself.

Getting into the building is easy enough. Leo and I slip in without too much hassle as a group of young twenty-somethings leave the building, whooping and walloping about their Friday night activities. One of them even holds the door open for us, believing we live in the building. There's no elevator, so the winding climb up the stairs to the fifth floor admittedly gets my heart pumping.

As we approach Kseniya's apartment door, my hands begin to feel clammy and cold. I tried to play out the situation in my head during our drive over, but now that I'm so close to confronting her about what she's done, my mind is blank and I can't seem to find my courage. There are so many things I want to ask her. Did she really do it? Why did she do it? I guess there's really only one way to find out, and that means ripping off the Band-Aid, no matter how painful that might be.

Before I knock on the door, Leo gently takes my hand. "For the first little bit, I want you to let me do the talking."

"Why?"

"It's kind of my specialty. I want you to know the man you see in there... It's not who I am, just who I have to pretend to be."

I reach up and caress his cheek. "I know." And then, softer, "I know who you are, Leo."

I can almost read his mind. He's concerned about me seeing him in action. Getting to see this new facet of himself. But I've already given him my heart, whether he knows it or not. I never understood the concept of a ride or die until I met him.

I will take all his good and his bad, and I will love every bit of him anyway.

Leo steps forward. He doesn't bother knocking. That would ruin our element of surprise. Instead, he leans back and throws a hard front kick, the heel of his shoe driving into the doorknob with enough force to send the door swinging open.

Inside, a pathetic yelp of a man, the director himself. "Good Lord!"

"What's going on?" Kseniya cries.

Leo enters quickly and I'm hot on his heels, closing the door behind us so we can have some privacy. I can already tell this conversation is about to get heated, and for very good reason.

I'm almost appalled at what I see. Before us, Kseniya and the director are frozen mid-embrace. She was sitting across his lap, her lipstick marks staining his cheeks, his lips, his throat, and even a corner of his shirt's collar. Kseniya is in a similarly compromising position, her top missing and her bra half unclasped. Apparently, we've caught them in the middle of their affair.

"What the hell is going on?" she shrieks. "Nikita? What are you doing here?"

"Stop talking," Leo says. I've never heard him so menacing. His voice is deep and rich, the sound vibrating through the air, the walls, even through my rib cage. He's a panther on the prowl, his eyes set on a pair of squawking geese. "We know it was you."

"What are you talking about?" the director demands. His eyes widen when he realizes who he's talking to. "Wait a second... Mr. Nicolaevich?"

"The two of you have been working together to sabotage the other dancers," Leo says. "First Vanya, and then, when the part didn't immediately fall to you, you decided to go after Nikita."

The director looks like he's about to piss his pants. His face is turning an unhealthy shade of green, and he can't stop quivering like a little mouse caught in a corner. Kseniya's reaction intrigues me the most. I have known her for many years, always so sweet and kind. It's one of the reasons I never suspected her until it was too late. She has worn her mask of practiced politeness for so long and so well that the look of pure, unadulterated hatred in her eyes takes me by complete surprise.

Her whole face darkens. There is so much heat behind her gaze I swear she might burn a hole straight through my head. Her lip curls up into a sneer, baring her teeth like a rabid dog preparing to lash out.

"You've got it all wrong," she says, sickly sweet, but I can tell she's furious by the way she grinds her teeth and clenches her fists.

"We found the security footage," I lie smoothly. My heart beats rapidly in my chest. This is all a part of the game plan, our bluff. Leo has assured me over and over again that this is going to work, as long as I remember to keep cool. "We've got video of you sneaking into the building to sabotage our shoes. Planting that toolbox in my locker."

Kseniya, no longer the sweet little puppy I always believed her to be, turns her attention to the director. It's obvious to me that he isn't the one calling the shots, but her. "You told me you deleted those tapes. You fucking idiot!"

"I thought I did!"

"So you're confessing?" Leo asks.

Slowly, Kseniya rises from the couch. I think she's trying to be threatening, but I know Leo would never let her do anything to harm me or himself. She's too small to put up a fight, but maybe she's stupid enough to try.

"Do you have any idea what it's like?" she whines. "All I've ever wanted was to be a soloist. Years upon years upon years of hard work—and for what? To be a part of the ballet corps yet again? To play some no name bit role everyone will forget about the moment I step off stage? It's my turn to shine, dammit! I'm tired of waiting."

"That's part of the job," I argue. "We all have to work our way up the ladder. I was right there with you. I know exactly how you feel."

"No, you don't." I can't tell if the tears in her eyes are of sadness or anger. Either way, they're not going to work on me. "My whole life, I have dedicated myself to my craft. You have no idea how lucky you are, Nikita."

"Lucky?" I scoff.

"Your mother is the ballet master. She pays so much attention to you, helps you improve. I bet when the two of you go home, she helps you practice even after hours. That's why you're such a brilliant dancer. How am I supposed to compete with that? I'm nowhere near as good, and there's no way I can be. Not when you have a leg up.

"That's why all of the other dancers are so jealous of you. You have a master helping you every step of the way. It isn't fair. I could have been a principal soloist had you not been Inessa's favorite."

I chew on the inside of my cheek. "You think I'm her favorite? You couldn't be more wrong. My mother hates me. Have you not heard the way she breaks me down every single practice? Don't for a fucking second think this is about nepotism, because believe me, Inessa would love nothing more than to bury me beneath her heel. Don't assume to know me."

"Bullshit—"

"How could you do it? How could you put fucking *razors* in my shoes? How could you hurt Vanya?"

"Oh, shut up!" she snaps at me. "Nobody's buying your goody two shoes act. You wanted to be a soloist for years. I did what I had to do. I snuck in and sabotaged her shoes while this incompetent fool made sure to scrub the security footage." She glares at him. "At least, he was supposed to."

"How long have you two been together?" I ask, not bothering to hide my disgust.

"A year," the director says, the slightest hint of pride in his tone. "We're in love—"

Kseniya gags. "No, we're not, you old fart. Holy crap, men really will believe anything, huh?"

"I was willing to work for it," I grumble. "Not sleep my way to the top." Resisting the urge to cuss her up and down, I turned to Leo. "Did you get all that?"

He pulls his phone from of his pocket, revealing that it's been recording our conversation the entire time. "We have her confession. All we have to do now is go to the police, or worse."

Kseniya frowns. "What do you mean, *or worse*?"

"We all know how much our reputations mean to us," I explain. "Word travels fast in our circles. All I'd have to do is have Leo upload this audio to an email and CC every single person at the Bolshoi. Everyone from the janitors to the patrons will know what you've done and how you tried to pin the blame on me."

For the first time since we arrived, Kseniya finally seems to understand the gravity of the situation. Her face pales and her eyes widen. Her bottom lip trembles, but her crocodile tears have all but dried up. We have her right where we want her, and the director is just an added bonus.

"You're going to *blackmail* me?" she shrieks. "You're bluffing. There's no way someone like you could—"

"I told you. You don't know me. I can and I *will*."

The director fumbles, his hands visibly shaking as he wipes his slimy palms on the front of his shirt. "What do you want, then? To make this go away."

"First of all, I want my name cleared," I tell them.

"How do you expect to do that?" the director asks.

"The police are investigating," I remind them. "They'll get this information anonymously."

"You can't do that!" Kseniya cries.

"I can and I will," I repeat. "I want my role back. I will dance the Sugar Plum Fairy on opening night."

Kseniya grinds her teeth so hard I can hear them squeak from across the room. "I fucking hate you," she grumbles. "You weren't supposed to—"

"What?" I challenge. "Fight back?"

I stare down my nose at her, savoring the sweet feeling of well-earned revenge. I have nothing more to say to this woman. Never once did I think she was capable of such atrocious behavior. I really did think of her as a friend, one of the very few I had.

Leo turns to me and places his hand on the small of my back, gently guiding me toward the door. "You two have a wonderful rest of your night," he says calmly, coolly. In that moment, I *see* him.

God, I think I'm in love with him.

We leave the building hand in hand, returning to his car parked by the curb. He hands me the phone, the audio file staring me straight in the face.

I've been staring at the screen so long I don't realize Leo's been watching me the entire time. The tense silence in the air is thick enough to slice with a knife.

"How do you feel?" he asks me.

I don't know how to put it into words. Relieved? Angry? "Tired," is what I end up saying. I turn in my chair slightly to look at him. "Will you be there? To watch me on opening night? I just want one chance to show the world what I can do, and then I think I'm done."

He holds my gaze, serious and intense. "Are you sure, Nikita?"

I nod. "I want one final hurrah. To go out on my own terms. One final, perfect performance before I retire my pointe shoes."

"But what will you do after?"

"I'm sure I'll figure it out." Truth is, I already have a clue or two, especially with this life growing inside of me... I reach across the center console and take his hand. I don't think I'll ever stop marveling at how perfectly our fingers weave together, different threads meant to make the same beautiful tapestry. "As long as I'm with you, I'm sure I'll land on my feet."

"I know you will," he says, pressing a kiss to my knuckles. "My sister-in-law already got us tickets to see opening night, well before I met you. It must have been fate."

"So you'll be there?"

"I'll be cheering so loud for you, there will be no question who's causing a ruckus."

Just as I break out into a massive smile, Leo's phone rings and breaks through our perfect little moment of victory. His lips press into a thin line, obviously irritated by the disruption, but I shake my head.

"It's okay. Answer it."

He offers me a sweet smile, a little secret just for me that I can tuck away and treasure forever. "Talk to me," he answers. I'm not too sure who he's speaking to, but judging by his serious expression, I'd bet a pretty penny this has to do with the Bratva. I won't pry, though. I'm sure it'll take some practice, but if we can keep our work lives in our personal lives separate, I think our futures will be nothing but smooth sailing.

"Got it," he says. "I'm on my way." When he hangs up,

he gives me an apologetic look. "I've got to take care of something. Work."

I nod understandingly. "Do what you got to do, handsome."

"I'll drop you off at the penthouse. It shouldn't take me long."

CHAPTER 28

LEO

Once I know Nikita is safely tucked away at home, I hurry back to the taxi depot where my brothers have managed to find three of the four night shift members who, until recently, had us all turned around.

Vlad. Georgi. Kostya.

They are bound to individual chairs in the basement storage room. This place in particular brings back memories, though they aren't exactly what I describe as fond. A few years ago, when my brother Andrei was making a power play to take over Moscow from the Antonov Bratva, we kidnapped Sandra Antonova, their heir apparent, and kept her down here in this exact room.

I'm glad that particular chapter of our lives ended up working in our favor. I never would have expected Andrei to fall in love with her, let alone risk everything we worked toward just so they could be together. A real Romeo and Juliet story, minus the tragic ending. Now our houses are united, and we rule this city together with an iron fist.

It's chilly down here, more so than usual because we're deep into the winter months. Being underground is basically like walking into a freezer. The earth is cold and constantly seeking heat, sapping it from whatever poor creatures decide to linger too long. *I'm* having a hard time down here, even with my bulk and insulated winter coat. I can't imagine how frigid our guests must be now that we've stripped them down to nothing more than their underwear, their hands bound behind them, ankles strapped to the legs of their chairs.

My brothers are already there by the time I arrive, muttering quietly amongst themselves. Andrei hangs back, as he always does. He's a relaxed sort of leader and prefers to work from the shadows and let his brothers do all the dirty work. Not only does this keep him safe from potential attack, but it also gives him a better view of the whole picture.

He nods when he sees me, crossing his arms over his chest.

"Was the traffic bad?" he teases. "You're normally the first to arrive."

"I was helping my girl take care of something."

"*Ooh,*" Roman says. "You mean the beauty to your beast?"

I ignore my younger brother outright. "Where did you find them?"

Samuil cracks his knuckles. "Caught Vlad trying to catch a train to Finland. I guess he didn't realize we'd pick him up on the CCTV outside the station."

Damian tosses his chin toward Georgi and Kostya. "And these two were just about to board a ship to Turkey."

"How much money were you able to recover?"

"Seventy-five percent, if my math is right," Andrei says, "though I'll leave the final calculations to you."

In the grand scheme of things, a twenty-five percent loss

isn't that big of a deal. What *is* a big deal, however, is the principle of the matter. I'm not willing to compromise. A crime has been committed here, and I must dole out punishment.

I approach our three captives with an air of indifference. There's no point in letting them see my fury. Because if they see what's really boiling underneath the surface, they'll know they have the upper hand. They'll know they managed to get to me. My pride simply won't allow it.

"Where's Arman?" I ask, speaking slowly as I gauge their reactions. The three of them are understandably shifty, unable to look me in the eye, but judging by the blankness in Georgi's expression, I can tell he doesn't have the answer I'm looking for.

So that leaves me only two of the men to work with.

"You would be wise to cooperate with me. The sooner you tell me where he's hiding, the sooner we'll let you go."

Vlad's face lights up. "R-really?"

"He's lying." Kostya spits at my feet. "Don't believe a word out of this fucker's mouth."

It seems I've discovered the leader of this band of brothers. I stand before Kostya and study him. He's brutish like Samuil, cold and hard like me. It's going to take forever to get him to crack. Not ideal. Right now, time is of the essence. Arman could be halfway across the globe by now. Someone needs to start talking...

That's why I need to start with the weakest link.

"Samuil," I say, "take Georgi out for a walk, would you?"

My brother stomps forward, heavy footfalls like war drums against the solid cement floor. Predictably, Georgi starts to squirm in his seat, desperately looking around for an escape he won't find.

All Samuil has to do is grab the back of Georgi's chair and start to drag him out, the legs of the chair screeching against the floor as he starts to whimper.

"W-wait! Wait, no—I don't know where he is! I *swear*!"

His cries go unheeded. I'm sure my brother won't kill him—it's one of Sandra's policies. Since our family joined with the Antonovs, we've had a very strict *murder-free* rule set in place unless it's to save a family member's life. But she never said anything about shelling out strategically placed, painful bruises.

Not that they know that, though.

"Stop it!" Vlad exclaims. "Leave him alone. He doesn't know anything!"

He's an exposed nerve, and now it's time to stab him where it hurts. "But you do, don't you." It's a statement, not a question.

"Don't say anything," Kostya warns.

"It isn't fair, is it?" I continue. "Your brother gets to go free, spend his fortune while you three will be six feet underground come morning."

"Shut up!"

I approach Vlad slowly, pinning him with my glare. "Is that what you want? A coffin instead of a Christmas present?"

"C-Come on, Leo, let's just... We've got families to think about."

"And I don't?" I ask coldly. "Let me ask you this: if I stole from *your* family, what would you do?"

"I... I'd..."

Kostya lurches in his seat, but he doesn't get very far. "Vlad, for the love of God, *stop talking*."

"I'm a reasonable man," I say. "Always have been. I think I proved that with your early Christmas bonuses. We just want the money back. It'd be too much of a hassle to dig four unmarked graves. Besides, I don't want to welcome in the new year by killing you and your brothers."

Vlad visibly swallows, his Adam's apple bobbing harshly. "The money. That's really all you want?"

I shrug a shoulder. "That, and your heartfelt apology. Oh, also, you're all fucking *fired*, but yes. The money's all we want."

"St. Petersburg."

Beside us, Kostya hisses. "Dammit, Vlad! You had one job!"

I arch a brow. "St. Petersburg? What's he doing all the way up there?"

"Look, don't hurt him, okay? He didn't even want to go through with the idea. It was all me. He's got his wife and kids there. Living with a cousin of hers."

"Do you have an address?"

"Yes, but... *Swear* you won't hurt them."

"I don't hurt women or children."

"And Arman?"

"I'm inclined to forgive him. After we've had a talk."

Kostya throws his head back and groans. "They're going to kill us. They're straight up going to kill us, you blubbering idiot."

"They were going to kill us if we didn't say anything. At least *this* way, we have a chance."

I have no idea what's come over me lately, but I chalk it up to Nikita's influence. I place a hand over my heart. "You have my word. No harm will come to any of you."

Vlad's head drops forward, a heavy sigh dragging itself from his lungs. "Fine. Fine, I'll tell you where he is."

~

By the time I get back to the penthouse, it's well after midnight. I find Nikita passed out on the living room couch, curled up in a blanket. The television is on, but the volume is muted. She's managed to hook up her phone to my Smart TV and was in the middle of watching an old recording of *The Nutcracker* ballet taken several years ago. The only reason I can tell it's old is because the footage is grainy and the costumes look incredibly dated, though beautiful, in its own classical way.

I watch Nikita for a moment, more than a little amused at how easily she's acclimated to her surroundings. I love that she's already comfortable here. She looks *good* laying on my couch, wrapped up in my throw blanket.

There's almost a sense of pride swelling in me, my caveman brain coming to the forefront. I'm territorial, suddenly eager to build her a home from scratch with my two bare hands. I want to scoop her up and put her in my bed where I can keep her safe and warm.

For now, though, I'll settle for carrying her to the bedroom where she can get a proper night's rest. Now that we've gotten her problem squared away and her role has finally and rightfully been returned to her, I doubt she wants to dance with a kink in her neck.

Nikita yawns and holds onto me as I pick her up, one arm braced around her back and the other beneath her knees. "Did you take care of business?" she mumbles against my chest sleepily.

"Not quite. I have to make a quick trip out of the city."

This wakes her up, her eyes suddenly wide open. There are sleep lines on her face from where her cheek was smushed against the couch cushion. "Really?"

"Don't worry. I won't be gone long. I'll be back in time to see you dance."

She runs her hand over my chest, smoothing the wrinkles on my shirt. "You'll be safe, right? It's not dangerous?"

I kiss her forehead. "No, sweetheart. It's not dangerous. It's just a... talk."

I can tell by the look she gives me that she isn't quite convinced, but she doesn't press the issue. "Just promise to be safe."

"You have nothing to worry about, Nikita."

"*Promise* me."

I kiss her tenderly as I lay her down in my bed—our bed now, I suppose with growing glee—before looking deep into her brilliant blue eyes.

"I promise."

CHAPTER 29

LEO

"Ah, road trips," Roman says with a mischievous grin. "When was the last time we went on a vacation together, just you and me?"

I get into the car with a grunt. "This isn't a vacation."

"Do I get to pick the music since I'm in the passenger seat?"

"I prefer to drive in silence."

"And *I* prefer not to spend the next couple of hours driving with a psychopath. You don't listen to anything *at all?*"

I sigh heavily. Why couldn't Andrei send Samuil or Damien with me? At least Samuil's quiet, and Damien and I don't get along well enough to bother having meaningful conversation. Of all my brothers, why did I have to be stuck with the chatterbox of the family?

"There's duct tape in the trunk," I tell my brother.

"What for?"

"To seal your mouth shut."

Instead of getting offended, Roman just laughs. "Dear God have mercy, this is going to be a *long* trip."

~

It's roughly seven hours from Moscow to St. Petersburg. I suppose we could have sent one of our lieutenants to retrieve the funds, but this needs to be kept under wraps. We don't need anybody knowing that an employee managed to pull a fast one over on the Bratva. This is a get-in, get-out kind of mission. Clean and precise.

I somehow manage to endure an entire day in the car with my brother. How I managed not to strangle him to death with his own seat belt is, frankly, nothing short of a Christmas miracle. Not to sound dramatic, but I almost fling myself out of the damn car when we finally pull up to the house—anything to get away from his constant jabbering.

"Focus," I snap at him. "We're here to do a job."

Roman dares to give me a mock salute. "Aye aye, captain."

"Take this seriously."

"I'm always serious, Leo. It's just that my face is so charming people forget I am."

I roll my eyes. "Stay with the car. Keep it running. This is going to be quick."

"It better be. I've got to pee really bad."

"You're the least serious gangster I've ever had the displeasure of meeting in my entire life."

He flashes a toothy grin. "I love you too, big bro."

Finding my way into the house is easy enough. It's an older building, a shadow of its former self during the mid-Cold War era. All white bricks and a heavily shingled roof. I hear voices inside. The sound of children playing. It's for their sake that I want this taken care of as quickly as possible. I meant what I said before, about how I don't hurt women or children. It's unconscionable.

All it takes is a hard yank on the back door before it squeaks open on its hinges. It leads directly into the kitchen. The lights are off, save for the one over the stove, casting the entire room in a soft orange glow. I smell peppermint and priyaniki gingerbread cookies, as well as the more traditional herbal scent of kulebyaka, a sort of salmon pie, lingering in the air.

I take in the whimsical, pale-yellow wallpaper and the decorative porcelain plates mounted to the walls. The old oak cupboards are in need of a paint job. Leftover raspberry tarts sit in a pile on the kitchen counter, the sink full of dirty dishes set aside for later.

Somewhere deeper inside the house, I hear laughter. Joyous conversation. Apparently, I've caught Arman and his family after just having finished dinner. I decide to take a seat at the kitchen table, patiently waiting. I can hear his kids, both of them young and brimming with life. They talk about what they want most from Old Saint Nick, about what they're looking forward to learning in school in the new year.

As I take in my surroundings, I realize what a humble existence they must live. All that money he stole from us... surely, he could have afforded a nicer place for them?

Someone approaches, the tap of a pair of crutches reaching my ears. A child emerges from around the corner, stepping into the kitchen only to freeze. The girl looks no older than ten. She has startling blue eyes that remind me a lot of Nikita. She stares at me, torn between confusion and fear. Slowly, I bring a finger to my lips.

"Would you mind getting your father for me?"

She nods slowly. I don't blame her when she quickly

whips around and rushes away. "Papa! Papa, there's a strange man in our kitchen!"

Rapid footsteps follow quickly after, Arman rushing in to see what she's talking about. The moment our eyes lock, he understands. Resignation washes over his expression. He doesn't try to run, nor does he attempt to defend himself.

"I was wondering when you would show up," he says sadly.

"Dear, what's—" His wife stops behind him, her hand clutching his shoulder in surprise when she spots me. "Oh, dear God—"

"Relax," I say. "I mean you no harm. I just want to talk with your husband, man to man."

Arman gently pats the back of his wife's hand. "Put the children to bed."

"But—"

"Do it. Quickly."

His wife disappears in the blink of an eye, whispering under her breath for her children. The shuffling of feet, hushed comments, the creaking of old floorboards. The next thing I know, Arman and I are alone. His posture is that of a man defeated. He knows as well as I do that his time has run out. Instead of running away, or maybe even attacking me, he slowly makes his way to one of the kitchen cupboards and retrieves two glasses. He goes to the refrigerator and pulls out a small bottle of premium vodka, probably intended for a special occasion.

He pours us each a glass and then sits across from me at the table. He helps himself to his drink. Maybe as a show of faith that he isn't trying to poison me, or maybe because he needs a little extra liquid courage to get through what's next. I don't follow suit, however. *I* need a clear head.

"I guess this means you found my brothers?"

"Yes."

"Are they alive?

"Would it matter?"

He pours himself another drink, his hands visibly shaking. "Of course it would," he answers. "You have siblings of your own. You know what it's like to worry for your family."

"That I do."

"What's going to happen?"

"What do you think is fair?"

Arman hits me with a withering look. "Enough of your games. No sense in stretching this out. Do whatever you want to me, but please leave my wife and children out of this. Everything I did, I did for them."

I think momentarily about his daughter. Her crutches. Then I mentally crunch the numbers. Working solely as the night shift manager at the taxi company doesn't exactly bring in an impressive salary. We do offer a benefits package for our more senior members, but it's a far cry from living in the lap of luxury. Especially if there are medical bills to consider.

"If you're going to kill me," he says, "can we at least do it outside? I don't want my family to have to see it."

"I'm not going to kill you," I state firmly. "And for what it's worth, your brothers are all alive and well."

The tension in his shoulders melts. "I'm glad to hear it."

"This is what's going to happen. You're going to give that money back, and, in the spirit of the holidays, I'll let you live."

"I can't give the money back."

"Why not?"

"I spent it already."

I stare at him for a moment, trying to discern whether or not he's lying to me. I suppose he doesn't really have any reason to. He already knows how much trouble he's in, so why make things worse?

"I had medical bills to pay. I was behind on rent. My credit's shot, so no bank will approve a loan. It was never my intention to steal from you, but I had no choice."

"How did you even know about the Bratva?"

"It wasn't that hard to figure out. All your odd comings and goings. Your taxis have reinforced trunks with expanded cargo holds. Your people are careful, I'll give you that much, but sometimes mistakes happen. In the years I've worked for you, I found all sorts of incriminating evidence. Baggies left behind, weapons forgotten."

"But you never went to the police."

Arman shakes his head. "That would have been an immediate death sentence."

I huff. "You're probably right."

"And then my father let it slip that he was paying an arm and a leg every month for protection. I don't think he meant to say it. Dementia, you see. All it took was a bit of questioning and I was able to piece everything together. I realized who you and your brothers were and I figured it couldn't hurt to skim a little off the top. Cook the butcher's books a bit. Never enough to raise any red flags, but just enough that we could get by."

I strum my fingers on the kitchen table, listening intently. "Very clever," I tell him. "A commendable effort. It takes a lot of guts and a lot of smarts to pull a fast one over me."

Arman works his jaw. "So what's going to happen now?"

I can feel the beginning of a headache slowly growing in the back of my skull, bringing with it a dull, throbbing pain. What *is* going to happen now? He's made it clear he doesn't have the money. No amount of threatening is going to change that fact. I'm not going to kill him, either, because dead men can't pay their debts.

For a brief moment, I think about Erik Belov. The desperation in his eyes, all the begging he did for a little extra time. And then I think about Nikita and everything her father's situation put her through. Could I bear to do that to Arman's daughter? Maybe I've grown a bit of a soft spot because, no. No, I couldn't do that to her. Why should children suffer for the mistakes of their fathers?

"Here's what's going to happen," I say, speaking slowly and clearly. "Someone very important to me is expecting me home soon. We don't need to drag this out unnecessarily. I'm not forgiving your debt, but I won't punish you for it, either. You're going to spend Christmas with your family, enjoy your time together. And come the new year, you're going to come back to the depot to work off all the money you took."

Understandably, Arman looks confused. "You want me... to come back to work?"

"Would you rather I dump you in a ditch somewhere?"

"I just..." He runs a shaky hand through his hair. "Are you going to go back on your word?"

"I don't joke and I always keep my promises. Does that sound like a reasonable compromise?"

"Absolutely," he says quickly. "Thank you, Leo. Honestly, thank you so—"

"I don't believe a damn word out of his mouth!" his wife hisses from around the corner. She enters in a hurry, an old wartime pistol in hand. It looks like a family keepsake. Judging by her poor stance and jumpy nature, I don't think she knows how to use it.

Which makes her dangerous.

"Now hold on a minute," Arman tries to warn. "He said—"

"I know what he said. I heard him, but I don't trust him."

"Wait—"

Bang!

A sudden sharp pain spreads through my chest. There's a ringing in my ears, so loud and high pitched I feel disoriented. Instinctively, I bring a hand up to my chest. When I pull away, my palm is painted red with my blood.

The rest of the world suddenly fades away, darkness encroaching on the edges of my vision. I knew Arman didn't have what it took to shoot a man in cold blood, but I never accounted for the wife. That's a mistake I'm definitely going to regret.

I fall to my knees, a sudden coldness gripping me tightly. All I can think about is Nikita dancing across the stage with a bright beautiful smile on her lovely face, floating on air. And I'm going to miss it.

CHAPTER 30

NIKITA

Leo isn't back yet, but I'm not worried. He promised he'd be safe, and I've never known him to break his promises. Besides, tonight is opening night. I need my wits about me and for my heart to remain calm. I have to make sure this performance is nothing short of perfect. I want it to go down in history as one of the most beautiful, enchanting, and breathtaking moments in ballet...

And then I will retire with grace, happy to go wherever Leo wants to go. I will tell him that I'm pregnant, and I will get to see that smile bloom across his face as he realizes that our baby has been growing in my womb since the first night we met. The night he saved me.

It's been my dream to be a prima ballerina since I was a little girl, true, but dreams can change. People can grow. Leo has shown me there's so much more to life than just dance. Ballet will always hold a special place in my heart, but I'm eager to move on. An exciting new adventure awaits me, and I may not know exactly where I'm going, but I think that's part of the fun.

The director and Kseniya are nowhere to be found by

the time I arrive at the Bolshoi. Good. The police have hopefully arrested them already, although I haven't heard anything. I walked straight in, ignoring all the strange looks of my colleagues, going straight to the changing rooms where I find my costume ready and waiting. I have my own room, and I'm quite frankly thankful for the privacy as I get dressed and put on my makeup.

My costume fits like a glove, the glittering fabric hugging my curves. Thank the stars, it'll be a little while longer before my pregnancy starts to show. The tutu is structured with layers of fluffy tulle, sparkling sequins sewn into snowflake patterns on its surface. I've got a pair of white point shoes with satin ribbons just for this occasion, already broken in to fit my feet just the way I like.

I can hear everyone outside warming up. The orchestra is tuning up, too. From what I overheard from Pavel as I entered the building, it's a full house tonight. Over a thousand people have come to watch the opening night of *The Nutcracker* at the Bolshoi. There's an excited, electric buzz in the air; the promise of a magical escape through a landscape of snow just a few minutes away.

I'm struggling to get my hair just right. You'd think after years of practice putting my hair up in the bun would be a cinch. Naturally, because it's such an important day, my hair has decided to have a mind of its own. No matter what I do or how much hairspray I use, little hairs keep poking out in the weirdest of ways. I try to slick it back with a brush, but for some reason it ends up bumpy. When I try to tie it back, my elastic breaks, so I have to reach for another with a sigh.

"Do you need help?" Inessa asks.

I don't know when she slipped inside, but I frankly don't

have the energy to deal with her right now. I reach for a bobby pin. Maybe that'll help.

"What do you want?" I ask curtly.

She's silent for a moment, which is most unlike her. It's very jarring to see her so tongue-tied. She looks a little worse for wear, now that I've had a second to take her in. Her hair is dull, there are dark circles under her eyes, and her shirt is covered in wrinkles like she hasn't done the laundry in a while. Inessa is a far cry from her usual put-together self.

"Kseniya called in sick at the last minute," she says. I think to myself, I bet she did. "I was trying to call you to come. You never answered."

"Blocked your number."

I'll admit I feel a bit cruel being this cold. It goes against my very being. I have only ever wanted to treat others the way I would want them to treat me, but after those terrible things my mother said to me I don't know if I want to spare her the effort.

"Where have you been?" she asks, sounding almost like a concerned parent. Better late than never, I guess.

"Around," I answer vaguely.

"Your father has been worried sick about you."

I feel my anger flare, irritation licking through my veins. I'm nowhere near as upset with Dad as I am with her. "I'll call him later."

"But he—"

"Don't try and use him to manipulate me," I snap. "It's not going to work. If you have something to say to me, then say it and get out."

Inessa presses her lips into a thin line. I'm pretty sure it's been a long time since someone dared speak to her like I am. It feels *good*. Overdue. I wonder if she likes getting a taste of her own medicine, to see all her nastiness reflected back at her through her daughter—one she apparently never wanted to begin with.

"I wanted to apologize."

I break out into laughter. "Apologize? Seriously?"

"What I said out of anger... It wasn't right."

"But it was the truth, wasn't it?"

She pauses for just a little too long. "Of course it wasn't the truth."

"I don't believe you." With my hair finally fixed and my makeup perfectly in place, I reach for the Sugar Plum Fairy's beautiful tiara and set it upon my head, pinning it to my head with clips. Even through all of my spins and fouettés, this thing is so secure there's no way it's going to fly off mid-routine.

"Look, Nikita—"

"I'm retiring after this."

Mother looks genuinely horrified. "What?"

"This is my first and only performance. I'm sure you'll find another dancer for next season."

"Don't be absurd. If this is your way of getting back at me—"

"It's not. This is something *I* want."

"But all those years of training will go to waste."

"That's certainly your opinion. I don't see it that way."

Inessa clenches her fists. "Listen, Nikita. You're being ungrateful."

"This is *my* life," I say with an embittered sigh. "I'm tired of letting you tell me what to do. Sorry I couldn't live out your dream for you, but that's not what I want for myself."

For the first time in my life, my mother looks like she's on the brink of tears. I've struck a chord with her, dashed her dreams—no matter how twisted and manipulative they might be. I pity her. Truly, I do. She couldn't have the career she wanted when she was in her prime, and now she can't have it through me. I have to remind myself that's not my problem. I'm in control now, and I want to do what makes me happiest.

"Go out there and watch me dance. Not as my ballet master. Not as my mother. But as one ballerina to another. That's all I ask of you."

Without another word, I push past her and start toward the stage. I stretch and warm up in the wings, ignoring all the stares and the gossip. There's something surprisingly liberating about knowing I'll never have to see or deal with these people again. I'm buzzing with excitement now that none of it weighs on me. I'm here to dance my heart out, and there's really only one person in the crowd whose opinion I care for.

I'm in the zone, my mind humming with adrenaline. I know every step by heart, every musical beat and pause.

And then it's finally my time to shine.

I step out on cue to a smattering of polite applause, but that's not good enough for me. By the end of this song, I hope to have everyone out of their seats cheering my name.

My muscle memory kicks in—every turn, every step, every delicate gesture of my hand. I enter a sort of hypnotic state, moving about the stage with the command and confidence all my years of training have instilled within me. I float on the notes of the music. I spin beneath the lights, lost in my own little world full of paper confetti snow, toy soldiers dressed up in their uniforms, and a backdrop that looks so sweet I could eat it.

I feel like I'm floating. There's no weight to my steps, only the gentle glide from motion to motion. I feel magical, as all Sugar Plum Fairies should. There's a delightful tingle in the tips of my fingers, in my chest. I am lighter than air and nobody can stop me as I spread joy from the stage and into the theater just beyond. I may be breathless, but I keep going, driven by pure adrenaline.

Time dilates. I'm in a little world of my own, one I almost wish I could live in for the rest of my life. For the first time in years, I finally feel *free*. I am free to enjoy this moment in history. There will never be another performance like this. Not by me, not by anybody. What I'm creating here on stage is a unique experience, never to happen again—which is all the more reason to savor it.

When the music finally comes to an end and I hold my final pose, it takes me a while for my brain to catch up to the sound of applause. It's *thunderous*, practically shaking the entire theater. People cheer and whistle. Their smiles and looks of awe send a shiver racing down my spine. I bask in the glory, warm and fuzzy all over.

I did it. I was perfect. And when I look up to the box seats to my right I see—

Leo isn't there.

My heart sinks, confusion swirling inside me as I try to keep my smile in place while I take a deep bow. I don't understand. He said he'd be here. Did something happen? That has to be it. It's the only reason I can think of that would keep Leo from following through with his promise.

There's still a good deal of the ballet left. I have no choice but to stick it out through the pas de deux, through the finale before I can finally leave the stage to try and call him. My stomach is in knots, anxiety bubbling in my chest. I know Leo through and through. There's no way he would miss this. Maybe I got his seat wrong. Maybe he's watching from a different section of the theater.

By the time the ballet comes to an end and the curtains close, I all but elbow my way back to the change rooms where I quickly strip out of my costume and get dressed. It's chaos behind stage, the area flooded with patrons and admirers, all with flowers and program copies for signing.

"You were amazing," someone tells me.

"Truly fantastic!" someone else exclaims.

I thank them all, though I'm obviously distracted. Nausea keeps twirling in the back of my throat, and I break into a cold sweat, but I push it all down one last time. I can't let anything hold me back anymore. Not now. There are a flurry of flashing cameras and people shoving gifts into my arms. When I look out into the crowd and see a pair of red-headed twins, my heart leaps into my throat. Sandra and Charlotte.

I make my way over to them, hopeful that Leo is somewhere nearby. "Where's—"

Sandra puts a hand up, her expression grave. "You need to come with us," she says.

"I don't understand."

"We need to go to St. Petersburg," Charlotte explains. "Leo's been shot."

CHAPTER 31

NIKITA

I'm a nervous wreck by the time we arrive. I still have glitter in my hair, my bun so tight I have a headache. It didn't feel real when the twins invited me on to their private jet, taking off from a private airfield on the outskirts of Moscow only to land in St. Petersburg in under an hour and a half.

"How did it happen?" I ask them. "Is he alive? Why won't you tell me anything?"

These were only a few of the questions I pelted them with for the duration of the flight. I don't know these two very well, but it's obvious in their eyes how much they care about Leo.

Charlotte seems particularly sympathetic, offering me the occasional, "We don't know much, but Leo is strong." Not that it did anything to soothe my nerves.

I practically fling myself from the car when we pull up to the hospital, running into the emergency room at full speed. I'm just about to give the poor nurse behind the reception desk a hard time when I spot Roman, along with the rest of Leo's brothers. There's blood on his shirt. I stomp over, equal parts terrified about what I'm about to see, but also determined to get to Leo no matter what the cost.

"Where is he?" I demand. I dare to grab Andrei by the collar. I don't care if he's the one in charge, or the head of the Bratva. Right now, I need answers. If I have to throttle them out of him, then so be it. "Tell me what's happened before I lose my damn mind."

"We have him in a private room," Andrei answers, his words dripping with barely contained anger. I don't think it has anything to do with me, but the situation itself.

"Take me to him."

"Not yet."

I feel like my head is about to burst. "What do you mean not yet?"

"There's something you should know," Roman says. His eyes are downcast, his shoulders slumped. I don't appreciate the way he takes forever to answer.

"Just tell me," I rasp. "Please, I need to know. Is Leo okay?"

"The doctors were able to get the bullets out," he says slowly. I nearly vomit then and there. Bullets? As in more than one? "The surgery was complicated, but the bullets thankfully missed everything vital."

I shake my head. "So what's the problem then? That's good news."

"They had to put him under anesthesia for obvious reasons," Charlotte says softly. "But Leo reacted poorly to it."

My legs are jelly, barely able to support my weight. My brain is having trouble processing this information. "Fucking *tell me*," I hiss.

"He's in a coma," Sandra finishes for her twin. "The

doctors have no idea when he's going to wake up. *If* he'll wake up."

The news hits me like a runaway freight train. I'm suddenly overwhelmed with a terrible dizzy spell. The room spins and the floor seems to fall out from beneath me. This is too much. I try to form a sentence, but my brain shuts off. My body reacts all on its own. Before I know what's happening, my vision turns black and my whole body feels like it weighs a ton as I crash to the floor.

When I come to, it's to the smell of disinfectant and filtered air. I squint against the soft lighting from the panels above, noting the scratchy fabric of the hospital bed beneath me. My vision is fuzzy, and I have a terrible pounding in my head. The artificial lighting makes it difficult to tell how much time has passed. For all I know I could have been out for days.

"What happened?" I croak.

Beside me, someone shifts. Charlotte. "Oh good, you're awake. You really had us worried there."

"She's in stable condition," the doctor says. She's busy inspecting my chart, her brows knitted together in concentration. "But your blood sugar was quite low. I'm waiting on a few more tests to come through in the meantime."

Well, I already know what the tests will say. They will reveal a truth I've been holding on to for too long. But my man is not here. And I need him back. I need Leo awake so I can tell him. It can't be too late. It can't end here. Oh, god, I can't do this alone...

I attempt to sit up, but my limbs still feel incredibly

weak, like I'm working against twice the gravitational pull. "I want to see Leo."

The doctor clicks her tongue. "Not until I get the rest of your bloodwork."

"Just get me a juice box or something," I urge, not wanting to waste any more time. "It was a freak accident, that's all."

"Ms. Belova, I don't mean to concern you, but you are rather pale right now. I don't think it's wise to rush this process. May I ask how much you weigh?"

"About a hundred pounds, but that's perfectly normal for someone like me."

"Someone like you?"

"She's a professional ballerina," Charlotte answers for me.

"Until recently, it was perfectly normal for me to be working out for eight hours a day, six days a week. But I always make sure to eat balanced meals. The Bolshoi even has an in-house nutritionist to make sure we're eating properly."

The doctor nods her head. "And when was the last time you had your period?"

I hesitate. I understand the doctor is just trying to cover her bases so I answer, "Honestly? I'm pretty irregular. There are some months when I don't get it at all." Which isn't a lie. It wasn't the absent period that got me into that pharmacy. It was the nausea. I never get nauseated.

"No doubt due to your intensive training," she murmurs. "Ms. Belova, I'd like you to take a pregnancy test."

"Is that really necessary?" Dammit, now's not the time for this kind of reveal.

"As you said, you eat balanced meals and you have a

very active lifestyle. I need to rule out all the possibilities in order to determine what caused your fainting spell. Is that alright with you?"

I shrug a shoulder. I've never been one to argue with a medical professional, but I might as well let her do this so I can get her out of my hair. I already know what it's going to say.

"Okay, fine."

"The test will be quick," the doctor assures me. "I'll be right back."

When the doctor leaves, I run my hands over my face, exhausted. Just when I thought everything was returning to normal, the world had to throw me one last curveball.

"How long was I asleep?" I ask Charlotte who had stepped out while the doctor questioned me.

"Only about an hour. The rest of us went to check on Leo."

I set up right. "Is he—"

"Still comatose? Yeah."

I groan, torn between crying and crying some more. "How did it happen?"

"From what Roman told me, he was letting someone off the hook. A guy who owes us a lot of money. There must have been a misunderstanding because the guy's wife shot him."

I can barely hear her over my racing heart. "He was letting someone off the hook?"

"I know, surprised me too. I've never known him to let someone off the hook before." Charlotte flashes a small grin. "That is, before he met you."

"Do you think this happened because I—"

"Don't feel guilty, Nikita. Don't do that to yourself. We

know the risks involved in this life. You can't blame yourself."

"I want to see him."

"I know. And you will. But you have to look after yourself first."

I chew on the inside of my cheek. I suppose that at this moment, Charlotte kind of has a point. I can't worry about Leo if I can barely get out of bed to see him myself. I can already imagine his disappointment if he found out something happened to me.

"How do you do it?" I asked her weakly. "Your whole family is involved in this *world*. Aren't you afraid of something happening to them? How do you deal with all the *what ifs*?"

Charlotte leans back in her seat and nods, offering me a kind, understanding smile. "I'd be lying if I said I wasn't terrified around the clock, but you get used to it. You'll have to get used to it, if you're serious about Leo."

"I am serious about Leo."

"Are you sure that's wise?" She puts her hands up, almost as if an anticipation of the defensive retort on the tip of my tongue. "I just mean you have to be a special kind of woman to be involved with someone like him. You need to understand that as long as you're together, anything—even death—is a possibility."

I swallow hard at the sticky lump lodged in the back of my throat. "I know. I've already accepted that. I love Leo, and that's never going to change."

Her eyebrows shoot up. "You love him? Does he know?"

"I haven't told him yet, but I'm pretty sure he does."

"I hope you understand this means you're in it for the long haul. Through all of the ups and downs, all of the scares. Because they *will* happen again."

I nod. "I can handle it."

Charlotte giggles. "I know. Anyone ballsy enough to grab one of our pakhans by the shirt like that will have no trouble fitting in."

"You don't think he's mad about that, do you?"

"Nah. Though I should probably tell you never to do it again. Seriously. It's not a good look, if you know what I mean, letting himself get throttled by a woman half his size."

I laughed softly. "Okay, I promise."

The doctor returns with a small box of supplies in hand. "Ready?"

"As I'll ever be," I reply as steadily as I can manage.

CHAPTER 32

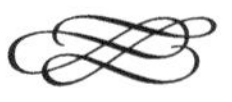

NIKITA

I never knew what it was like to have a big family, but one of the great things about being welcomed into this one is I'm never alone.

If it's not Roman or Charlotte keeping me company at Leo's bedside, then it's Andre and Sandra as well as their twin toddlers, or Samuil and Damien who tend to pop in whenever they have the spare time. They've welcomed me into the fold with such ease I'm starting to wonder if this was meant to be. They may be gangsters, but there's nothing scary about them. Not once have they made me feel like an outsider, and for that I'm grateful.

But the moments in between, when we are alone, I can truly appreciate the quiet. Today is Christmas Eve. I've been praying for Leo's speedy recovery, and the doctors have confirmed he's doing very well healing-wise, but there's still no telling when he's going to wake up or what state of mind he'll be in when he does. The real danger, they tell me, is if he stays under too long, we could be looking at possible brain damage.

I try not to think about that, though. I need to try and stay positive.

Besides, Leo is the strongest man I know. If anyone can make it out of this unscathed, it's him. For now, I just have to be patient. I have to hold on to that tiny seed of hope that he'll wake up soon. And when he does, I have some very important news to share with him. News confirmed by my bloodwork and the ultrasound, that is...

"Ooh, did you see this one?" Roman asks as he shows me the article pulled up on his phone. "They're calling you the *Angel of the Bolshoi*. Credit where credit is due, Nikita, you sure have a flair for the dramatic."

Charlotte cackles as she throws an arm over his shoulder. "Looks like you've got your work cut out for you."

I laugh softly as I flip through the taxi depot's ledger, making sure to carry all my ones and double check that each decimal is in the correct place. I never knew what a natural I was when it came to accounting.

There's obviously a lot to learn, but when I happened to overhear Samuil struggling to keep things in order in Leo's absence, I couldn't help but offer a hand. And since we've moved Leo to a facility in Moscow to continue his recovery, it's been easy enough to do. Turns out, I'm a natural at it. I made it perfectly clear I want nothing to do with *cooking the books*, but I'm perfectly happy to handle the legitimate side of the taxi company's operations. Keeping track of expenses and income isn't too difficult.

Naturally, there was some hesitation from Andrei and Sandra. They don't know me as well as Roman or Charlotte, but when I discovered an inputting error that saved them thousands, their reservations about bringing me onto the team quickly dwindled.

"You'll still need to get your certifications," Andrei told

me, "But I suppose it's fine as a temporary measure. Just until Leo wakes up."

It's a small blessing, I suppose, that they're all incredibly hopeful about Leo's recovery. They talk like he's going to wake up tomorrow morning, making plans like he'll be there without fail. It's certainly better than the alternative doom and gloom, though sometimes I wonder...

I tell myself it's because it's Christmas Eve. While everyone is preparing to celebrate Christmas morning surrounded by family, plenty of food, and a mountain of gifts, I remain adamant about staying by Leo's side even as he sleeps. The nurses have assured me over and over again that he'll be in good hands if I decide to go home for a bit of rest, but it wouldn't feel right. What if he wakes up while I'm gone? I don't want him to be alone.

My hand falls protectively to my belly. I'm not ready to lose hope. Not by a long shot.

"It's getting late," I murmur, smiling at Roman and Charlotte. "Why don't you two head on back?"

"And leave you here?" Roman replies with a chuckle. "I don't think so. Besides, we can't give you our gifts if you send us home."

"Gifts?"

"My sister wanted to give these to you," Charlotte says, reaching into the tote bag resting beside her. She pulls out a stack of thick books and hands them to me. I browse through them curiously, realizing they are informational books about pregnancy.

It's kind of weird that Leo's entire family were the first to hear about the baby, but hey... at least I know I'm not alone. I will never be alone, no matter what happens. I just want him back, though. I need him back. Our child needs his father.

I'm moved by the thoughtful gesture. "Thank you so much."

"I have one too," Roman says, reaching into the inner pocket of his suit jacket. He pulls out an envelope. "This is from me and my brothers. We obviously don't know if we're getting a niece or nephew, so we figured we should steer clear from buying any clothes. But I'm sure you'll find good use of our gift."

I rip open the envelope and pull out a check. My eyes nearly bug out of their sockets. I don't think I've ever seen that many zeros before a decimal place in my entire life. "Roman, this is too much."

He shakes his head. "I won't hear any of it. You're one of us now. We'll take care of you just as we care for all our family."

"I'm pretty sure this is the GDP of a small country."

He winks at me. "All I ask in return is that you name the kid after me if it's a boy."

A genuine laugh rises from my chest. It feels good. It's the first time in a while I've felt relatively okay. "I'll consider it," I say. "Although, I don't know if I'll be able to get Leo on board."

"Roman's a shit name," comes a low, dry croak.

Leo.

A gasp escapes me. I turn and look down at the hospital bed. Leo stirs, his eyes opening ever so slightly. There's confusion in his gaze as he looks around at his surroundings. He attempts to sit up, but I'm quick to place a hand on his shoulder to placate him.

"Take it easy," I say quickly. "Roman, go get the doctor. Charlotte, call your family. Tell them Leo's awake."

They vacate their chairs, in a hurry to leave the room. I stay by Leo's side, threading my fingers through his and giving him a squeeze. Tears sting my eyes, but they are tears of pure joy.

"What happened?" he asks, his voice raspy from disuse. His brows steeple together. "Nikita, what's going on?"

I caress his cheek, doing my best to keep it together. I sniffle, giggling with an almost manic sort of glee. "Everything's okay, just relax. Roman says you were shot."

Leo groans. "Oh. Arman and his wife. It's coming back to me." He reaches up slowly and combs his fingers through my hair. "How long have I been out?"

I glance at my watch. "It's Christmas," I tell him, teary-eyed.

Leo seems confused at first, and rightly so. He's missing a few weeks of time. He's quiet for a long moment. I'm not too sure what he's thinking, but when next he opens his mouth, he surprises me. "I missed your show."

I laugh softly, treacherous tears streaking down my cheeks. I don't bother to brush them away. Leo does it for me, stroking the pads of his thumbs beneath my eyes. "It's not a big deal."

"It is to me. I said I would be there."

"I'm just happy you're—" My throat closes up, a terrible burn in my lungs. I can't stop myself from crying this time. "I was so scared for you, Leo. I thought I was going to lose you. When Charlotte and Sandra told me you've been shot, I..." My heart rails in my chest. "I thought you were going to die."

"It's going to take a lot more than that to kill me."

"You don't understand. I thought you were going to die before I ever got the chance to tell you..." My voice quivers, wobbles. "I love you, Leo. I love you."

He regards me with the same soft adoration he always does. It's a look, I realize, reserved only for me. It makes me feel special. Like I'm the one exception he treasures above all else.

"Nikita Belova, I love you too. Now and always."

I'm smiling so hard my cheeks hurt. I'm so elated I feel like I could fly to the moon. Instead, I settle for leaning in and pressing my lips to his as gingerly as I can handle. I'm mindful of his recovering wounds, but Leo doesn't seem to care. He reaches out and wraps his arms around me, pulling me to his chest where he holds me tight. He kisses me hungrily, our lips slotting into place—a perfect fit.

We bask in each other's warmth and the safety of each other's arms. I never understood what people meant when they said heaven on Earth, but when I'm with Leo, I understand completely.

When he pulls away, he asks, "What's this about naming someone Roman? I wasn't sure if I heard right."

"It's my Christmas gift to you." I reached for his hand and slip it between our bodies, pressing his palm against my belly. "I found out a few weeks ago, but you were still asleep."

It's amusing getting to watch his mind work. I can practically hear the gears turning in his head, connecting the dots one by one until his eyes finally widen with realization.

"You're pregnant?" he murmurs.

"I know it's probably a lot to spring on you, but—"

"No, this is..." He pauses for a second. "How far along are you? Like... The math..."

I can't help but giggle. "Remember that night you plucked me off the side of the road in the middle of a snowstorm and took me to your cabin and I begged you not to be some kind of homicidal maniac?"

"Oh, wow. That far along."

Miracle of miracles, Leo smiles so wide and bright I feel

like the whole world has stopped. It's a true smile, one of pure joy and happiness, along with a healthy dose of pride. I have never seen anything more brilliant. His elation is contagious, stirring inside me with such overwhelming power I can't help but smile too.

"I'm going to be a father," he says to himself in disbelief. He laughs, the sound rich and sweet. "I love you, Nikita. Like you could never imagine."

"I love you, too, Leo."

And then, very seriously, he says, "There's no fucking way we're naming our kid after Roman."

I throw my head back and laugh. This is the best Christmas ever.

CHAPTER 33

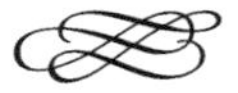

LEO

It's safe to say my stint at the hospital has thrown a wrench in my family's holiday plans. I almost feel a little guilty that they have to rearrange things, no matter how many times they tell me they're happy to do it. We end up celebrating Christmas roughly a week after I wake up and I'm finally discharged, gathering together at Andrei and Sandra's home.

It's a boisterous affair, plenty of music and tipsy conversations over eggnog by the fire. Their Christmas tree is still up, so big even Samuil looks small when standing right next to it, the top of it scraping the ceiling above. It's decked out in all sorts of fancy ornaments as well as string lights and silver tinsel. The air smells heavily of peppermint and gingerbread, along with the crackling logs of the fireplace.

Everyone's here, gathered together in celebration. Nieces and nephews, cousins, and even my sister-in-law's extended family. Her own parents, her uncles, and their wives as well. The Antonov and the Nicolaevich families together under one roof, united as one. There's discussion of business, but Sandra insists on keeping it to a minimum. I suppose even organized crime needs to take a break every now and then to smell the roses.

I've been given some space on the couch to rest and recuperate. I'll admit the medication the doctors gave me to deal with the pain makes me feel a little loopy. Even still, I have never been surer about what I'm about to do next in my entire life. Reaching into my jacket pocket, I run my fingers over the edges of the ring box, my heart thudding with quiet anticipation.

The kids open gifts, ripping into boxes and pulling apart ribbon with their eager little hands. Nikita sits beside me, watching with a smile on her lips as she watches the little ones with a glint in her eye. She's going to make a fantastic mother; of that I have no doubt.

"What are you thinking about?" I murmur against her ear.

"Thinking about next year," she says. "When we have a little one of our own."

I press my lips to her temple, breathing in the scent of her shampoo. I'm excited beyond words. But before we get there, I have a very important question to ask her. Now isn't the time, though. I have the entire evening planned out, so I'm just going to have to be patient.

"Ballet shoes!" my niece exclaims with a delighted gasp. "They're so pretty!"

"Your Aunt Nikita helped me pick them out," Sandra tells her kid with a chuckle. "You keep telling me how you want to try ballet, so your classes start in the new year."

"Thank you so much, Mama! Thanks Aunt Nikita!"

"Would you like to try them on?" Nikita asks.

"Only if you teach me a few moves."

Nikita laughs, her eyes twinkling. "Sure thing, sweetheart. Here, pop them on. Let's see how they fit."

"Am I going to get up on my toes?"

"No, these are just ballet flats, not pointe shoes. It takes many years of training before you're allowed to get up on pointe. But don't worry, if you keep practicing, you'll definitely get there."

My niece takes her hand and tugs her over to the kitchen where there's more space to move around. She giddily slides across the tile. "Papa, look!"

Across from me, Andrei chuckles. "I'm watching, baby."

Pride rises in my chest as I watch Nikita teach her first, second, and fourth positions. Patient and calm, her instructions are easy to follow. Her sweet voice is encouraging, and her genuine love of ballet shines through with ease. She teaches my niece the proper way to turn, how to fix her posture, how to pose. Within a matter of a few minutes, my niece is brimming with unmatched confidence. This is what all good teachers do, and Nikita is a natural.

Seeing how good she is with children only solidifies my resolve. I can't wait to ask her, but first, dinner.

"Have a good night!" Nikita calls over her shoulder as I walk her to our parked car. We feasted for hours on a juicy turkey, the creamiest mashed potatoes, and an assortment of smaller dishes I honestly can't remember anymore because I've eaten myself into a food coma.

It's a little before midnight and we've slowly begun filtering out of Andrei and Sandra's home. The festivities may be done, but I have one last thing I need to take care of before Nikita drives us home.

The drive back to Moscow is a sleepy one. There's something nice about being able to drive down the streets with little to no traffic on either side of us. The stars are out and twinkling above us, the moon round and bright. I keep tapping the ring box in my pocket, almost like a reassurance that it's still there. I keep having the intrusive thought that I might accidentally drop it somewhere.

"Are you okay?" Nikita asks me softly. "You're really quiet tonight."

"I'm always quiet."

She giggles. "More so than usual, I mean."

"I'm fine," I say, offering my hand over the center console. She takes it without hesitation, giving my fingers a light squeeze. "How are you doing? You said earlier you had a headache?"

"I'm better. I think I ate too much gingerbread."

"I told you not to dip it in the cranberry sauce."

"Look, cravings are cravings, okay? I can't help it if the baby wants it."

I feel myself smiling, the corners of my lips tugging upward. It's such a strange sensation, but I'm definitely getting used to it. Smiling doesn't feel so much like work where Nikita is concerned.

By the time we get back to the penthouse, I can tell Nikita is just about ready for bed. Her eyes are droopy and she's yawning wide.

"I'm going to hop into the shower," she says as she strides past me, dropping the keys on the table by the door. "Feel like joining me?"

When she turns to check on my answer, I'm down on one knee with the box in my hands, the lid popped open to reveal the diamond engagement ring tucked safely inside. Through the balcony windows, snow flutters down from the skies above, highlighted by the silver light of the moon.

A part of me wanted to jump the gun and pop the question while we were at dinner with my family, but I decided it was probably best for me to ask when it was just the two of us. I've never been a man concerned with spectacle. I care for my family deeply, but I want this just for us. I want to show Nikita she's the only one on my mind, that we can have this private moment together.

"I have no speech prepared," I tell her honestly. "I spent every day since waking up in the hospital thinking about how I was going to do this, but I don't want this to sound forced or disingenuous. Nikita, if you ask me to give you the world, I would. From the moment I first saw you, I knew you were special. It wasn't until later that I realized you're not just special, you're my entire universe. I want to spend the rest of my life with you. I want to spend every waking moment doing what I can to make you happy. Will you—"

"Yes!" she exclaims, practically throwing herself at me before I have a chance to finish. She wraps her arms around my neck and kisses me fiercely, our lips crashing together like two powerful magnets. "Yes, I'll marry you."

It isn't like me for my hands to shake, but they do—uncontrollably—as I pluck the ring from its box and slide it onto her finger. A perfect fit. The diamond sparkles like starlight, reminding me so much of the night I first met her on the roadside. Seeing it on her hand does something to my brain chemistry. It's a formal proclamation to the rest of the world that out of everyone, this woman—this beautiful, kind, amazing woman—is all mine.

"Let's skip the shower," I murmur against her lips.

She arches a brow and grins. "Straight to the bedroom?"

I nod in agreement. "Straight to the bedroom."

CHAPTER 34

NIKITA

"You're positively glowing," Dad tells me over our drinks.

Coffee for him, a cool glass of iced green tea for me. Leo is very particular about making sure I don't overdo it with the caffeine. Our daughter isn't even here yet and he's already so protective. He is going to be such a great father.

I rub my belly instinctively, so round I have to sit a little ways back to make space between myself and the edge of the table. I'm well into my third trimester now, and it's admittedly getting a little difficult to move around freely. Dad and I have been meeting every couple of weeks at a local cafe—conveniently owned by one of Leo's brothers, Damien. I try not to pry in their business, as per usual, but you can't even throw a rock without hitting a business under the Bratva's protection or ownership.

Leo has strange comings and goings, oftentimes leaving in the middle of the night and returning in the wee hours of the morning. I've admittedly gotten used to it, though there's always a small part of me that worries he might get hurt. It's one of the reasons I had Roman buy him a Kevlar vest to wear beneath his suit.

Just in case, I'd told him.

Leo, sensing my concern, complied without argument.

"How have your meetings been going?" I ask.

"Really good, actually." Dad smiles, the corners of his eyes crinkling. "Next week will officially be six months. They're going to have a small little get-together, kind of like a ceremony? They'll be handing out commemorative tokens. I'd love it if you could come, Nikita."

I reach across the table and take my father's hand. "Of course I'll come. Just name the time and place. I'm really proud of you."

"I'm not going to lie, I thought my gambling addiction was going to destroy me for a while there. Thank you for believing in me."

"You put in the hard work. I always knew you could do it; you just needed a little push."

"Things have really been looking up. I even landed a new job."

"Dad, that's wonderful!"

"Yeah, it's at a restaurant. As an assistant manager. I really enjoy the work."

"I'm really glad to hear it."

"How's Leo been treating you?" my father asks, changing the subject.

He asks this question every single time, and every single time my answer is the same. "He treats me like a queen," I answer honestly. "You have nothing to worry about, Dad. Leo's taking really good care of me and the baby."

He takes a deep breath, nodding slowly. I know it's easier said than done, and I appreciate how understanding he's been. It was a difficult conversation, telling Dad about Leo and me. Given their history, I was sort of expecting him to blow up. Get angry. But I think he can tell how good Leo is for me, how good we are for each other. We're all eager to start these new chapters of our lives, so why poke the hornet's nest when there isn't any need?

"How are you liking your new apartment?" I asked him.

"'It's good. A little weird, living without your mother after all these years, but I'm excited about this next step now that the divorce has been finalized. It's a fresh start I think we both need."

"Good. That's good."

"She's been asking about you."

I chew on the inside of my cheek. Inessa and I haven't spoken since opening night of *The Nutcracker*. It isn't like me to hold on to my resentment, but I would be lying if I said I had fully forgiven her. We sent a few texts back and forth so I could organize a time to come collect my things, but that's about it. From what I hear, she has taken on the role of the director at the Bolshoi, her predecessor incapable of returning due to his crimes.

From what I've heard, a lot of things have changed at the Bolshoi. They've hired additional security guards who are rotated out more frequently, as well as a more secure network of security cameras. People can't just come and go as they please. The chances someone will be able to get away with sabotage like Kseniya in the future will be slim to none.

"She just wants to grab a bite with you," Dad says. "I can be there, too, if you want. When she heard you're expecting... I don't know. She's been different."

"Different? How?"

Dad shrugs. "I've noticed she's trying to be more patient. Gentler. Just in the way she's interacted with me throughout the divorce proceedings. I think she regrets what she said a great deal, and knowing the baby's on the way... I have a feeling she wants to make amends. Keep you in her life. Although you're more than within your right to say no. I certainly wouldn't blame you."

I take a deep breath in through the nose, savoring the smell of freshly ground coffee and buttery pastries. It's a lot to think about. First and foremost, I need to think about what's best for the baby. If Dad thinks Inessa is making an effort to change, then I'm inclined to give her a chance. I make a promise to myself that the moment she pulls any toxic, abusive shit—it's over for real.

"Maybe. I just need a bit more time."

Dad smiles. "I understand."

"I'm not saying never. I want to put things behind us, too. I'm just not ready yet."

"I'll let her know. I'm sure she can respect that."

The little bell over the cafe door jingles, signaling someone's arrival. When I turn to see who it is, I spot a familiar figure out of the corner of my eye. He's hard to miss, clad in all black from head to toe. Most of the guests give him a wary glance, but I am filled with nothing but love and adoration when I see Leo with a bouquet of flowers in his arms. White lilies—my absolute favorite.

"I have to go," I tell my father. "Same time next week?"

Dad nods respectfully in Leo's direction. Leo nods back. It's the most interaction the two are willing to participate in, and I'm frankly fine with it. As long as they can be civil, I'm happy.

"Sure thing, sweetheart."

I get up from the table and join Leo, smiling at the

flowers as he wraps a protective arm over my shoulder and presses a kiss to my hair. "These are beautiful. What's the occasion?"

"I wasn't aware I needed an occasion to spoil you."

"How were things at work?" I ask as he guides me out to the car waiting by the curb. "Some big business meeting, right?"

"It went well," he answers. "Though I was very eager to get back to you."

I giggle. "Did you miss me that much? Such a big baby."

Leo snorts. "I always miss you," he says, unflinching. "But also because I have a surprise for you."

"Another surprise? You really are spoiling me. What is it?"

"Get in the car and you'll see."

I'm not too sure where he's driving us, but I don't particularly care. I'm just happy we get to spend some time together. I haven't been asking for details, but I can tell work has been busy for him. Lots of meetings with his brothers, lots of talk about negotiating new deals. It must be exhausting, being so high up the chain of command. Leo never complains, though. He's always so strong and resilient, no matter what comes his way.

We drive around for about fifteen minutes, arriving in a neighborhood I don't recognize. It's an up-and-coming area, complete with many modern buildings and flashy boutiques. We pull up to the outside of a storefront. There looks to be plenty of space inside, though it's completely empty.

"This is the surprise?" I asked as he helps me out of the

vehicle. He's always there to offer me his hand like the gentleman he is.

"You'll see, you'll see."

To my mild confusion, we walk right up to the door. He pulls it open. When we get inside, the air is knocked from my lungs. Floor to ceiling mirrors wrap around two of the walls, wooden ballet barres drilled into the sides. The floors are made of special tiles, ones I recognize from all my time spent training at the Bolshoi. They have a matte finish, designed for added grip perfect for dancers.

Leo flicks the light switch, revealing the space to me in all its glory. Eggshell white walls, a small seating area arranged like a theater on raised platforms. It's a dance studio.

"You mentioned you were interested in teaching ballet," he says casually. "This is yours, if you want it. There's still a bit of work to be done, but I can have the contractors prioritize this job so it's ready for you by the time the baby gets here. You can choose to work straight away or take all the time you need to adjust—it's really up to you."

I can't help but gawk at him. "You're giving me a dance studio?"

"Does it make you happy?"

I throw my head back and laugh. "Happy? Leo this is amazing!"

He smiles wide, gesturing toward the window. "I know a guy who can put your studio name up on a big sign outside. And whatever equipment you need, you just let me know and I'll put the order in. Whatever you want, it's all yours. I know how much dance means to you, so I want this place to be perfect."

I grab the lapel of his jacket and hop up on my toes,

tilting my head upward so I can kiss him sweetly. "I love it," I say against his lips. "You're a dream come true."

EPILOGUE

NIKITA

Five Years Later

Piano music plays over the studio's speakers, which have been mounted to the corners of the room to make sure there's ample space to move. I don't need some clunky grand piano in the way taking up precious real estate. Do I miss having a live performer play music during classes? Of course. It's a wonderful experience to be able to tell the pianist what adjustments to make and when, but Leo hooked me up with a very intuitive surround sound system. It's honestly the next best thing.

"And everyone in first positions please," I say to my students.

I make sure to check each of the girls' forms. Good posture is everything, the foundation of every young ballerina. There are even a few boys in my class, and I always make sure to pay extra attention to them. I know they can be a little self-conscious at times, but they've shown signs of great promise. I'm protective of all of them, eager to watch them learn and grow into brilliant dancers.

When the music finally comes to an end, I clap my hands twice. "That's great! Well done everyone. That's all for today's class. Remember to change into your street shoes. You don't want to wear your ballet flats on the sidewalk. And don't forget the next week will be our recitals, so be sure to tell your parents to bring you a little earlier so they can get good seats."

"Thank you, Miss Nikita," the kids say in chorus together.

I watch them shuffle off in their pink leotards and tutus, chattering amongst themselves about homework and the latest episode of their favorite TV show. Parents are waiting outside, some of them pressing their noses to the glass to watch their kids during class. Slowly but surely, the children file out while I start the cleanup process. It's almost a guarantee I'm going to find a forgotten lunch box or backpack, so I get to organizing quickly.

While working, I notice Anya, my sweet little girl, holding on to the barre, anxiously nibbling her bottom lip as she stares at her toes.

"Honey?" I call out, making my way over to her. I place my hand on her little back. Feels like yesterday she was big enough to fit in my arms. We just celebrated her fifth birthday a few weeks ago with all of her aunts and uncles and cousins. "Is something the matter?"

"I don't want to do my recital," she says, chewing on the inside of her cheek, a habit I have no doubt she picked up from me.

"But you've worked so hard, honey. And just yesterday you were saying you were so excited for it."

"Changed my mind," she mumbles under her breath.

I take a seat on the floor beside her, tenderly brushing a few of her loose hairs away from her face. She takes after her father. Dark black locks and dark eyes. She has my nose, though, as well as my smile. When the two of us team up together against her father, Leo never stands a chance.

"Will you tell me why you changed your mind?" I ask my daughter patiently.

"I'm scared," she confesses. "I have bad dreams about tripping. What if I fall? What if everyone laughs at me?"

I wrap my arms around her and give Anya a big hug and kiss. "Have you ever fallen before?"

"Once."

"And can you tell me what happened?"

Anya shifts her weight from foot to foot. "Um... Nothing?"

"Did someone laugh?"

"No."

"So what makes you think anyone will laugh again?"

She shrugs. "I don't know."

I kiss her little cheeks. I can tell there's something she wants to tell me, but she might be too afraid to do it. Call it a mother's intuition, but she's not telling me something. "Anya, honey, can you tell me what you're thinking?"

"Promise not to be mad?"

"Of course, I promise. You can tell me anything."

She's quiet for a moment, her eyes suddenly distant like she's searching for the right words. It's the same look Leo gives me when he's deep in thought about something.

"I don't think I want to do ballet anymore," she confesses, averting her gaze. "But I know you love ballet. I don't want to make you sad if I quit."

I hug my daughter even tighter and giggle. "Oh, honey, that's totally okay!"

"Really?"

"I'm not going to make you do something you don't enjoy. That takes the fun out of it. If you want to dance, then you should dance. It'd be cool to get to do it together, but that doesn't mean you have to. I'll still love you to the moon and back either way."

Anya cracks a small smile. "I love you, too, Mommy."

"Where's *my* hug?" a deep voice reverberates through the dance studio.

Anya and I turn to see Leo entering the building. He tucks his sunglasses away in his pocket and smiles, opening his arms just in time to catch our daughter as she jumps toward him.

"Daddy!" she exclaims. "I'm quitting ballet!"

Leo glances at me. "Oh?"

Anya puffs her chest out with pride. "I want to be an accountant like you!"

He kisses her forehead. "Color me flattered, duckling."

"I like math more than dancing."

"Does this mean I don't get to see your dance recital?"

My daughter looks at me. "Can we do my dance just for Daddy?"

"I think that's a great idea, honey."

Leo ruffles our daughter's hair. "I get an exclusive show from two professional ballerinas? I guess today is my lucky day."

"Go sit, Daddy, go sit!"

He takes a seat in the front row just off to the side while I get busy resetting the music. It's an easy piece set to the music of *Twinkle Twinkle Little Star*. I choreographed it myself, taking into account my student's shorter legs and need for more balance.

I take my spot beside Anya, and we move together in

time with the melody. I think it's adorable how serious Anya looks, her lips pressed into a thin line as she concentrates on remembering what move comes next. Her movements are a little clumsy, but I think it's the cutest thing in the world.

When the music comes to an end, we take our bows. Leo applauds and cheers, the sound filling the space with ease.

"Beautiful!" he says, stepping down to scoop both of us up. He kisses Anya's cheeks. "That was wonderful. Truly magnificent."

Anya giggles. "Daddy, stop! That tickles!"

He sets her down. "Go grab your things, duckling. I'm taking you and your mother out to dinner."

"Can we get ice cream?"

"Is water wet?"

Anya skips off excitedly. I'm about to go grab my things, as well, but Leo's arm remains firmly circled around my waist. He dips me back and kisses me hard, peering deeply and lovingly into my eyes.

"I love you," he tells me.

"I love you, too."

"Does she really want to be an accountant?"

I giggle. "I guess the apple doesn't fall far from the tree."

Anya, exhausted from the day, falls asleep in the backseat of the car. Leo takes great pleasure in being able to pick her up and carry her to the elevator, our daughter's little cheek pressed against his shoulder. She drools against the fabric, but Leo doesn't seem to mind in the slightest. When we get up to the penthouse, he takes her straight to her room and tucks her into bed, placing a loving kiss on her forehead before joining me in the hall.

"She's growing up so fast," he mumbles warmly. "One day I'm not going to be able to pick her up anymore."

"That's why we should enjoy it while it lasts," I whisper back.

He brings my hand up to his lips and kisses my knuckles. I don't even have to ask what he's thinking. I know him so well I can practically read his mind with a single glance. The hunger in his eyes is undeniable. We're of a single mind, the two of us.

"We're going to have to be quiet," I say, smirking.

"I can think of a couple creative ways we can manage."

"Is it my turn to be tied up, or is it yours?"

Leo leans forward and all but growls. "*Yours.*"

EXTENDED EPILOGUE

LEO

Eleven Years Later

"Y-you're not going to break my kneecaps or something, are you, One-Eye?"

I stare down my nose at the guy. He's scrawny, like a rat. His two front teeth protrude outward, which definitely lends itself to his rodent-like appearance. His hair is greasy, too, like he's just climbed out of the sewer to personally stink up my office.

"No one's breaking anything," I mumble tiredly. "But I *will* be confiscating that car of yours."

"B-but I—"

"You owe us a significant amount of money, and I've been more than generous with my deadline. There's no reason for you to be driving around in a Bugatti." I scoff. "Seriously, what were you thinking? Driving a luxury car all over Moscow like you've got the cash to spare."

"Look, I just need more time—"

"Give me the keys."

"I don't—"

I glance at Samuil. "You can either give me the keys to your stupidly pricey vehicle, or my brother can hang you upside down by the ankles until you do."

My phone dings with a text message from my wife.

Anya's back from her date.

It sounds like it did NOT go well.

I pinch the bridge of my nose and sigh. I knew that kid, Christoff, was a piece of shit the moment I saw him. It wasn't even because I was in protective father mode. The boy looked like trouble—and I *know* trouble. Baggy purple tracksuit, gaudy gold chains—probably fake—and those stupid patterned bucket hats I see kids wearing all the time. My darling Anya deserves so much better than a loser like him.

But she's sixteen and free-spirited, the latter of which she most certainly got from her mother. While I had my reservations—and obviously, for good reason—I wasn't going to be the bad guy by doing something as stupid as forbidding her to see him. That probably would have blown up in my face. The last thing I need right now is to give Anya a reason to act out against her parents.

I glare at the quivering man in my office. He looks like he might piss himself. Even after all these years, I'm proud to say I've still got it. "Give me the keys," I grumble. "Someone else's kneecaps need breaking."

~

When I get home, I find my wife with her ear pressed against our daughter's bedroom door. "Honey, please talk to me. I just want to know what happened."

"Leave me alone, Mom!"

Ah, teenagers.

I approach and place a hand on the small of Nikita's back. "What's going on?"

She kisses me in greeting, a quick peck on the cheek. "I thought you said you had a meeting."

"I wrapped it up early."

Nikita gives me a dry smile. "Let me guess, you threatened to break someone's kneecaps?"

I shrug. "If it works, it works. Now, tell me what happened."

My wife runs her fingers through her hair, exasperated. "I honestly don't know. She was so excited about going on this date, but then she showed up not even thirty minutes after she texted me that she'd arrived at the movie theater."

"Do you think they broke up?"

"Sounds like it, but—"

On the other side of the door comes the sounds of sobbing, muffled by what I can only assume is a pillow. It hurts my heart to hear Anya cry. I have to get to the bottom of this. If that little shit hurt her...

There *will* be hell to pay.

I knock on her door. "Anya, it's Dad."

"Go away!"

Nikita places her hand on my forearm and shakes her head. "You know what? Let's give her some space."

"But—"

"We need to respect her boundaries. If she isn't ready to talk, forcing her won't solve anything." My wife takes my hand and gives my fingers a squeeze. "Let's go have dinner. When she's ready, or if she's feeling hungry, I'm sure she'll come down."

I grind my teeth. I don't particularly like the thought of

leaving my little girl alone and distressed, but Nikita makes a good point. Sometimes a good cry can be a cathartic experience. "Okay, duckling, your mom and I are right downstairs if you want to tell us what happened, okay?"

We don't get a response, only more sobbing.

Nikita and I descend the stairs together, hand in hand. The first part of dinner is a quiet affair. I help set the table while Nikita throws various ingredients into a big pot. We're having goulash tonight, a recipe she's developed over the years and mastered to perfection. She pours us each a large bowl, hot and steaming, and even sets out a third in front of the empty chair across from us.

"Do you think she'll come down?" I murmur.

"She will," Nikita says. I have learned to never doubt a mother's intuition.

It only takes a few minutes for the delicious scent of the fragrant, spicy sauce to reach upstairs, and a few minutes more to lure Anya out of her room. She descends the stairs slowly, each footstep a heavy stomp. My daughter does, eventually, join us at the table.

Her eyes are red-rimmed and her nose is all stuffy. She picks up her spoon and takes a slow, angry bite.

"He was cheating on me," she mutters bitterly.

My fingers twitch. I ought to beat him into next Sunday. I'd probably do it, too, if it weren't for the fact that Nikita now has a hand on my knee beneath the table. A soothing gesture that silently tells me to *calm down*. My wife knows me too well.

"How did you find out?" Nikita asks.

"I showed up at the movie theater, but I didn't see him anywhere. I tried texting and then calling, but he wasn't replying." Anya swipes her forearm beneath her nose. "And then I saw him in the arcade area with another girl."

I give Nikita a sideways glance. "Maybe they're just friends?"

"They were *kissing*, Dad."

"That little fucker."

"Leo," Nikita warns. "Language."

My daughter sighs heavily, running her hands over her flushed cheeks. "I'm so embarrassed. I thought... I really thought we had something special."

"Do you want me to call your uncles?" I ask, dead serious. "We can roll up and teach him a lesson or two."

"*Leo*."

Anya shakes her head. "No, you'd probably end up killing him."

"He hurt you."

"Yes, but... I don't know. Hurting someone else just because they hurt you... That's a shitty way to live, you know?"

I lean back in my seat, in awe of my daughter's maturity. I'll admit maybe my response wasn't the sanest, but what good father isn't willing to knock a few heads to protect their child?

"I just wanted something like you and Mom have."

Nikita smiles sweetly. "You'll find it one day, honey. Your soulmate is out there somewhere, but love isn't the kind of thing you can rush."

"I'm impatient."

I can't help but chuckle. "Yeah, you get that from me. But your mother's right. If it's meant to be, it's meant to be. Don't waste your tears on this loser. You deserve the world, the universe, and beyond. If he can't see that, then he isn't worth shit to begin with, okay?"

Slowly but surely, Anya manages a small smile. I'm glad what we're saying seems to be getting through to her. "Will you tell me about how you met again?" she asks. "I love that story."

Nikita smiles at me. "How about you start this time?"

I grin. "Let's see, it was a dark and stormy winter's night..."

The End

Printed in Great Britain
by Amazon